Only With You

Hayden Falls
Book Two

By:

Debbie Hyde

Debbie Hyde Books.

Cover Design by: Debbie Hyde
Couple Image by: fotostorm @ Istock
Background Photo: Carrie Pichler Photography (Facebook).
Photographer Website: https://carriepicherphotography.weebly.com
ISBN: 9798827708636

To my awesome friend, Pit. Thanks, Man, for all the grilling tips. Baby Back Ribs all the way! (Yeah, I know your name is Cal, but you'll always be Pit to me. The Best Toon Blast leader EVER!)

And to The 406! Facebook Group. Thank you all so much for your help with stories from Montana! Thank you, Tim Reiter, for letting me make the post. If you liked or commented on the post, or shared a story, check the Acknowledgments page.

Chapter One

Miles

*I*t has been one long week. My shift at the fire station ended at 8 am this morning. With all the errands I had to run today, I was exhausted. I should be home catching up on some sleep, but I wasn't about to bail on my friends tonight.

Meeting up at Cowboys on a Friday night was the normal thing to do around here for most of us. Well, we could go to O'Brien's Tavern across town, but I didn't like some of the people who hung out there. It was better for me to be here at our little country bar rather than the Irish Pub. Besides, tonight was a special night. There's no way I'd miss it.

Jake Campbell and his band were on stage. The dance floor was full. The pool tables were taken. I casually take it all in. My eyes settle on the group of women at the table across the dance floor. From where my friends and I were sitting on the upper level, we have a clear view of the entire bar. My gaze lingers on the five women for a few minutes. They're having fun.

"You ready to get married?" Spencer asked.

I snap my head toward my best friend. Spencer Murphy is sitting across the table from me. His question jolted me from my thoughts.

"More than ready," Aiden replied. His eyes drift to where mine was a few minutes ago.

Of course, Spencer was talking to Aiden. Aiden Maxwell was my other best friend. The three of us have been friends since we were toddlers. Aiden was getting married next Saturday. His fiancée, E, it's short for Etrulia, is among the five women at the table I was staring at just now. Aiden and E are the reason we all were here tonight. This was kind of a bachelor/bachelorette party for them. Since neither of them wanted anything big, we decided on a night out with friends.

"It's about time." Levi Barnes raises his bottle of beer at Aiden, prompting the rest of us to do the same.

Levi works at the fire station with me. He and I have had each other's backs many times on calls, last night being the latest. Thankfully, his twin brother, Luke, who also works with us, wasn't here tonight. Luke is annoying. The two aren't identical, but they're close enough. Levi's right though. It's about time Aiden and E got married.

"I'm glad you came back, man. E was miserable," Leo Barnes said.

Leo is Levi's older brother. He and his twin, Lucas, work at the Sheriff's Office with Spencer and Aiden. Those two are identical. Lucas is at the bar with a few of his friends tonight. He's a jerk but nowhere near as bad as Luke is. When you have all four of the Barnes brothers together, it gets confusing really fast.

Leo is also right. E was miserable. We all felt Aiden's absence in Hayden Falls. It wasn't the same around here without him. Thankfully, after six years, my friend was home. The world was right again. Well, for the most part, things were right. Some hurts could never be mended. I've been secretly nursing one for years.

"Can I get you guys another round?" Shelly, one of the waitresses here at Cowboys asked.

"Yeah." I raise a finger. "This round is on me."

As tired as I am, this should probably be my last drink for the night, or I won't be able to drive myself home. The guys continue to talk, but I'm not following the conversation. Casually, I look around the bar. I don't want people thinking I'm staring. With a mind of their own, my eyes drift back to the table of women. Five beautiful women who have been best friends since the third grade. It doesn't sit right with me that practically guy in here glances their way a few times.

Noah Welborn, the bar owner, delivers drinks to the women as Shelly returns with our beers. Four of the women get a beer and shot. That's the beginning of trouble. Finally, he sets a pina colada in front of E. That's not right.

"Hey, man!" Aiden's on his feet, with his arms held out, shouting at Noah. "What's wrong with you?"

The entire bar goes quiet and turns to look at my loud friend. The band is still playing, but Jake doesn't sound like he's sure of the lyrics he's singing. It got awkward in here really fast.

"What, man?" Noah holds his arms out as well, the serving tray is still in one, as he shouts back at Aiden. "There's no alcohol in it. Do you think I'm stupid?"

"You are stupid!" Aiden narrows his eyes and jabs a finger toward Noah.

Noah rolls his eyes and shakes his head before going back to the bar. Gradually, everybody goes back to their conversations. E sighs and shakes her head at Aiden. My overly protective friend needs to relax. Spencer and I have the same idea. We grab Aiden's arms and pull him back down to his chair.

Everybody in town knows that E is about two months pregnant. Even if she had ordered an alcoholic drink, there's no way Noah would have given it to her.

"You need to chill out," I tell Aiden. "Even if Noah was stupid, E's not."

"You're right." Aiden nods his head. "I can't help it. It's just…" He sighs and runs a hand through his hair.

"We get it, man." Spencer pats our friend's arm.

The rest of us nod. We do get it. E's psycho ex had stalked her for a year, and he had hurt her twice. Nearly every male member of our community showed up last month to save her and apprehend the jerk. That's one man I hope never gets out of prison.

"Pit! Four! Stop it!" Noah shouts across the bar.

All five of us groan but look over to the pool tables anyway. The town clowns are so drunk they are sword fighting with pool sticks.

Noah should probably add the cost of new pool sticks to their tabs. The girls at the table beside them are leaning against the wall laughing. It might be for support. I'm not sure. They look as drunk as Pit and Four are.

Levi and I laugh. I wave a finger at the other three.

"That's y'all's department. We, firefighters, are going to sit right here," I say with a smile.

Levi and I lean back in our chairs, happy we're not cops. The two town clowns acting out is also normal around here. Pit and Four do something crazy almost every weekend. Noah has to kick them out at least once a month.

"Sometimes, I hate my job," Aiden mumbles.

The three wonderful deputies of Hayden Falls reluctantly get up and head over to the pool tables to take care of this nonsense. I'm not sure who is giving them the hardest time. Pit and Four, or the four girls at the table next to them. I've never seen these girls before. They must be from one of the surrounding towns. I was right, three of the girls are seriously drunk and have to hold onto something for support. It looks like the fourth one is their designated driver. At least they were smart enough to plan ahead, unlike Pit and Four.

Spencer, Aiden, and Leo have to escort the girls out to their car. The sober girl wasn't able to handle her friends on her own. When the guys sit back down, for the most part, everything goes back to normal. Pit and Four are no longer sword fighting, but they are arguing over how to play pool. Idiots.

Movement across the dance floor catches my eye. I'm no longer tired and sleepy. Pissed off is what I am. Slamming my hand down on the table with a loud bang, I bolt out of my chair.

"I don't think so," I mutter through clenched teeth.

Anger fills every pore in my body as I hurry down the steps. Without apologizing to the dancers, I storm across the dance floor. With more force than necessary, I push my way between the table of women and the one man I hate the most in this world.

"Keep walking, Crawford." I cross my arms over my chest and glare at him. I'd rather punch him.

"I was just talking to the ladies." Phillip grins at me.

I swear this fool pushes my buttons on purpose. He's a little older than us, but I cannot stand this man. During high school, I caught him making out with Aiden's ex-girlfriend at the waterfall one night. A week later, he took the girl I had just started seeing up there. We've been mortal enemies ever since.

"And now you're finished." I nod my head once, confirming the matter for him.

"You should stay on the other side of the bar." Aiden steps up beside me.

"Or go home," Levi adds.

"The ladies didn't seem to mind." Phillip tilts his head to the side and grins at the women behind us.

"We mind." Spencer moves to my other side and a little in front of me. He knows I won't hesitate to knock this fool out.

"Keep moving." Leo has his arms folded across his chest too.

I figured Spencer and Aiden would follow me down here. Aiden's fiancée and Spencer's little sister are sitting at the table behind us. Surprisingly, Leo and Levi joined me as well. We form a solid wall around the table of women.

"Bye, ladies." With a sly grin in my direction, Phillip waves to the girls and walks away.

At least the jerk left. Now, we were going to have to turn around and face these five women. I can dream they'll be grateful for our interference but it's pointless. At least one of them won't be happy. The moment I turn around, a hand slaps me in the chest.

"Who do you think you are?" she shouts.

Chapter Two

Katie

"You had no right to do that." I poke Miles Hamilton in the chest for good measure.

Truth was, and I'll never admit it to him, my hand stings from slapping his chest. Firefighters work out. They have muscles, a lot of muscles. They are annoying. Well, this one firefighter is for darn sure.

"None of you need to be talking to either of the Crawford brothers." Aiden moves around the table and wraps his arms around E.

"Nothing happened." Sammie tosses up both of her hands.

"He only said 'hey' before Miles stormed in," Ally said.

"None of us really paid him any attention anyway," E adds.

"We were talking wedding details with E." Beth leans against E's side. She's had a little too much to drink tonight.

"Okay, Bethie." Spencer grabs his sister's arm. "Let's get you home."

"Come with me." Beth grabs E's hand as Spencer pulls her away from the table.

Beth doesn't seem to comprehend things are different now. E can't go home with her on a whim anymore. E's pregnant and living with

Aiden. They're getting married next weekend. She needs to go home and rest.

"I'll go with you," I say and hop off my stool.

I give Ally, Sammie, and E a hug before turning to push against the wall of one Miles Hamilton who's standing in front of me. Not that the wall moved much, but still, I managed to walk past him.

"Will you guys see to it that Ally and Sammie get home safely?" Spencer calls out to Leo and Levi. Both nod their heads in reply.

I don't look back. In a little too much haste, I follow Beth and Spencer out the door. I've taken only two steps and my heel sinks into the dirt just outside the door. Strong hands reach out, preventing me from falling.

"I got you," Miles says.

Why did he have to follow us out here? He's the last person I want to talk to.

"I've got myself." I try to snatch my arm away but fail to do so.

"Just let me help you get to Spencer's truck," Miles said.

"I can walk," I insist.

When I reach the truck, Miles is still behind me. His hands rest on my hips to keep me steady. I'm not some porcelain doll who needs to be protected all the time. I jerk forward trying to put some distance between us. Naturally, I fail at this too.

"Why do you have to be so stubborn?" Miles whispers in my ear.

Seriously? He is totally insane. He knows all the whys. I whirl around to face him. My chest heaves with each breath I take. His steel-gray eyes bounce back and forth between mine. I will not cry. I will not cry. I WILL NOT CRY.

"I hate you," I whisper as my eyes fill with tears.

This is too close. I can't take it. Spinning on my heels, I jerk the door open and climb into the backseat of Spencer's truck. Beth leans her head back. Reaching over the seat, I rub her shoulder. Anything is better than looking at the confused man standing in the parking lot.

"Will you stay the night?" Beth asked. She's had way too much to drink tonight.

"If you can't, I will," Spencer said without taking his eyes off the road.

7

"It's fine," I assure him. "I can stay."

"Oh, you can show me photos of the wedding flowers." Beth's words are a little slurred, but I can make them out.

"Sure." I go along with what she's saying. "I'll show them to you when we get to your apartment."

I don't know why she acts like she hasn't seen the photos. E and I both have shown her several times this week the flowers E picked. That just proves how drunk Beth is tonight.

My mother and grandmother opened Petals, the local flower shop, thirty years ago, long before I was born. I've taken on more shop responsibilities since last summer. Of course, I have always been a part of the business.

When I was a baby, one of the back rooms was a nursery and playroom for me. Later, it became an after-school study room where my friends and I did our homework. Now, it's a small kitchenette and breakroom. Other than my family, we have one part-time employee, Bailey Larson. She's sweet and amazing. During our busy months, we do have a few delivery boys that help out. Hence the reason we needed a breakroom. Well, it was my reasoning when I convinced my mom to remodel the room.

Naturally, Petals is doing the flowers for E and Aiden's wedding next Saturday. E is one of my best friends. We met toward the end of third grade. She was already friends with Beth. I was already friends with Ally and Sammie. The five of us were on the same relay team for Field Day that year. We've been together ever since. It was great because I didn't have a sister. Now, I have four. Even though we aren't related by blood, we're sisters just the same. I do have one annoying little brother, but he doesn't count. Of course, I can't tell mom that.

When we get to Beth's apartment, Spencer insists on escorting us inside. I know he's a cop, but he takes this protective big brother thing way too seriously. That might not be true. Since I don't have an older brother, I don't really know.

"Thanks, big brother." Beth pats Spencer on the arm. "You can go now."

Spencer sighs deeply. Lifting his eyes to the ceiling, he shakes his head. He's probably praying for patience too. Beth can be a handful sometimes.

"Bethie, you need to stop doing this." Spencer points his finger at her.

"Someday, I will." Beth stumbles down the hall to her room.

"Don't worry. I'll watch over her." I give Spencer a sympathetic look.

"I wish I knew what she's hung up on, and why she gets like this." Spencer runs his hand through his hair.

He's really worried about his little sister and with good reason. We all are worried about her. Beth has gotten worse the past couple of months. Thankfully, she doesn't drink like this if she has to work the next day.

"I'll talk to her and see what I can do," I offer.

Maybe our dear deputy will relax if he knows someone is helping Beth. I know what gets her like this, but I can't tell him. Sadly, the situation responsible for Beth's actions is getting worse. My friend may drown her sorrows in alcohol for a long time to come.

"Thanks, Katie." Spencer holds his hand out. "Give me your keys."

"Why?" I narrow my eyes and lean back.

"Since you're staying here tonight, Miles and I will drive your car over," he replies. "I already have a key to Beth's car."

Reluctantly, I dig my keys from my purse. I hate doing this, but mine and Beth's cars are at Cowboys. If I don't give him my keys, I won't have a way to work in the morning. I already have a change of clothes here. I won't have to go home and shower first.

"Thanks." I hand him my keys and lock the door behind him.

After he leaves, I hurry to Beth's room. She's already passed out on the bed. I remove her shoes and tuck her in. My heart breaks for Beth. Maybe she could process things and move forward if she would admit to herself what the problem is. I leave a glass of water and a bottle of ibuprofen on the nightstand for her.

"You're a fine one to talk," I mumble to myself as I turn Beth's light off.

Unable to sit still, I pace the living room floor until Spencer comes back with my keys. It takes about thirty minutes because they bring Beth's car first.

Thankfully, Spencer is the one who brings my keys to the door. While he walks back to Miles' truck, I make the mistake of looking at the annoying man sitting behind the wheel. I could feel his eyes on me before I looked his way. Big mistake. I'm not too drunk tonight. It's just enough to heighten my emotions. Blinking back tears, I close the door and lean back against it. We all have secrets in Hayden Falls. Miles Hamilton is mine.

Chapter Three

Miles

As tired as I was yesterday, I still tossed and turned last night. It's a good thing I have today off because my tail is seriously dragging this morning. I need coffee, but I don't feel like making it. Instead, I hop in my truck and drive to town.

On the drive to the town square, my mind replays everything from last night. It wasn't the first time Katie Matthews told me she hated me. She's been saying it for almost five years, and I don't know why.

Parking in one of the spaces around the gazebo, my eyes drift over to the flower shop. It's after ten. Katie is already there. The image of her tear-filled blue eyes flashes before me. It's the same image that jolted me awake a few times last night.

I release a long breath. Running a hand through my hair, I reach for my baseball cap with the fire department's logo on it from the passenger seat. The mixed emotions I have right now are driving me insane. I don't know what's happening to me, or how to make it stop. This woman has me tied up in so many ways. I don't like how I feel right now.

My eyes dart between the flower shop and Beth's Morning Brew. I came here to get a cup of coffee so I could settle down and fully wake up. Instead, one glance at Petals has me an even bigger jumbled mess than I already was. If I could fix things with her, I'd do it in a heartbeat.

With a shake of my head, I push the truck door open and head to the coffee shop. Maybe once I get some caffeine in me, my head will clear and all these emotions will go away. I just can't close my eyes until I get a grip on this, whatever this is. Closing my eyes brings back those tear-filled eyes from last night. I've only seen Katie cry one time and that was nearly five years ago.

"Hey, Miles. What can I get you?" Beth asked.

"I thought you were off today." I narrow my eyes and tilt my head. Beth doesn't get drunk when she has to work the next day.

"I got breakfast at the diner and decided to come in." Beth shrugs like it's no big deal. "You want your regular house blend with cream and sugar?"

"Yeah." I glance over my shoulder out the huge front window. "And a Peppermint Mocha," I add.

After paying, I move to the side and wait. I don't really have a plan here, but I have to do something. With both hands, I reach up and adjust my baseball cap.

"Here you go, Miles," Beth calls out as she sets my drinks into a to-go tray.

"That's not my order." I point to the tray with three cups.

"Yes, it is." Beth smiles sweetly.

"Beth, I ordered two drinks." I hold up two fingers. Surely, she can count.

"Yes, but you paid for three," Beth said as she continues to smile at me.

"Why would I do that?" I'm totally confused here. Maybe she's seriously hungover this morning after all.

"This is your coffee." Beth points to the cup with my name written on it. She points to the next cup. "This is a Peppermint Mocha with extra whip cream and extra peppermint pieces." She then points to mysterious cup number three. "This is a Salted Caramel Latte."

"And why do I need a Salted Caramel Latte?" I hold both hands out.

"Bailey is working today," Beth replies.

She leans her head to look toward the flower shop. Beth knows what I'm doing. I sigh and nod my head. If I had shown up without a drink for Bailey, I would have felt like a jerk.

"Thanks, Beth." I grab the tray. "You're the best."

"Miles," Beth calls out before I get to the door. Thank goodness no one is in here right now. "I don't know what's going on, but don't hurt her."

The door chimes as four girls walk in. It's not like Beth's Morning Brew to stay empty for too long on a Saturday morning even with a chance of snow. Beth watches me instead of greeting her new customers. Since I don't know what's going on either, I simply nod my head before walking out the door.

Petals is located on the opposite side street of the town square from Beth's coffee shop. It's a short walk, but my steps slow as I get close to the flower shop. Katie hates me, so this kind gesture could backfire on me. Since Bailey is here too, I'm probably not going to get any answers to my burning questions today. Still, maybe this will be the start of a truce between Katie and me. I hate fighting with her.

Walking into the flower shop, I find myself surrounded by red roses. I've never seen so many in one place. Of course, there are other flowers and plants here too. Balloons line a section of the wall in the back corner with numbers on cards attached to them. The smell is sweet. I guess this explains why Katie reminds me of flowers.

"We'll be right with you," Katie calls out from the back workroom.

Slowly, I make my way to the counter where the cash register is. I haven't been inside Petals in years. During middle school and the first two years of high school, I use to deliver flowers for Katie's mom. It wasn't a steady job or an official one. However, it was a nice way for a teenage boy to make a little spending cash. The tips were really good.

Katie and Bailey are arranging flowers at a table in the room behind the cash register. The room they're in is as long as this one. The coolers are in the back on that side. The office, restroom, and breakroom are at the back of this side. Katie's standing on this side of the table with her back to me.

"Hey, Miles." Bailey sees me and waves.

Katie stands up straighter and her back stiffens. Maybe this was a bad idea.

"Hey, Bailey. Katie," I greet her, but Katie doesn't turn around.

"What can we do for you?" Bailey wipes her hands on a towel as she walks to the counter. "Do you need to order your girlfriend some flowers for Valentine's Day?" She wiggles her eyebrows at me.

Katie's back stiffens even more. Slowly, she looks over her shoulder at me. I don't have a girlfriend. Everyone in town knows this.

"No," I reply. My eyes never leave Katie's. "I brought you ladies a coffee."

"Oh, wow. That's sweet." Bailey smiles up at me. "Thanks, Miles."

I hand Bailey the Salted Caramel Latte. She takes a sip and sighs.

"Oh, my favorite." Bailey sounds as though she may melt on the floor. Her reaction makes me smile. Women and their coffee.

Katie sets the bow she was making on the table. Cautiously, she turns toward me, but she doesn't walk over. She doesn't smile or speak either. The door chimes as a new customer walked in.

"Hey, Grace," Bailey says happily.

She hurries around the counter to hug Grace. Grace Wentworth owns the book store and lives in the apartment above it. Katie slowly walks to the counter. Our eyes stay locked on each other.

"Good morning." Grace walks up beside me.

I'm not sure if she's talking to me or Katie. I look down at Grace as she sets her purse on the counter. Her eyes are bright, and she has a cheery smile. She's usually shy and quiet.

"Morning," I greet her.

"Your order is ready," Katie says to Grace before disappearing into the back cooler.

Katie makes two trips to bring out three Valentine's Day arrangements while Bailey rings up Grace's order. Leaning on the counter, I wink at Grace. She shyly tucks her hair behind her ear. The blush on her cheeks is cute.

"You have a lot of sweethearts," I tease.

14

"No, silly." Grace giggles. "Two are for the book store and one is for my grandmother."

That's what I figured. Grace and her older brother, Elijah, were raised by their grandparents after their parents died in a car accident when they were kids. Grace and her grandmother are very close.

Grace didn't date a lot. You hardly ever hear a rumor of Grace dating. The few rumors of her love life were just that, rumors. Oh, she's pretty, and several guys have asked her out. As far as I know, Grace had turned them all down. I have seen her glance at someone a few times though. Sadly, he's clueless. I should pop him in the head to get his attention. Nah. Doing that would get me twisted up into a pretzel. I could drop him a few hints though.

"I'll have to come back for one of them." Grace picks up two of the arrangements.

"No need. I can carry one over for you." Bailey picks up the third arrangement and grabs the door. The book store is only about fifty yards away.

Now that we're alone, Katie still doesn't speak to me. The counter between us might as well be a football field. Picking up her drink, I give it a little shake.

"Peppermint Mocha," I tempt her. "Extra whip cream. Extra peppermint pieces."

Katie sighs and wraps her hand around the cup. I don't let go. A moment of vulnerability flashes in her eyes. It's quickly replaced with the challenging tilt of her head.

"Why are you doing this?" Katie asks.

"Can't you just say thank you?" I ask.

"Thank you," she says with an untrustworthy tone. "You usually aren't nice to me."

"That's not true." My eyes lock with hers again as I walk around the counter.

"Don't, Miles." Katie takes a couple of steps backward into the workroom.

"Don't what?" I stop a few inches from her. It wouldn't take much to reach out and touch her, and I want to touch her.

"We hate each other," Katie mumbles as her eyes drop to the floor.

15

"Do we?" My chest heaves with each breath I take.

"You know we do." She bravely looks up at me.

The lift of her chin is all that's brave about her. Her breathing is as hard as mine. Her eyes blink rapidly. Is she fighting to hold back tears? I need to find out what that's about. It rips me in two seeing her like this.

"Why, Katie?" I whisper, leaning closer toward her.

"You know why," she replies and looks away.

"I don't." I shake my head.

I have no idea what I did to cause her so much pain and hate. Being this close to her makes me want to pull her into my arms where she belongs. The bell above the door jingles, causing us both to freeze.

"It's snowing," Bailey calls out.

With the spell between us now broken, I step back. My eyes roam over her from head to toe. When our eyes meet again, I know I've had all I can take of this for today, maybe for a few days.

"I'll see you next week," I tell her.

Grabbing my coffee off the counter, I leave the flower shop an even bigger mess than I was before. Nothing in me has settled down. There's only one thing I can think of that will help relieve this pent-up energy. It's what I should have done to start with. Getting into my truck, I make a beeline to the gym.

Chapter Four

Katie

Firefighters are the worst. Before Bailey can ask me any questions, I rush into the office and lock the door. Why did he have to show up here today? Why?

I was doing good at not remembering last night. Usually, throwing myself into my work had a way of settling me. Having Bailey here this morning was seriously helping me keep my mind focused. Her stories about her brothers were hilarious. Her brother, Matt, was our local family doctor. Who knew the good doctor had a sense of humor? Drew worked at the H. H. Maxwell Ranch. He was more outgoing than I thought. Everything was great. Then that blasted firefighter had to show up and ruin everything.

Every sip of this Peppermint Mocha makes me think of the man I vowed to hate forever. If Beth hadn't made me this drink, I'd throw it in the trash, preferably in front of Miles. It is a good drink though. It would be ashamed to waste it. At least that's my argument for keeping it.

Taking another sip of the sweet goodness, I close my eyes and lean my head back against my desk chair. The image of those steel-gray eyes bouncing back and forth between mine torments me. His soft tender voice surrounds me. Any other woman in this town would fall for his charms. I've seen plenty do it. But, not me. I sniffle and push a finger into the corner of my eye. Not me. Not me. Not me.

A light knock on the office door pulls me from my thoughts. I shouldn't have left Bailey to deal with everything in the shop alone. I just needed a few minutes to get myself together, not that I really am.

"Katie," E calls out from the other side of the door. "Are you okay?"

I wasn't expecting her today. Panic shoots through me. What could be wrong? In a rush, I open the door.

"I'm good. Are you okay?" My question rushes from my lips.

"Yeah." E gives me a tight smile. "I just came to check on things."

Her smile is totally fake. Since she's holding a cup of coffee, I'm assuming Beth told her about my visitor this morning. Miles Hamilton is one subject I can't talk about. We need a happier conversation.

"Great." I plaster on a fake smile too. Looping my arm through hers, I turn us toward the workroom. She didn't mean her wedding flowers, but I'll play it off this way. "Let me show you."

On a table in the corner of the workroom sit the blue, white, and silver bows and vases for E's wedding. In the cooler are the flowers I've been working on. There weren't a lot of blue flowers available this month on such short notice. That's why I'm trying to dye some white flowers blue. Several vases are filled with water and a nontoxic blue food coloring. One side of the cooler is full of white flowers. One test flower is in each vase.

This is my first attempt at dying flowers through the stems. I found a *YouTube* video and wanted to give it a try. We started testing yesterday. If this doesn't work out as well as I hope, we still have time to dip the flowers.

"This is amazing." E carefully touches each flower.

More white roses, mums, daisies, hydrangeas, lilies, and orchids wait to be added to the blue water. We're testing them all to see which ones do the best. Each vase has a different amount of coloring in them to try and get deeper shades of blue. Blue was E's favorite color, but she could never decide on a shade. She loved them all. It was the reason I was trying to get as many shades as possible. A few may still need to be dipped to get the richer blues. Whichever flowers do the best, those are the ones we will use.

"It's turning out better than I thought." I pick up the rose to check its coloring. "All of these were added yesterday."

The plan is to add the remaining flowers on Tuesday. Twenty-four hours is recommended for dying. That time frame does give them a nice light blue color. I will pull a few at this stage but leave the rest for forty-eight hours to see what happens. On Thursday and Friday, Bailey and I will finish putting together E's wedding arrangements. She didn't ask for anything crazy. Simple and blue were her only requests. She gave me complete freedom to design everything. It would be nice to have more customers like that. I loved coming up with new designs.

Mom is coming in on Monday to help us with our Valentine's Day orders. That should be enough help to pull off the holiday flowers and the wedding. Leave it to my friend to want to get married on Valentine's Day.

"Thank you for doing this." E holds her arms out for a hug.

"Anything for you." I happily step into her hug. "If this fails, we can always go with pink and red. I have plenty," I tease.

E scrunches up her face and shakes her head. Those are not her colors.

"I'll go with all white with blue bows first," E said. We both laugh.

"So." E drags the word out as we walk back into the workroom.

I know what she's asking, but we can't talk about it, or rather him. E's pregnant and getting married in seven days. She's been through a lot lately. My friend doesn't need my messed-up issues.

"I can't." I shake my head.

"It's okay." E squeezes my hand. "When you're ready."

I nod my head. She has no idea how much her patience means to me. If anyone understands how hard it is to talk about things, it would be E. We didn't push her to talk about her problems. Last month, after she got out of the hospital, we had a girl's night at the house she shares with Aiden. He spent most of the evening at his parent's house so we could talk.

That night, E opened up and told the four of us everything about the abuse she went through from her childhood to her crazy ex. There were even some things she hadn't told Beth. She seems freer and happier now. She sure deserves it. Maybe it would help me if I talked my troubles out. I'm just not ready to do it.

"So." I look into the shop. "Where's Aiden?"

"Oh, please." E waves her hand. "I can walk to Petals by myself."

Bailey falls over on the work table laughing. I cover my mouth with my hand in an attempt to hide my laughter.

"We're talking about the same Aiden Maxwell here, right? I mean, girl, it's snowing out there." I can't hold back my laughter any longer.

Bailey raises her head. "He dropped her off at the door." She falls over the table again.

"He's at the hardware store." E covers her mouth with both hands. Her body shakes with laughter.

I'm so happy for my friend. She has everything she's wanted since middle school. E never told us she was in love with Aiden, but we all knew. She finally got her cowboy. In September, she would be a mother. Too bad all of us couldn't have our dreams come true. The bell over the door chimes again. Aiden walks in and wraps his arms around E from behind.

"Are you ready to go, Sunshine?" Aiden kisses the top of E's head. "The snow is getting heavier. I need to get you and our little sunbeam home."

It's adorable how Aiden refers to their baby as a sunbeam. I fight back tears every time I hear him say it. E nods in reply and gives me another hug.

"I'm here," she whispers in my ear.

"I know," I whisper back.

"You two should consider closing up early." Aiden waves a finger between me and Bailey. "The roads are becoming a serious issue. Several accident reports have already come in at the station."

"You really should go home," E agrees. "We all can come in next week and help out so you won't be behind."

"That sounds like a good idea," I give in easily. After seeing Miles this morning, I do need some time alone.

"Bailey, do you need a ride?" Aiden asked.

Her phone dinged with a text. Bailey rolls her eyes and shakes her head.

"No. Drew is already on his way to pick me up." Bailey waves her phone.

Bailey's lucky. I feel a little jealous. I don't have an older brother to look out for me like that. Bailey has two. My little brother is in high school. The troubles of the world don't weigh on him yet. I do have my mom and grandmother though. My phone on the table rings. Mom's picture lights up on the screen.

I swipe to answer the call. "Hey, Mom."

"Hey, Sweetie," Mom says. "You should close up."

"Yeah, we're doing that right now." After assuring her I'll call before I leave, mom lets me end the call.

Bailey's brother shows up as Aiden and E walk outside. I wave bye to them and watch as they walk across the street to their truck. There's a red truck parked next to Aiden's. I already know who it belongs to. Aiden talks with Miles for a few minutes before he gets into his truck and drives away.

It looks like I'm a stalker today. As much as I need to go, I can't force my feet to move. The falling snow settles on Miles' shoulders and the baseball cap he's wearing. He looks almost magical as he walks around the front of his truck to get in. He pauses and his head snaps in my direction. I hate him, but I can't help watching him from a distance. With a deep sigh, I break our eye contact. Flipping the open sign to closed, I lock the door and head out back to my jeep.

Chapter Five

Miles

For seven days I did my best to avoid the town square. The first few days were easy because of the snow. The fire department was busy rescuing stranded travelers. When things settled down, on my days off I slipped up to the diner an evening or two to grab a take-out order before heading home. That was it. I didn't even go to Beth's for a cup of coffee. If I didn't make coffee at home or the station, I suffered the days without caffeine.

Avoiding Katie was driving me insane. Our interactions seemed to affect her as much as they did me. She had a lot on her plate this week with Valentine's Day and E's wedding. Since my presence upset her so badly, staying away was my only option for now. Aiden and E were important to all of us. The last thing I'd do was mess up their wedding day. However, staying away from her had me on edge.

Today was the wedding, and I couldn't avoid her any longer. Once this wedding was over, I was going to become a thorn in Katie Matthews' side. She's been hating on me for years, and I was going to find out why.

I wasn't sure if I wanted to hug my best friend's bride, or if I was mad at her. Even if I was mad at E, I'd never act on it. Aiden would kill me. He has a super serious caveman primal protection over his little bride. Can't say I blame him though. Aiden waited a long time to win his girl.

I'm not sure if it was a curse or a blessing yet, but somehow, I was the one who got to escort Katie down the aisle. She closed her eyes and swallowed hard when she took my arm, but she never protested the line-up. At first, I thought it was a coincidence. The looks E keeps giving me and Katie made me question it. Does E know why Katie hates me? Could I take a chance and ask her about it?

After the pictures were taken and the cake cut, our cute little bride gave out dances. Everyone mostly swayed in small circles with E. Morning sickness could hit her without warning. I was proud of my friend. As rough as those moments were for E, no matter where they were, Aiden was right there with her. Seeing Aiden's devotion to E caused my chest to tighten. Would the rest of us be blessed enough to find what they have?

"How are you feeling?" I asked E when it was my turn to dance with her.

"Happy," she replied.

The gleam in her eyes and the smile on her face were enough for everyone to know how happy she was. My eyes moved from E to the couple dancing behind her. My blood boiled, and I wanted to rip the jerk's head off. Katie was dancing with Jessie Calhoun. I think I could handle it if it was Four dancing with her. Katie would never take Four seriously. Jessie, on the other hand, was a problem. I like Jessie, I just don't like him around Katie. The man charms every woman he passes in town. A growl rumbled in my chest.

"Are you okay?" E asked.

My eyes dart back to her. "Yeah." It's a lie.

E looks over her shoulder at Katie and Jessie. She sighs and gives the slightest shake of her head. It was so small, I almost missed it. When she looks up at me again, her eyes were filled with concern, or sympathy, I'm not sure which.

"That doesn't mean anything," E loudly whispers.

Okay. E has to know something. I wasn't planning on bringing this up with her today, but I'm at my wit's end.

"Why does she hate me?" I asked.

"I don't know what she's upset about." E chances another glance at Katie. "But, I don't think she really hates you."

Well, it wasn't the answer I was hoping for. I didn't get an answer as to why Katie was upset but hearing the hate part may not be real gave me a little hope.

"If you knew, would you tell me?" I shouldn't even ask this question.

"Miles, I promise you, I don't know." E shakes her head. "If I did know, I'd tell you I knew, but I'd never betray Katie like that."

I nod my head and let the matter drop. It's good Katie has loyal friends. I'd be the same way if it was Spencer or Aiden. Speaking of Aiden. He's standing at the edge of the dance floor. His narrow eyes go from me and his sweet bride over to Katie and Jessie a few times. *Don't worry, my friend, I'm not about to upset your bride.* I can't believe my friend sometimes.

"Smile and wave at your husband please." I slightly turn us so E is facing Aiden. She does as I ask.

"I'm so sorry," E apologizes. Her little giggle is cute.

"You are the safest person on this planet," I tell her.

I can't help but laugh at my friend watching us from a few feet away. It looks as though he needed to move closer to his bride. Hopefully, Aiden can see that his wife is fine. If the fool comes over here and tackles me, we'll be wrestling on this dance floor. I might lose, but he would know I was there.

"You should dance with her," E whispers as the song ends.

That's a good idea. It's also dangerous territory for me. Maybe with all these people watching, Katie won't make too big of a scene. If she turns me down, I'll end up in Megan's stupid gossip blog as scorned or something.

Before I can reply to E, Four pushes me aside to dance with the bride. Aiden is going to kill this fool one day. Sure enough, the groom has his arms folded across his chest and glaring holes into the older Calhoun brother. Someone should tell my friend the shade of red on his face doesn't go with his tux. It's not going to be me though. Hopefully, he'll figure it out.

24

At least the younger Calhoun brother is walking away from Katie as I cross the dance floor. Jessie is a huge flirt which makes him a serious problem for me. An even bigger problem is about to step in. Luke Barnes.

Before Katie can accept Luke's request to dance, I slide between them. In one smooth movement, I take her extended hand in my right one. With my left hand on her waist, I twirl her out onto the dance floor. I ignore Katie's yelp of surprise and narrow my eyes at Luke.

Luke Barnes is nothing like his twin brother. He chases every woman he sees. He can have them all, just not this one. He's a great fireman, but that's all I'll give him. The stories he tells at the station about his weekend hookups are disgusting. His idea of showing a woman a good time is nothing but wild make-out sessions at the falls or the lake. I never want to hear about his hotel flings again. Seriously, the man needs to grow up.

"What are you doing?" Katie looks around nervously.

"This is called dancing." I move us to the far corner of the dance floor.

"We don't dance." Katie tries to twist away, but I hold her firmly in place.

"We've danced plenty of times," I whisper next to her ear.

Invading her space like this is a bad idea. The breath she sucks in is not lost on me. She remembers. How could she not? My hand on her waist slides to her lower back. Her floral scent wraps around me. Memories of holding her like this can't be held at bay any longer.

We've never…we can't," Katie stammers.

"Never in public," I agree. My voice lowers as I pull her closer and nuzzle my nose into her hair. "And we sure can."

"We hate each other," she practically spits the words out.

"I don't hate you," I tell her. One of us needs to admit it.

"Well, *I* hate *you*." She tries to pull back again. I give her a little room this time.

"Why?"

"You know why," she hisses.

"I don't, Katie." I shake my head. "You got mad at me about something, but you never said what. You just started lashing out at me."

"Stop," Katie pleads. She won't look me in the eye.

"Come on, Buttercup. Talk to me," I whisper in her ear.

Her body goes stiff. "Don't call me that."

Buttercup has always been my nickname for her. It was what she called Daffodils when she was a little girl.

"You used to *love* it when I called you Buttercup," I remind her. "Summer nights. A blanket on the ground. An ocean of stars above."

"Stop it," her voice cracks. "Why are you doing this to me?"

"I need answers, Katie." My arm around her waist tightens, pulling her closer.

"You need?" She huffs out a strangled laugh. "I needed…"

I wait, but she doesn't finish her sentence. Why won't she talk to me?

"Tell me what I did so I can fix it," I plead.

I've never begged anyone for anything until now. The canyon between us guts me. I hate it.

"You can't fix this." Her eyes finally lift to meet mine.

A single tear escapes from the corner of her eye. I wipe it away with my thumb. More threaten to follow. Crap. I didn't mean to make her cry. I only wanted answers.

"We can't do this here." Katie sniffles. "E and Aiden."

I nod my head. She's right. No matter what this is between us, or how much I want answers, we can't ruin our best friends' wedding.

"Okay." I lead her out the side door and to the end of the hall where the restrooms are before anyone notices the tears in her eyes. "I'm sorry, Buttercup."

When I press my lips to her forehead, more emotions than I can control wash over me. Nothing is better. I've only made things worse.

"Freshen up and go back to the reception." I motion toward the restroom. Thankfully, no one is in the hallway.

The jerk in me doesn't stick around to make sure she's okay. I have to get out of here. This is Aiden and E's special day. It's not a day for answers. Without looking back, I hurry out the back door of The

Magnolia Inn and get into my truck. Instead of going home to an empty cold house, I take a long drive. I've got to find some peace before I completely lose my mind

Chapter Six

Katie

Two weeks. That's how long I've managed to avoid Miles. We have now started on week three. Every Monday morning since E and Aiden's wedding, Miles has shown up at Petals with mine and Bailey's favorite coffee. Bailey thinks it's sweet. I think it's annoying.

I don't know what he thinks happened between us when we danced. I don't even know what passed between us, but trust me, it's nothing good. It can't be good. I won't let it be. Things need to stay exactly as they are. Hate is the only thing I can allow myself to feel where he's concerned.

Come to think of it, I didn't even agree to dance with the annoying fireman. He, doing as he pleases like always, stepped in and hijacked my dance with Luke Barnes. Closing my eyes, I lean my head back against my desk chair. What am I complaining about? I didn't want to dance with Luke. That's one playboy I never want to be tangled up with. Am I only fueling my anger here? Probably. But it's necessary. I can never forgive Miles.

My office door is open allowing me to hear the bell over the front door jingle. Bailey happily greets the new customer. From the laughter I hear, it's more than one customer. Bailey taps on the door and gives me a weary smile. She's not as happy as she sounded a few minutes ago.

"You wanna take this?" Bailey points toward the shop.

With an exasperated sigh, I get out of my chair. Bailey is perfectly capable of handling customers. It makes no sense for her to need me. I know it's not Miles. I've hidden every time he's shown up. Yeah, that's a coward's move, but I'm not ready to face him. The laughter I heard was from women, so this shouldn't be a problem.

That's what I thought anyway. When I stepped into the shop, my eyes landed on a woman I never wanted to see again. Well, calling her a woman is a stretch. Brittney Douglas was leaning over the front counter looking through a floral arrangement book Bailey had given her. Her friend Holly Laine was beside her pointing out her favorites. This had to be a joke. Brittney has never been here, and I didn't want her here now. I was prepared to throw her out until a movement across the shop caught my eye. Brittney's mother was looking at the arrangements on the far wall. I liked Mrs. Douglas. She was the only reason I slapped on a fake smile.

"Hello, ladies." I walk behind the counter and face the vile woman and her friend. "How may I help you?"

"Holly is getting married this summer." Brittney gives Holly a one-arm hug. "And Mama insists that you're the best."

"She is the best," Mrs. Douglas insists. She sets a pink and white arrangement with a sheer bow on the counter. It's small but cute. "I have to have this one for my kitchen table. You know pink is my favorite color."

"Yes, Ma'am. You do have great taste." I happily ring up her purchase. I keep a few pink arrangements on the shelves with her in mind.

"Is this *all* you do?" Brittney's tone grates on my nerves. She taps the sample book with a long manicured nail.

She didn't get those nails done here in Hayden Falls. There's no way Kennedy Reed would let someone walk out of her salon with those gaudy things. Perhaps I could poke Brittney's eyes out with them.

"No. Those are just suggestions." My words are sharp. I can no longer maintain a fake smile for this woman.

"Oh, good." Holly sighs with relief. "I do like a few of these, but I've found several on *Pinterest* too."

"When is your wedding?" I ask Holly. It's best for me to ignore Brittney. "I need to see if I have an opening."

"July 20th," Holly replies with a smile.

"Let me get my datebook," I say before hurrying to my office.

Why did that evil woman have to come here today? Grabbing the datebook, I hold it to my chest. I don't have to check it. There are no weddings scheduled yet for July.

"Are you going to do it?" Brittney slips into the office and closes the door behind her.

"I don't want to," I reply honestly. "But, I don't want to lose Mrs. Douglas."

Brittney's mother has been a customer here since the first day my mom and grandmother opened Petals. I can't take my loathing for her daughter out on her.

"Holly won't be a problem." Bailey glances over her shoulder. It's not like anyone can see us in here. "I'll do my best to help run interference with Brittney."

"Thank you." I don't know what I'd do without Bailey.

With dread in my heart, I go back out front and schedule Holly's wedding in the books for July. I give her a deadline of June 10th for her final decision and deposit. That's enough time to order anything she needs if we don't already have it. Something tells me she's going to want a lot. Even if Holly turns out to be easy to work with, I'm sure Brittney will still do everything she can to make my life miserable. If Holly misses the deposit deadline, I'm off the hook.

I should have closed up early after dealing with Brittney, but I didn't have a good enough reason. How would I explain to my mom that I went home because a woman I despised showed up? My personal feelings couldn't interfere with this business. I've worked hard since last summer proving to my mom I could handle managing the shop. I wanted to be here at Petals, unlike my earlier dreams of leaving this town. Someday, I hope mom passes the shop to me. I want to make her and my grandmother proud of me. They're all the family I have, along with my little brother.

My next customer seriously pulled on my emotions too, but in a different way. Macy Hamilton, Miles' mother came in just before closing. Through the winter, when there wasn't a holiday or a scheduled event, we closed around four in the afternoon. Weddings and prom time could have me here way past closing.

"Hey, girls." Mrs. Hamilton gave me and Bailey a hug.

"How are you?" I don't have to fake my smile this time.

"Great. I'm just running errands. There's so much to do." Mrs. Hamilton wasn't complaining. She loved being a mom. The way she cared for Miles and his sisters was really sweet.

"What brings you by today?" I ask. "Would you like a cup of coffee? Bailey just made a fresh pot."

"Thank you, but I don't have time. I actually have a cup from Beth's in the car." Mrs. Hamilton walks with me to the counter. "I stopped by because I'm planning a party at the end of the month, and I wanted you to do the flowers and balloons."

"That sounds like fun." Baily hands me the datebook.

"Ben is going to be fifty this year." Mrs. Hamilton beams as she talks about her husband. "I have to do something big. He'll hate it, but the girls said we're doing this."

"I think it's an awesome idea. When is the party?" I open the datebook. I already know her husband's birthday.

"March 30th, and we're doing a surprise party at The Magnolia Inn." Mrs. Hamilton's expression goes from happy to concerned. "I want to keep things simple. E's parties are amazing, but I don't want to work her too hard."

"Oh, working parties with E is one of my favorite things to do. But don't worry, we'll keep as much off of her as possible," I assure her. "Beth, Ally, and Sammie will pitch in too."

Mrs. Hamilton's phone rings. She scrunches up her face and holds up a finger. While she steps away to take the call, Bailey and I pull out a few party idea books and the balloon list. After ending the call, Mrs. Hamilton rushed up to the counter.

"Oh, girls. I'm going to have to come back." She's in a panic state.

"Mrs. Hamilton, what's wrong?" I rush around the counter and put an arm around her.

"My friend in Walsburg was rushed to the hospital. Her son thinks she's had a stroke." Mrs. Hamilton trembles. "I have to go. I need…"

"Are you able to drive?" I ask. She nods her head. "Okay. You go to the hospital. If you have errands you weren't able to finish, I'll do them. I can even go by your house and stay with Chloe until you get home if you need me to."

Chloe is Miles' little sister. She's a Junior in high school. She's about seven years younger than Miles. He used to tease her saying she was a late surprise. She probably was.

"Are you sure?" Mrs. Hamilton's voice trembles.

"Absolutely," I say firmly.

This is what we do in Hayden Falls. If someone needs help, we pitch in. The people of this town may gossip, spread rumors, and fight amongst themselves, but when it matters the most, we band together.

"Thank you, Katie. I'll be right back." Mrs. Hamilton rushes out to her car.

Bailey has already closed up everything by the time Mrs. Hamilton comes back in carrying four boxes from Sweet Treats Bakery. Bailey waves on her way out the door.

"Is Chloe having a party?" I tease.

"No, but make sure she does her homework and eats a decent meal. A bag of chips is not dinner." Mrs. Hamilton takes a deep breath. I would laugh at that but her situation is too serious.

"It's okay. I'll take good care of Chloe." I rub her back to offer her some comfort.

"These." Mrs. Hamilton points to the boxes she set on the counter. "They are for Miles and the guys at the station. They had to assist with a bad accident on the interstate a little while ago. I was trying to cheer them up."

Oh my. The fire station. I can handle this. I have to handle this. There's no way I can break my promise to her.

"It's fine. I have this and Chloe." I walk her out to her car. "You drive safe and let me know when you get there."

"Thank you again." Mrs. Hamilton hugs me before getting into her car.

It would probably be best to get all the details before I volunteer for something like this in the future. The last place I want to go is to the fire station. I can do it. I can drop two boxes of cupcakes and two boxes of donuts off without having to talk to Miles. At least, I hope I can.

Chapter Seven

Miles

*D*ays like today gut out a man's soul. I hate working car accidents. A raging fire is a force to be reckoned with and one I'm trained to handle. The devastation from a car accident will haunt you for days. No amount of training will fully prepare you for car accidents. The six-car pileup on the interstate today had taken hours to work. It was going to take more than a shower, ibuprofen, and coffee to make this day go away. Someone dropped down in the recliner next to me, but I didn't open my eyes.

"You alright, man?" Levi asked.

"Are you?" I didn't have to ask. We're all feeling the aftermath of the accident.

"No," Levi replied in a low voice.

Levi was by my side the entire time today. He had seen everything I had. Three people lost their lives today because one guy decided to be a speed demon and switched lanes too sharply in a curve. Some people should never be allowed to have a driver's license.

The Hayden Falls Fire Department is mostly made up of volunteers. We only have eight full-time employees plus the Fire Chief, Mike

Foster. Most of the guys are still here hanging out in the dayroom and kitchen area. A few of the guys went straight home. The rest are trying to get themselves together before they head home to their families. Even Luke is sitting quietly at one of the kitchen tables. He's never quiet.

A woman's voice and light laughter outside the door catches my attention, and everyone else's. Looking over my shoulder, my eyes narrow as Katie walks in beside Chief Foster. One look at us causes her laughter and smile to fade. What is she doing here? She's never been to the station. Our gazes meet for a moment before she drops her eyes to the floor.

"Katie brought us some cupcakes and donuts." Chief Foster sets two boxes from Sweet Treats on one of the tables.

Katie shyly follows the Chief across the room with two more boxes. Wow. That was sweet of her. The guys surround the tables and begin to devour the sweet desserts. I need a different kind of sugar. Taking her by the arm, I pull Katie into the hallway.

"Thanks." Sadly, I'm at a loss for words right now.

"Actually, they're from your mom. I told Chief Foster but I guess he didn't hear me."

Mom? This sounds like something she would do. I look around but don't see her.

"She got an emergency call. Her friend in Walsburg was rushed to the hospital," Katie answered my unspoken question.

"So, you volunteered to bring us pastries?" I raise an eyebrow.

"I did." She nods her head. "And when I leave here, I'm going to go stay with Chloe until your mom gets home. I don't know where your dad is."

My dad and uncle went to Denver for a few days. My uncle's rodeo buddies were meeting up and he didn't want to make the trip alone. Her offering to help my family stirs something in my chest. Hope could bring a man to his knees.

"Dad and Uncle Glenn will be home tomorrow." I'm not sure how to process everything she's telling me. That accident has my mind in too many places. "Why are you doing this?"

If she hates me so badly, why help my family? Oh, I'm grateful. I just don't understand it.

"Helping?" She sounds shocked I asked. "It's…"

I hold my hand up to stop her. "Please don't say it's what we do in Hayden Falls."

"But…" she starts, but I place a finger to her lips.

"I need a little more than that right now." I take a deep breath and close my eyes. "Please just let me believe it's because you care."

"I do care," she whispers. My eyes snap open. "I do," she says and looks away.

Taking her chin in my hand, I force her to look me in the eye. I need to see this. Yeah, there's something more in her eyes. This isn't just a neighbor's kindness.

"That accident was bad." Her eyes glance toward the dayroom where everyone else is, but I don't release her chin.

"Yeah," I confirm. There's no way I can tell her how bad it was.

"I'm sorry," she whispers.

For once, there's no arguing, no hateful words falling from her beautiful pink lips. Her eyes are watery but not because I made her cry. She hates me. She's been avoiding me, but right now, I don't care. She won't admit it, but she cares. I can see it in her eyes.

Cupcakes and donuts are sweet, but I need more today. I'm probably going to lose some limbs here, but it's worth the risk. I need her. Before she comes to her senses and plunges us into an artic river, I pull her into my arms and hold her as if my life depended on it. Maybe today it did.

The protest I expected rests in the background. It's faint, but I feel it there. However, the push, the slap, the punch in the stomach never comes. When her arms wrap around my waist, I sink into her. I miss this. I miss her. One of my biggest regrets was keeping her a secret years ago. I shouldn't have done it. The teenage boy I was didn't know what else to do. The man I am now needs to figure out what went wrong and fix it.

The warmth of her body seeps into mine, taking away the numbness. Death is being replaced with life. This is what I needed. Unsure of how long we have to peacefully exist together like this, I tighten my hold on her. Her floral scent envelops me. Flowers and sugar fill my nostrils. It's perfect. She's perfect. Wait. Sugar? That's a cupcake.

Opening my eyes, I find a cupcake being waved near my face. I'm going to hurt somebody. My eyes move from the cupcake to glare at the fool holding it.

"Last one," Levi smirks at me.

Katie startles and rushes out of my arms. The sheriff has four sons. Maybe he won't miss one. If this was Luke, I'd already be all over him. I happen to like Levi.

"Thanks." I snatch the cupcake, not really wanting it.

"Your girl did good." Levi grins at Katie.

"I'm not his girl," Katie snaps, lifting her chin.

"Yeah," Levi drags the word out. "Keep telling yourself that." Not waiting for the fallout he created, he goes back to the dayroom.

"Ugh!" Katie throws her hands up and heads for the exit.

"Wait!" I call out. Setting the cupcake on a table in the hallway, I hurry to catch up with her. "Don't leave like this."

"Like what?" she snaps. Anger flashed in her eyes. "Like I have some sense?"

What? This is making my head hurt.

"Katie, you're not stupid." Grabbing her arm, I turn her to face me. "I don't understand you sometimes, but you're far from stupid."

"I have to go." She jerks her arm from me and storms out the door.

When she reaches her jeep, I catch up with her again and snatch the keys from her hand.

"Hey! Give me those!" Katie shouts.

Her attempts to take the keys from me are fruitless. I don't hold back my feelings. After the day I've had, I couldn't mask my emotions if I tried. I'm tired of doing it anyway.

"No." I pocket her keys and push her back against the jeep. My eyes bounce back and forth between hers. I look like a madman, but I can't control it. "You can't leave like this. It's too dangerous."

"You're dangerous." Her eyes narrow as her chest heaves.

"And don't you ever forget it." I rarely ever snap. Today is just one of those days.

"Let me go," she demands.

"No." I lean into her space and cup her face in my hands. "I can't. I can't let you leave when your upset." Shaking my head, I pin her body with mine. "I can't clean you up off the side of the road. It's hard enough when it's a stranger. I *can't* do it with you."

That took the fight out of her. She huffs out a breath and looks away. I don't release my hold on her. I can't risk her darting off.

"Everything okay here?" Chief Foster asks behind me.

"No," I admit. "She can't leave angry."

"Okay, son." Chief Foster pats my back. It's not comforting. "Drive her home."

"I can drive," Katie insists.

"You can drive tomorrow," Chief Foster said calmly. "Miles is driving you home today."

"Mom went to the hospital for a friend. She's going to stay with Chloe." My eyes stay focused on Katie's face.

"Okay. You drive her to Chloe, and Levi will follow you so you have a ride back." Chief Foster folds his arms across his chest and waits.

"But I can drive." Katie's voice drops, but she looks the Chief in the eye.

"He needs this, Katie. Give it to him." Chief Foster nods his head once.

Her shoulders drop, but she nods her head in agreement. "Okay."

Even though I've won this battle, it feels like I'm losing the war. I release her and slowly take a step back. She scurries around and gets in the passenger seat. I won't sleep tonight but knowing she's safe will ease my mind a little.

"I got him." Levi steps forward and puts his hands on my shoulders. Chief Foster goes back inside. "Take a few deep breaths. You can't drive upset either, my friend."

He's right. After a few deep breaths, I nod my head. Katie will hate me even more for doing this. Knowing she's home safe will be worth the backlash I'll get from her later. Once my emotions are no longer raging, I get in and drive her to my parent's house. I'll make sure Katie and Chloe are okay, and then I'll call mom to check on her.

Chapter Eight

Katie

I'm going to kill Megan Sanders. Okay. Not kill, but seriously maim. She needs to mind her own business. The way that girl has her nose in everybody's lives, she can't have a serious day job. A gossip blog cannot support her. She needs to get a life. The girl is insane.

Flames at the Fire Department

Emotions were running high at Hayden Falls Fire Department yesterday. Our favorite firefighting Hero had his hands full. He was so close to our little floral beauty you couldn't get a petal between them.

Could all those angry words shouted around town by those two for years be a farse? Did something stem between them when we weren't looking? Are the flames from them truly from anger? Or, are they a steamy secret hidden in plain sight?

Hayden Falls, I guess we will have to keep our eyes on these two for a while.

After reading Megan's horrendous post, I tossed my phone on my desk. Calling her wouldn't do any good. Whenever someone does that, she laughs and posts another article. The crazy woman thrives on gossip. There's no way I'll pick up the phone and feed her obsession. There's also no way I can show my face in town today. I don't have to walk out into the town square anyway because everybody is coming here. We've had three customers in less than thirty minutes just to look around. They are fooling no one. These people don't want flowers. They're only here to look at me.

This is all Miles' fault. If he hadn't gone all caveman yesterday, I wouldn't be gossip blog headline news and the freak show for the day. Were these nosy busybodies knocking on the door at the fire station today too? Of course not. Our wonderful firefighting Hero's shift ended at 8 am this morning.

I'm sure Chief Foster would put everybody who showed up at the station in their place. I don't have that luxury here. I had Bailey, but she can only do so much. Maybe I could get Lucas Barnes to detour people away from Petals for a few days. The east side of the square was his section when he was on day shift. I still don't understand the program the city council talked Sheriff Barnes into. Maybe I could use it to my advantage here. No, it wouldn't be right to ask Lucas to intervene for me on something like this. I was just going to have to tough it out.

The bell over the door jingled again. Ugh! Plopping my elbows on the desk, I dropped my head into my hands. Customer number four and it's not even 10 am yet. This is ridiculous. Maybe I could put a sign on the door saying *a fee is required upon entry*. Or maybe, *one question will be answered per purchase*. That last one might not be a bad idea. Mom would lose her mind though, so it's a no.

At least Miles can go home and escape this madness. After yesterday, he sure needed some peace. No, I'm not going soft here. I'm just not a heartless person. Even though that's the persona I publicly display where he's concerned. Privately? Well, I refuse to talk about that.

After Miles left me at his parent's house yesterday, I focused mainly on Chloe for a while. She finished up her homework at the kitchen table while I fixed dinner. Spaghetti was one of Chloe's favorite meals and easy enough to fix. She filled me in on everything happening at school. Talking with her helped to settle my nerves. Arguing with Miles takes a lot out of me.

When Chloe went upstairs to get ready for bed, I settled on the couch with my phone. I was going to read an eBook but decided to search for the accident the fire department helped with. Seeing those mangled vehicles broke my heart. A couple of them were unrecognizable. It explained why every member of the fire department was walking around like zombies yesterday. I could feel their pain, Miles' pain. I don't know how they do their jobs.

"Hey. Hey." Beth taps on the door before walking in.

"Hey, Beth." I wave and slouch down in my chair.

"Oh, girl. You need this." She sets a large coffee on my desk.

"Thanks." I take a sip and almost spit it out. "Beth! This is *not* a Peppermint Mocha."

"No, girl." Beth sits down in the chair in front of my desk and points at the cup in my hand. "That is an Irish Cream. Extra on the Irish."

"This is *not* just coffee," I point out.

"Irish Cream is not supposed to be *just* coffee," Beth informs me.

"How much whiskey is in this?" I ask.

"Just a double shot." Beth shrugs like it's no big deal.

"You've read it." It's not a question. I know she's read Hayden's Happenings.

"I read it every morning and if it's good, I'll read it again before going to bed." Beth takes a sip of her coffee. I wonder if she has an Irish Cream too.

"Will you be reading it before bed tonight?" I set my cup down. I don't care what she says, there's more than a double shot in this cup.

"Girl, please." Beth flips her hand at me. "I've read it five times this morning."

Her laughter has me dropping my head into my hands again. This is not funny. The doorbell jingles again. This day is getting worse by the minute.

"Miles Hamilton, huh?" Beth sounds like a gossiping teenager. That high pitch is her nosy voice. "You, my dear friend, have been holding out on us. I need the details."

"So do I," Sammie says from the doorway.

"Me too." Glancing up, I find Ally peering over Sammie's shoulder.

"There's nothing to tell." I cross my arms and pout.

"That's a lie," Beth said.

"Yes, it is." Sammie walks over and leans against the desk.

"Yeah," Ally agrees.

They're right. It is, but I can't tell them the truth. No one can ever know what happened between me and Miles.

The doorbell jingles again. I groan and shake my head. Can't a national disaster strike so I can go home?

Ally, still standing in the doorway, looks over her shoulder at the new customer and frowns. "That would be Ms. Taylor."

Oh, no. I slap my hand to my forehead. Be careful what you wish for. That woman *is* a national disaster.

"We need a girl's night so we can continue this conversation," Beth suggested.

A girl's night sounds great, but we certainly do not need to continue this conversation. The matter needs to die right here. Sadly for me, it will never happen in this town. This will go on for days. Maybe I could talk mom into letting me take a vacation to the Bahamas for about a month.

"Friday night at Cowboys?" Ally asked.

They're all agreeing. I'm about to give in and say yes, but Ms. Taylor's loud voice from the other room grates on my last nerve.

"No." I point at Beth. "I can't wait that long. It's tonight."

A Wednesday night out drinking is uncommon, but we're doing this.

"Okay. We'll all meet at Cowboys around six." Beth sounds pleased.

My eyes fall to the cup of Irish Cream coffee on my desk. I'll have to make a pot of coffee in the breakroom and coffee this drink down after Beth leaves.

"No." I lift my chin. "We're going to O'Brien's Tavern."

The other three nod their heads. We rarely go to the tavern. No one will be expecting this. That's why it's perfect.

"Okay. O'Brien's it is," Ally said.

"You will tell us everything, right?" Sammie grins at me. "Or, do I have to ask my dad?"

Well, her father is the Fire Chief, but he can't tell her everything. Oh, she would get a replay of what happened at the station, but she wouldn't know the whys. She can never know the whys. I've never told anyone the whys.

"No promises." I grin back at her.

Thankfully, my friends leave the matter be and head for the door. Now, I have to go out front and deal with Ms. Taylor. Plus, ever how many more nosy people show up before we close at four. Six o'clock at O'Brien's is looking really good right now. I just have to survive the next six hours until closing. It's going to be a long day.

Chapter Nine

Katie

$\mathcal{P}$etals had a revolving door today. I wanted to jerk the bell down and throw it in the trash. This was worse than a holiday. Sales were great though. I worked this little gossip nonsense to my favor. Bailey and I sweet-talked everyone who graced us with their presence. Several people chose an arrangement off the shelves or placed an order. The others bought a single rose or a balloon in their favorite color. Was it underhand of me to use this? Yes, it was. If they were going to gawk at me, they were going to pay to do so.

Unlike Cowboys, O'Brien's Tavern was on the outskirts of town. Ally and Sammie were waiting in the parking lot when I arrived. Since Beth was running late, we went inside and grabbed a table. O'Brien's wasn't really busy. There were about a dozen people here, including us.

We wouldn't be able to turn this into a real girl's night out with lots of drinking and dancing tonight. After all, it was the middle of the week and we all had to work tomorrow. However, getting together with my friends was relaxing, no matter the reason behind it. Let's face it, after the day I just had, I needed to relax.

We didn't have to wait long for Beth to get here. She was less than ten minutes behind us. We stared at Beth with our mouths open when she walked in. This was bad. Beth didn't appear to think so though. She was beyond excited. E, on the other hand, was fuming. She shouldn't be here and it wasn't because she was pregnant.

E dropped down in the chair between me and Sammie. Beth didn't notice there was a problem. She was already signaling the bartender over to our table. It was a slow night. I didn't see a waitress.

"What can I get you lovely ladies?" Duncan O'Brien asked as he tossed a towel over his shoulder. I don't know how he mixes an Irish and country accent, but oh how they work on him.

"We all will have an Irish Hot Whiskey." Beth held up her hands and wiggled in her seat.

Those were great back in December at the Tree Lighting Ceremony. We're all hooked on them now. I'm not sure if they're what tonight calls for though.

"Water." E huffed and folded her arms over her chest.

It wasn't often E Hayes, well she's E Maxwell now, got angry. Right now, I believe she could strangle Beth without any help.

"She needs more than water," Beth tells Duncan. "Just nothing with alcohol in it."

"Water," E repeats firmly.

"No problem, little mama, I have you." Duncan holds up his hands as if he's surrendering and goes to the bar.

"Are you okay?" I ask E.

"No." E shakes her head. She won't look at Beth.

"Beth, what did you do?" Ally bluntly asked.

"Nothing." Beth seems clueless. It's fake. She knows the issue. "Everything is fine."

"It's not fine." E slaps her hands flat against the table. "You caused me to lie to my husband."

Oh, no. This is worse than I thought. We need to call this night and leave right now. We can reschedule a girl's night for Friday at Cowboys.

"Aiden doesn't know you're here." Sammie looked from E to Beth.

"Hey." Beth held up her hands. "I didn't say where we were going."

"That's no excuse." I can't believe Beth would do this to E. "The Crawfords come here. You know Aiden doesn't like them."

Actually, both Crawford brothers are at the pool tables with a few of their friends. Beth has been out of control since the Tree Lighting Ceremony back before Christmas. Her drinking has gotten a little worse every week. But this, this is beyond wrong. Everyone in town knows how long it took for Aiden and E to get together. Undermining their relationship like this is one of the worst things Beth could do.

"I don't know what their little feud is about, but they need to get over it." Beth sits up straight as Duncan sits our drinks on the table.

"This is small town, USA." E taps the table with her finger. "In Montana, no less. Men don't just get over feuds here."

Usually, Duncan was as flirty as Noah Welborn was. It must be a bartender thing. Then again, it's also more than half the men in this town's thing if I'm being honest. Tonight, Duncan has an awkward smile on his face. I hand him my credit card and point to the check on his serving tray. We'll have this one drink and get out of here.

"Okay. Raincheck on girl's night." I raise my glass. The others raise theirs. Well, E twists the cap off her bottle of water and leans back in her chair.

"Hello, ladies." Phillip Crawford walks over and places his hand on the back of my chair.

"Nice of you to join us." Roman walks up behind Beth's chair.

"We're not *joining* you." Ally glares at Roman.

"We're going to drink this and go." I wave the Crawford brothers away but they don't leave.

"You just got here." Phillip's fingers brush against my shoulder. The slight touch causes my body to tense.

"Guys, why don't you go back to the pool tables?" Duncan suggests as he hands me back my credit card.

"I can take you home," I tell E, ignoring Phillip.

"No need." E shakes her head.

"You called him, didn't you." Beth huffs out a breath.

"Of course, she did," Aiden's deep voice says from behind us. His eyes shoot daggers into Roman.

"I don't want any trouble." Duncan steps between Aiden and Roman. "The last time you two came to blows in here, you destroyed half my tavern."

A bad situation turns far worse. Aiden is not alone.

"There will be no trouble," Spencer assures Duncan. He turns to Beth. "Little sister, we need to talk."

"Again," Beth whines.

Tonight, we'll let Spencer deal with Beth. As big brother, he gets the first chance at helping her. Soon, the girls and I need to plan an intervention or something. Until tonight, I hadn't realized how much Beth was spiraling out of control. The Beth we knew would never hurt E like this. This *I don't care* attitude of hers was a problem. We can't let our friend continue to drown in her troubles.

"Come on, Sunshine." Aiden put his arm around E. "Let's go home."

I stand up to go after them. I feel bad for how this played out tonight and needed to talk to Aiden. E had no idea Beth was bringing her here. When I suggested coming to O'Brien's Tavern, I knew E wouldn't be able to come tonight. She's perfectly content with staying home and cuddling up with her husband. Before I can get away from the table, Phillip steps in front of me.

"Why don't you stick around for a while? Let the little married lady go home." Phillip leans into my personal space. "I'll buy you a drink."

A drink? Is that what this idiot thinks a woman wants? Maybe it's all his small mind can comprehend. I don't know what's up with him lately, but Phillip Crawford has never talked to me like this before. We've spoken plenty of times in passing around town, but that's it. Has he run out of women around here to chase? Before I can tell this fool off, a body wedged between us.

"Stay away from her," Miles hisses through clenched teeth.

"You ain't man enough to handle her." Phillip gives Miles a cocky grin.

Phillip winks at me. Gross. Oh, no. He's only acting this way with me to rile Miles up.

"Back off." Miles pushes Phillip away.

Phillip starts to swing but I step in front of Miles, stopping him. Phillip holds his hands out and backs away.

"Another time, maybe," Phillip smirks.

I'm not sure if he's talking to me or Miles. Either way, the thought of this man near me turns my stomach.

Strong hands grab my hips and turn me toward the door. When we get outside, Aiden and E are already pulling out of the parking lot. Hopefully, he won't be too mad at her because of what we did. Maybe I can catch him in town tomorrow to take the blame for all of this. It was my idea after all, but Beth knew better than to bring our friend here.

Spencer and Beth are arguing outside his truck. My heart breaks for Beth. Her pain is something I know. I haven't dealt with my own issues. I'm not sure how we are going to help my friend, but we have to try. We're slowly losing Beth and that can't happen.

Spencer snatches her keys from her hand and tosses them in my direction. Miles reaches out and catches them with ease. He's here to help Spencer with Beth, not for me. Yet, he doesn't remove his other hand from my hip even after we reach my jeep.

"We need to talk," Miles whispers in my ear.

"We've said enough," I say over my shoulder.

His fingers on my waist move. It's not much but it makes my body aware of how close he is. The memory of those hands, and what they can do, haunt my nights. Alone in bed at night is the only time when I can't control my thoughts and memories. During the day, I fight them with everything I have in me.

"Tell me what I did." His lips are so close to my ear that I can feel the heat of his breath run down my neck.

"You know what you did." My voice cracks.

"I don't. I swear to you I don't. Meet me somewhere and talk to me," Miles pleads.

"I can't talk about it." I swallow the lump in my throat.

"Why?"

"It hurts," I admit.

"I want to fix this." Miles presses his body closer to mine.

This is too much. I can't think clearly with him this close. He makes me want to forget what happened. My body wants to turn around and wrap my arms around him, but I can't.

"You can't fix it." I reach for the door handle. "I want you to go away and leave me alone."

Instead of releasing me, Miles' arm goes around my waist pulling me back against his chest. My body betrays me and lets him hold me like this for a moment.

His lips brush my ear when he speaks. "That's not happening, Buttercup. You can never get rid of me."

When the coldness surrounds me, I know he's gone. With a jerk, I open the door of my jeep and hop in. Why? Why does he affect me like this? I hate him, and I want him at the same time. My mind is so messed up.

From my review mirror, I see Beth's car pull out of the parking lot behind me. Miles follows me all the way to my house. I breathe a sigh of relief when he doesn't pull into the driveway. Or, was that disappointment? See? My mind is seriously messed up where he's concerned.

Chapter Ten

Miles

Getting Katie to talk to me was like trying to catch a fly with chopsticks. That only happens in the movies. Just when I think I'm making progress with her, she pushes me away again. I don't know what to do, and I'm running out of ideas.

About five years ago, we were close. I've gone over that summer hundreds of times in my mind. The only problem I can see was the fact we kept our relationship a secret. I shouldn't have done it, but it was the only way I could see her. If I had fought harder, maybe we wouldn't be in this mess now. Katie had turned seventeen that June, and I was twenty that April.

I didn't go away to college as a lot of my friends had. Hayden Falls would always be my home and I had no desire to escape it. I've wanted to be a firefighter since I was a little kid. I didn't do this for what some people called hero worship or because girls thought firemen were hot. That could definitely be Luke Barnes' reason, but not me. I wanted to save lives. This was a serious career for me.

I did go to college in Missoula though. I took fire science and administration classes. Most of us at the station have gone to the fire academy to train. Yes, there really is a fire academy. Most people think that only applies to the police department. I took every training course I could get because this was a life-long career for me. Someday, I hope to be Chief.

Katie and I spent over a year sneaking around together. How we pulled that off in a town full of gossipers was beyond me. I thought she was it for me. Maybe she was, but I screwed it up somehow. If I knew what I did wrong, there might be a chance I could fix it, fix us. I missed her.

As much as I try, I can't figure this out. One Saturday night in early August, we slipped away to our favorite spot. I never took her to the waterfall or the lake. Well, not the main area of the lake where everyone else went. We had a special spot a little further down and on the other side of the lake. I wasn't just some punk kid who slipped Katie away for make-out sessions. She was worth more than that. I took her on dates to Missoula every chance we got, but never in Hayden Falls or the surrounding towns.

Sneaking around wasn't ideal and it couldn't go on forever. I had a plan on when it would end. June 10th of the following year would be the end of hiding my relationship with Katie. That magical day would be her eighteenth birthday. On that day, nothing nor anyone would be able to keep us apart. I was going to stand in the middle of the town square and declare my love for her in front of everyone. Sadly, it never happened.

The next weekend, Katie ghosted me. I didn't see her, and she wouldn't take my calls. At one point, I was so insane I knocked on her door. Her father cussed me out and ran me off. Mr. Matthews hated me, but I chanced his anger that night to see Katie.

It was the next weekend when I finally saw her. Two weeks of nothing with her. Two weeks from a magical night together at our spot. We didn't have the happy reunion I was hoping for. I didn't get an explanation of what happened either. No. What I got was a slap across the face. Words I never wanted to hear from her beautiful lips were thrown at me. She hated me and never wanted to see me again. Almost five years later and I still don't know why.

I should listen to her and give Katie what she asked for, but I can't. Call me stubborn. Every Monday morning for weeks now, I've shown up at Petals with a Peppermint Mocha and a Salted Caramel Latte. Bailey thanks me but Katie never does. She simply takes her drink and quietly locks herself in her office. Sooner or later, I'll wear her down and she'll speak to me. At least, I hope so anyway.

This weekend, Katie is in charge of the flowers and balloons for my dad's surprise birthday party at the inn. I'm hoping to use this to strike up a conversation with her. To sweeten the deal today, I even slipped into Sweet Treats and got a half dozen assorted donuts.

Katie was with a customer when I walk in. I quietly slip around the counter to the workroom and set the coffee and donuts on the table. She can yell at me later for being back here. Bailey immediately grabs her coffee and a chocolate-covered donut. She mouths the words *thank you* to me.

Bailey is never quiet. I raise an eyebrow, and she nods toward the front counter. Katie is talking to an irritated Brittney Douglas. I walk over to the doorway and lean my shoulder against the frame. Brittney is angry about some wedding flowers. Guess she found somebody crazy enough to marry her. In high school, she was a self-absorbed cheerleader. I thought she'd go off to college and never return. She was only gone a year. Never heard why she came back. I don't really care.

"This is what Holly wants." Brittney taps her fingernail on a picture.

"If it's in Holly's budget, I'll gladly do this. Just know the colors and designs in these photos will not blend with what Holly has already shown me. They will clash," Katie explains.

Holly? I should have known nobody was marrying Brittney. Holly Laine was a sweet girl. I never understood how she and Brittney were friends.

"Just do your job." Brittney huffs out a breath and rolls her eyes.

Katie sounds as if she's about ready to pull her own hair out. Seeing who she's dealing with, it's understandable. Hoping to give her a little break and a moment of happiness, I grab the Peppermint Mocha and take it to the counter.

"Here you go, Buttercup." I set the coffee on the counter in front of Katie and rub her back with my other hand.

"Hey, Miles," Brittney said in a sugary tone.

I glare at the woman and dip my chin in reply. I don't like how she's talking to Katie. It's best I stay quiet, or I'll pop something smart off to her.

"It's good to see you." Brittney smiles and bats her eyes.

Is this woman serious? I stare blankly at her. I can't even bring myself to speak to her. The last thing I need to do is to cost Katie a customer. It's the only reason I stay quiet. Brittney can go, but Holly doesn't deserve to lose her wedding florist. Oddly enough, Katie's back stiffens, and she steps away from my touch.

"Well," Brittney finally gets the hint. "I'll see you around." With a little wave and a sly smile, she's out the door.

I don't know who she was talking to, but it darn sure wasn't me. She'd be better off going to the bank and trying her luck with Roman Crawford. She sure chased after him in high school.

When I turn my attention back to Katie, she's trembling and breathing hard. She's on the verge of a panic attack or hyperventilating. This makes no sense. Brittney did have her frustrated, but how did an irrational customer turn into this?

"Katie," I say in a soft tone as I reach for her.

Katie spins to face me. She twisted up with so many emotions, I have no idea what she's feeling right now. She removed the lid from her coffee and throws it in my face. Thank goodness it had cooled down some. With all of my training, nothing prepared me for this. Bailey calls out, but Katie doesn't hear her. Before she can make it to the safety of her office, I regain my senses and catch up with her.

"What was that about?" I demand as I push her back against the wall.

"Go away!" Katie shouts.

"Not until you tell me what just happened." My voice is stern, but I'm not shouting.

Katie shakes her head and squeezes her eyes shut as tears begin to fall. What in the world? How do I help her?

"Why did you throw your coffee on me?" I ask. She struggles, but I hold her firmly against the wall.

"You." She sobs. "Her." Another sob. "You."

Okay. That tells me nothing.

"Me? Her who?" I cannot piece this together.

Katie's chest heaves with each breath she takes. She glances toward the front door of the shop. Surely, not. She did tense up when Brittney was here. She can't believe that meant anything to me.

"Brittney?" I ask in disbelief.

"I hate you," Katie cries. "I hate her." Her sobs wreck me. "I lo…"

She clamps her hands over her mouth and sinks to the floor. Bailey rushes to her side. I'm so stunned I can't move.

"Is everything okay?" a man asked.

I glance over my shoulder to find Lucas Barnes walking toward us. Can this idiot not see that things aren't alright? Some cop he is. I glare at him like the idiot he is.

"Katie?" Lucas steps closer to her.

Katie only cries. Bailey looks up and shakes her head at Lucas. He's talking, but I don't hear what he's saying. Unsure of what to do, I kneel in front of Katie. She's broken, and I want to wrap my arms around her. She's so hysterical, my touch will only make it worse.

The next thing I know, I'm being pushed out of the way. Levi is in front of Katie with a medical bag. He and I have had EMT training.

"Katie, it's Levi." He talks softly and reaches to touch her forearm. She looks up, and Levi nods. "I need you to take some deep breaths with me. Okay?"

He talks her through a few breaths before putting an oxygen mask on her face. Bailey helps Levi move Katie to the breakroom. Lucas grabs my arm and pulls me out the front door. Unsure of what's going on, I go willingly.

"You need to stop coming here." Lucas stands between me and the door of Petals. "If I need to put a restraining order on you, I will."

"Are you insane!" That snapped me out of my shocked state.

Sammie comes running by. Her apartment and art studio are above the jewelry store, one building over from Petals. She rushed into the flower shop without stopping to speak. I go to follow, but Lucas blocks my path.

"I will arrest you if I have to," Lucas threatens. He can throw that deputy tone away. It doesn't work on me.

"For what?" I shout.

"Nobody is getting arrested." Spencer takes my arm. He and Aiden walk me over to my truck.

"What happened?" Aiden asked.

"I don't know." I throw my hands up. "It has something to do with Brittney."

"Brittney Douglas?" Spencer scrunches his face up.

"Yeah, buddy, I'm as confused as you are." I lean back against the truck. There's nothing else I can do here anyway.

E comes running down the sidewalk. Aiden leaves us to catch up with his wife.

"Slow down there, Sunshine." He gives her a kiss before letting her go inside to Katie.

"Why don't you go home?" Spencer suggested. "We'll call you when we know what's going on."

Releasing an infuriated scream, I run my fingers through my hair and tug on the ends. How is this my life right now?

Levi walks out of Petals alone. That's a good sign. He wouldn't have left Katie if she wasn't okay. Hopefully, Sammie, E, and Bailey can keep Katie calm. It doesn't matter what I say or do, they're not going to let me go back in there.

"How is she?" I ask.

"I don't really want to call it a panic attack but it's close. She's an emotional mess though." Levi looks toward Petals and back to me. "It has something to do with you."

I never told him there was anything between me and Katie, but after the day she showed up at the station, he figured it out. Thankfully, Levi doesn't push matters or pry in people's business. It's one of the reasons he and I get along so well.

"I thought you said this had something to do with Brittney," Spencer said.

"That part I can't figure out." I cross my arms over my chest and lean against the truck again.

"What did you do to her?" Aiden asked.

"I don't know that either," I admit and point to my shirt. "And that's why I'm wearing coffee."

"Come on, man." Aiden motions toward the diner. "It's lunchtime."

As much as I don't want to leave, I have no choice. It's what's best for Katie. If I cause her this much pain, I'll have to stay away from her from now on. I can't be the reason she falls apart like this. I care about her too much. I may never get to say how I feel about her out loud, but I can't hurt her again. It'll destroy me, but I'll give her what she asked for that night at O'Brien's. I'll leave her alone.

Chapter Eleven

Katie

I hate Mondays. I hate people. I hate Miles Hamilton. Maybe all of it isn't really true. Hate has been simmering in me for so long it's now consuming me. I don't want to feel this way. It hurts, and I can't process it all anymore. Not that I was doing a great job of it to start with.

I've stopped reading Hayden's Happenings. It doesn't matter if I read the gossip blog or not. Everyone in town is talking about me. They don't whisper as quietly as they think they do. Nosy idiots. My emotional breakdown is the main topic this week. Next week, it'll be something else. I'm sure my best friends are reading everything, but they're not sharing it with me.

Just remembering what happened Monday at Petals breaks me all over again. That's why I'm sitting here today. If anyone had ever told me I'd one day need a therapist, I would have laughed in their face or punched them in it. Yet, here I am. Thankfully, I'm not alone.

E reaches over and takes my hand. "Take your time."

"My appointment is in five minutes," I remind her.

"Actually," she drags the word out. "You have thirty-five minutes."

"What?" I snap my head toward her. "You said we needed to be here at two."

E squeezes my hand again and gives me a small smile. Her eyes are full of understanding and love.

"This is your first appointment, and it's up to you if you continue with them or not. This one can be hard, so I gave you a little cushion time," E explains.

Relief washes over me. If anyone understands how hard this is, it's E. Rachel Montgomery is the therapist she started seeing last year after her ex-boyfriend attacked her. Our reasons for seeing a therapist are different. I wasn't attacked, but I'm holding onto a lot of pain.

When I broke down on Monday, E suggested I talk to someone who wasn't a close friend or a family member. Her wording it that way convinced me to do this. The word therapist makes me feel as though I'm insane. Who knows, maybe I am.

When I agreed, E didn't give me time to change my mind. She called Rachel and had this appointment booked within minutes. I wanted to refuse this one and reschedule for a later date so I could prepare myself for it. Due to a cancelation, this was the only open spot Rachel had for over a month. After what happened Monday, I probably shouldn't wait that long.

It takes me a full twenty minutes before I'm finally ready to go inside. By the time I have all of my paperwork filled out with the secretary, Rachel is saying goodbye to a teenage girl and calling me back to her office. Her office is decorated much as I expected. A desk, a chair for her, and a big comfy couch for me.

We start out my session with just me and Rachel. Introductions and pleasantries are passed. My voice is weak, but I manage those okay. After nearly ten minutes of sitting quietly and staring at the floor, Rachel decides to get E since I did approve her to join us. E sits down next to me on the couch and pulls me into her arms.

"Close your eyes and pretend this is girl's night. We're having a sleepover with movies and root beer floats." E rests her head against mine. A visual of her suggestion makes me smile.

"When you're ready, Katie, tell us about your Monday," Rachel says in a soft voice.

"I don't really remember everything that happened," I admit. "No one has told me anything."

"You don't have to remember everything, or what other people did or think about it. Tell me about *your* Monday. Let's talk about what you thought, did, and experienced," Rachel said.

Okay. I think I can do as she asked. With my eyes still closed, I snuggle closer to E and start talking. Rachel is so easy to talk to. Her soft voice relaxes me, and I freely describe everything I remember from the time I opened Petals on Monday. When we get to the part where I broke down, someone places a few tissues in my hands. I'm too broken to open my eyes.

"Why is Miles important to you?" Rachel's question throws me for a loop.

I don't want to answer her, but I do. "I loved him."

E shifts beside me, but she doesn't release her hold on me. I have never said those words out loud before. It's strange saying them now.

"How long did you two date?" Rachel asked. Looks like she's not shy about asking the hard questions.

"A little over a year," I reply.

"Why did you keep the relationship a secret?" Rachel asked hard question number two. How did she figure that out?

"I was sixteen when we first started dating. I was still a minor, and my father hated him." I pause and take a deep breath. "But, I don't know why."

My father was another subject I didn't like talking about. Truth be told, he hated everybody, his family included. Two years ago, he left my mom and hasn't been back to Hayden Falls since. It's okay. We're better off without him. My brother, Elliot, lashed out at first but even he accepts it now.

"What ended the relationship?" Rachel pushes me for more but not in a demanding way. We're on a roll here, so why stop now?

There's more than one answer to her question. I'm not sure I can do this anymore. Being here was a bad idea. I start to push away, but E pulls me closer.

58

"I know it's hard, but I'm here. You don't have to carry this alone anymore. Let me help you," E whispers.

Alone. She's right. That's exactly what I've been doing. It's too much. I can't keep doing this anymore. E truly cares for me, and she's trying to help. Will she still love me if she knows it all?

"Brittney ended it and I …" I pause. There's more, and it's the part I'm not ready to share.

"How did Brittney end your relationship?" Rachel asked calmly.

"It was a Saturday. I was supposed to see Miles later that night." I close my eyes again as the memories come back. "I was at the diner with my mom. Brittney and her friends were at the table next to us. When my mom went to the restroom, Brittney went into detail about being with Miles at the waterfall the night before. She spared nothing. She gave every sordid detail. She said he told her he loved her, and they would leave Hayden Falls together by Christmas."

E's arms tighten around me. More tissues are pushed into my hands as the shredded pieces I was holding are taken away.

"Did you see Miles that night?" Rachel continued to search for more about the situation. She's already sensed it and knows I am hiding something.

"No," I replied. "I couldn't."

"You never let Miles explain?" E asked.

Until this point, E let Rachel ask all the questions. Pushing away slightly, I sat up and looked her in the eye. She wasn't judging me as I expected people would. I shake my head.

"When you're strong enough, you should let Miles explain that," Rachel suggested.

"No," I snapped and wildly shook my head.

"Why couldn't you see Miles that night?" Rachel tilted her head. How can she sit there so calmly?

"I wasn't even in Hayden Falls that night." Defeated, I drop my head and let more tears fall.

"Breathe." E gently rubs her hand back and forth across my back. "Where did you go?"

This is the hardest part. This is the part I wished I could change. Sadly, it's the part I had no control over. Well, at least that's what I was told. My family and friends don't know my secret but a handful of strangers do. I doubt any of them remember it.

"I left the diner and just started driving. I think Brittney knew I liked Miles. I heard her laughing when I ran out the door." E started to speak, but I held my hand up. If I was going to share this, I had to do it now. "I had to pull over on the side of the road to throw up. I was an emotional mess and the pain was unbearable. I ended up in the emergency room in Missoula."

"I'm so sorry." E continues to soothe me by rubbing my back. "At least you caught the early signs of a panic attack and got help even if you didn't realize what it was at the time."

A panic attack? If only that was what it was. I glanced at Rachel. She was sitting calmly in her chair. Her face was unreadable. This wasn't her life so why would she show any emotions. Turning back to E, I swallow hard. If I'm going to give up my secrets, I'll give them to one of my best friends, to someone I trusted with my life.

"It wasn't a panic attack." I choke back a sob. Here goes everything. "I lost everything that night. I lost Miles. I lost me." More sobs wreck my entire body. "I lost us. Us, E. I lost us."

When she doesn't fully piece it together, my gaze drops to her stomach and back to her eyes. I can't see through my tears.

"Oh, Katie," E cries and wraps her arms around me in the tightest hug I've had in my life.

Chapter Twelve

Katie

$\mathcal{S}$tanding in the corner of the Grand Room at The Magnolia Inn, I watch as the Hamilton family and their friends shout *'Surprise'* at Ben Hamilton, Miles' father. I whisper along as they launch into the *Happy Birthday* song. The flowers and decorations around the room are beautiful. I must say, E and I did a fantastic job organizing this party. As proud as I am of this event, I feel out of place here.

Watching this family's happiness twists a knife in my heart. I have to turn away to hide my emotions. I've already checked the 50th birthday balloon display twice, but I do it again to have something to do. When I can no longer hide behind the balloons, I walk around the edge of the room going over the food and table centerpieces on my chart. Sadly for me, nothing is out of place.

Longing fills me as my gaze sweeps over the Hamilton family again. I wanted this to be my family. It was supposed to be my family. Sadly, I no longer have my connection to them. Tears prick my eyes as I turn away again. If I'm going to be here, I need to stay in the background. Slowly, I start making my way back around the room so

I can disappear to the kitchen. Before I can escape, Mile's sister catches me.

"Hey." Chloe throws her arms around me. "It's beautiful."

"Thank you." I hug her back, careful to not hit her with the clipboard in my hand. "How's school?"

"I'll be glad when it's over." Chloe sighs dramatically.

"Well, you have another year and college," I remind her.

"No." Chloe slaps her hand to her chest and falls against me. Maybe she should try acting. She's very good at it.

"Hey, Katie." Natalie, Chloe and Mile's older sister, rushed up to hug me.

"Hey, Nat." I plaster on a fake smile. I don't want her to see my pain. "I'm glad you could make it."

"I wouldn't miss it." Natalie's face beams with pride as we watch her parents dance. "Sadly, I won't be able to stay for Miles' birthday though."

Taking a deep breath, I nod my head. Miles' birthday is six days away on April 5th. My eyes automatically seek him out. He's across the room talking to Spencer and Aiden. Our eyes lock for a moment before he looks away and turns his back to me. Wow. That hurt.

"Excuse me please," I say. "I need to check something in the kitchen right quick."

Instead of going to the kitchen, I hurry down the hallway to E's office. She left it unlocked in case I needed a private escape today. I drop down onto the sofa and lean my head back against the cushions. Closing my eyes, I start the breathing exercises Rachel and E taught me. They help most of the time. It's only been two days since my appointment with Rachel. My issues aren't going to go away overnight, but I've had to do these breathing exercises for over thirty minutes a few times to calm down. I may one day heal from most of it, but one part will always be a hole in my heart.

E comes in and sits down beside me. Without speaking, she takes my hand in hers. Words aren't needed right now. After I spilled my secret, my friend didn't push or ask any more questions. To her, my well-being was more important than knowing the answers to questions

I'm not ready to answer. It's only been two days, and E is already the wall of strength I need.

Thursday, after the session with Rachel, E carried me to her house for a sleepover. There was no way I could go home. My mom and grandmother would have asked too many questions. Aiden went to his parent's house for a few hours so we could talk. Only, we didn't talk, and we didn't call our other friends to join us. E sat with me on their couch with root beer floats in hand and cried with me. She has such a loving nature. She's going to be a great mom.

"I thought I could do this, but I can't." I break the silence.

"You're healing, Katie. There's no time limit on when that happens. You don't have to hurry. You tried today and that's brave. Baby steps will get you to bigger steps," E said.

I stare at my friend in awe. How did the quiet shy girl become so wise? When I went home yesterday, she called twice and texted several times to just check in with me. All of my friends are great, but E is the one with the biggest heart.

"Baby steps," I agree. "I can do baby steps."

"Why don't you go back to Petals?" E suggested. "Marcie and Avery will help me oversee everything here."

"I hate leaving you." I want to stay, but I can't.

"Trust me, everything will be fine," she assures me.

It will be fine. No one at the inn will let her overdo it today. Besides, Aiden is here. I doubt E has to lift a finger around him.

"He looks good," I whisper.

"Yeah." E nods her head. "Mr. Hamilton looks great for fifty."

She winks, causing me to laugh. My friend has a loving and playful sense of humor. E is the perfect friend. After giving her a hug, I slip out the back door of the inn. My jeep is parked in the back driveway outside E's old apartment above her aunt and uncle's garage. We planned ahead in case today was too hard for me. I might be weak right now, but I'm not a weak person. Until I'm stronger, E taught me how to plan out escape routes in case I need them. Until she shared this tip with me, I didn't realize she was doing this all of last year.

Of course, this is my life and I can't plan escape routes properly. Stepping outside the kitchen door, I find Aiden, Spencer, and Miles out here.

"The flowers and balloons look great," Spencer said as I walked by.

"Thanks." I wave and keep walking.

"Do you need some help?" Aiden asked.

"No," I reply. "I'm heading back to the shop."

My eyes lock with Miles' and I pause. The happiness he displayed inside the Grand Room is gone. I've avoided getting this close to him today. Now, I can see the dark circles around his eyes.

Miles takes a step toward me. Aiden and Spencer grab his arms, holding him in place. He wants to talk. He's been begging me to do so. We need to talk, but it's too much right now.

"I'm not ready." I give my head a little shake. Hopefully, he'll understand.

Miles nods his head and looks away, but he doesn't speak. He probably doesn't really understand, but at least he's respecting my wishes.

"I'll walk you to your car," Aiden offers.

He puts his hand on my back and nudges me toward the path that leads to the back driveway. We don't speak until we get to my jeep.

"Thanks," I say as I reach for the door handle.

"Are you okay to drive?" Aiden asked. He's always the cop. "If not, I can drive you to Petals and walk back."

It's sweet of him to offer to do that. Aiden is a good man. This town was so wrong about him. I'm glad E has him. He gives me an odd look. He has to see through my fake smile. The way he's acting concerns me. Did E share my secret with her husband?

"You know?" I ask without looking him in the eye.

"I know you saw Rachel and this is serious," Aiden replied. "I don't know the why."

Of course, he knows I saw Rachel. E drove me to that appointment. She does nothing without telling him about it. I hope E keeping my secret isn't causing problems between them. When I go to open the door, Aiden puts his hand over mine. He waits until I look up at him.

"I don't like my wife keeping things from me, but I understand, and respect your privacy." He releases a breath before continuing. "Don't be mad at her. I had her promise me, that if your life was in danger in any way, she'll tell me so I can help keep you safe."

"I'm sorry I asked your wife to keep secrets from you," I apologize. "But, I promise you, my life isn't in danger."

"You have a lot of friends who want to help you." Aiden opens my door for me. "I'm Miles' friend, but I'm yours too."

"That means a lot," I tell him and climb into the jeep.

"Katie." His voice is tender, causing me to pause from starting the engine. "I'm not trying to interfere here and tell you what to do. You're obviously hurting and need time to work it out. Just know, and I'm not sure if it matters to you or not, but Miles is hurting too. He's not taking this lightly. It's not a passing thought or joke to him. More than his own pain, he's concerned about yours."

There's nothing I can say to that. I understand Aiden is trying to help us both. In the end, his loyalty will fall to Miles, as it should. I'm not sure how to process everything he just said. Miles knows nothing of the pain I feel. He wants answers I'm not sure I can ever give him. How do I tell the man I once loved that I lost our child, and I blamed him for it?

Turning to face Aiden, I nod my head. Words won't come right now. Tears will fall, but I'll hold them back until I'm locked away in my office at Petals. Thankfully, Aiden closes my door and lets me drive away.

I have a lot to think about. Technically, I know it's not Miles' fault I lost our baby. It's just been easier blaming him and Brittney for it. It gave my hurt and anger somewhere to go. I should have dealt with my pain years ago. Instead, I gave it a home where it rotted and festered. It grew and crumbled at the same time. I can't keep doing this. I'm only destroying Miles and myself. Can I forgive Miles for cheating on me? Can I forgive myself for everything I lost? If I was stronger back then, would it have changed things? I don't know, but things couldn't stay the way they were.

Chapter Thirteen

Miles

Dad's birthday party was a huge success. My entire family was pleased with the job Katie and E did to make it happen. It was the first time we were able to surprise my dad.

Since Katie's emotional breakdown on Monday, I've been forcing myself to stay away from her. I want answers. No, I need answers. Only, she's too fragile right now to give them to me. Avoiding her wasn't too hard when I didn't have to be around her. It was better when I could turn in the opposite direction from the flower shop or her house. Yesterday, there was no way to avoid her.

Every time I saw her at the party, I made sure to stay on the opposite side of the room. A few times I had to step outside to calm down. One of those times put us in close contact when she was leaving. If I had known she was leaving, I would have stayed inside.

The stolen glances I allowed myself to take of her had ripped me in two. Her smiles were few and they all were fake. Even when she talked to my sisters. Jealousy slammed into me when my sisters hugged her. I wanted to hug her but couldn't. That's when Aiden and Spencer ushered me outside. Both of my friends were watching me close yesterday. It was a good thing because I was on the verge of losing it completely.

Seeing her outside pulled at my need to be near her. My friends stopped me, and I didn't speak. I wasn't able to. The only words spoken between us were from Katie when she said she wasn't ready. Could I find hope in that? Would she talk to me one day soon? I need to know what I did so I can fix it. It's the only reason I'm not pushing. Waiting is hard though.

Today, a few of us gathered at Aiden and E's house for a small party. It was opening day for the MLB and Aiden never missed it. Of course, he was grilling steaks and burgers. It was sad that Aiden never got the pro career he had wanted. My friend gave up everything to save his little brother's future. That's a real hero in my book. I'm just glad Aiden came home. Hayden Falls wasn't the same without him.

I was going to skip this party in fear that Katie might be here. Aiden assured me she wouldn't be. She was having some kind of weird girl's day with Sammie and Ally at Sammie's apartment. Painting and wine. I have no idea how those work together. Beth was here, but things have been a little tense between her and E since the night at O'Brien's Tavern.

There were a few things Aiden Maxwell was serious and passionate about. Naturally, his cute little wife and their baby held the top spot. He protected them fiercely. Family and friends were next. Baseball and grilling rounded out his top five things.

Today, there was a little chill in the air, but the temperature was in the high sixties. Not bad for a spring day in Montana. It was a good thing because my friend had set up a big screen tv on the back porch so he could keep up with the games today and grill. His devotion to the game made me laugh. Baseball is kind of slow to me. I've never understood how he gets so worked up over it. Of course, I cheered him on in high school. He did the same for me during football season. I liked football and was good at it, but my heart wasn't in it like some of the guys were.

"Here you go." E hands me a beer.

She walks around the yard handing all the guys one. When she gets to Aiden, she pauses and gives him a kiss. It's not chaste. Those two have no modesty anymore. Happiness looks good on them. A few guys whistle and cheer. I smile and lightly chuckle.

On the way back to the kitchen, E stops near my chair. She looked at me like this yesterday during my dad's party. If I'm reading her right, she wants to say something. More than likely, she wants to lecture me about what she'll do to me for hurting her friend. Best friends did that, right? Girls did anyway. I can't recall a guy ever doing it.

"How are you holding up?" E asked.

Shocking. I wasn't expecting her actually say anything. I shrug because I don't truly know how I'm doing. I'm barely holding it together, but I won't admit it.

"Give her a little time." E pats my shoulder.

"Wait." I grab her wrist and jump to my feet.

I search her eyes. She looks away and then back to me. Something has changed here. I feel it.

"Hey, man!" Aiden yells out.

I wave him off and keep my eyes on E. Big Mistake. Aiden is on me within seconds. Well, he's not hurting me. He's standing behind his little wife.

"Miles, you're my best friend, but let my wife go." Aiden uses his cop tone.

Before Aiden goes all caveman and rips me apart with his bare hands, I release E's wrist. I hadn't meant to grab her like that.

"Sorry," I apologize to her.

"It's okay. You didn't hurt me." She looks over her shoulder at Aiden. "You need to stop doing this."

"Sorry, Sunshine." Aiden shakes his head. "That's not happening. It's built-in."

"E." I draw her attention back to me. I don't feel like hearing these two debating about her strength again. "I asked you before, and you said no. Forgive me here, but I have to ask again. Do you know why Katie hates me?"

She takes a deep breath and her shoulders drop. She doesn't have to answer. I already know.

"I do, but I can't tell you. She has to do it," E replies.

She told me at their wedding she would admit it if she knew, but she would betray Katie's trust. I won't push her for more and not just because Aiden is standing behind her. E can't give me the answers I desperately need but hearing her say this feeds my hope a little more. If Katie is talking about this to someone then maybe one day soon she'll talk to me too.

"Thanks, E." I nod to her and sit back down.

Propping my elbows on my knees, I drop my head into my hands. Two chairs pull up on either side of me. I don't have to look up to know who it is.

"You wanna talk about it?" Spencer asked.

Sitting up, I look between my two best friends. Not only had I kept Katie a secret from this town, but from them too.

"It might help," Aiden said.

"Are you going to tell me what you know?" I asked Aiden.

"I don't know the details." Aiden shakes his head. "All I know is, it concerns you and it's serious."

That's a shocker. I never expected E to keep something from Aiden.

"You really don't know what this is about?" Spencer asked.

"No." Taking off my baseball cap, I run a hand through my hair. Maybe talking about it will help. "I dated Katie for a little over a year about five years ago." Their eyes widen. "Okay. We dated for a little over a year, but we hid it."

Aiden wasn't here five years ago, but we talked on the phone every week. I had plenty of chances to tell him. Spencer was training to be a cop. He was too busy to notice.

"Why did you hide it?" Spencer takes a sip of his beer.

"Her age for one, but mainly because her dad hated me. He refused to let me date her. He would have had me arrested if he found out." I lean back and fold my arms. I shouldn't have been surprised. Katie's dad hated everybody.

"How does Brittney fit into this?" Aiden's face scrunches up. I'm pretty sure it's disgust because it's exactly what I feel when I think of that woman.

"I don't know that either." I shrug. "I can't make sense of any of this. Monday, Katie said it was me, Brittney, and she started to say something about herself, but she clammed up and dropped to the floor."

Aiden shakes his head again. "Sorry, man. I got nothing here."

Really? These two are paid to figure stuff out. Well, when the trained detective can't piece things together it must be bad. What am I missing here?

"Why did you and Katie break up?" Spencer is still digging for answers.

"One weekend we were great. The next one, she ghosted me. I couldn't find her. When I went to her house, her dad ran me off. The next week, I see her in town. She slaps me. She said she hated me and never wanted to see me again." I can tell them no more. That's all I know. I've gone over those two weeks so many times, but there's nothing more.

"Something happened on ghost weekend." Aiden is nodding at Spencer.

"Yep," Spencer agrees.

Seriously? That's all these two trained professional officers of the law can tell me? I knew that much. Our tax dollars are seriously wasted here.

"Maybe I should find Brittney and ask her." I throw my hands up.

"I wouldn't do that." Spencer points at me. He says that like an order, not a suggestion.

"That would be the biggest mistake you could make," Aiden agrees with Spencer.

I agree with both of them. Brittney is the last person I want to talk to. It's just that I'm at my wit's ends here.

"What am I supposed to do?" I ask.

"If you want honest answers, you wait for Katie," Spencer advises.

"I know waiting is hard, but if you talk about this with Brittney, you'll push Katie further away," Aiden said.

"Brittney Douglas will lie to you in a heartbeat." Spencer gets up and grabs us another beer.

"This is just speculation here." Aiden holds up a finger. He's in cop mode. About darn time. "What if Brittney lied to Katie about you?"

Huh? Does he mean as in a relationship? I never thought of that. Brittney was a little flirty with me Monday at Petals. It was the moment Katie tensed up.

"Oh, no." I slap my hand to my forehead. "I guess it's possible."

"It would be one way to tie you three together," Aiden said.

"But, I've never done anything with Brittney. We don't even talk." The thought of being near the hateful woman makes me shudder and turns my stomach.

"Like I said." Spencer pats my back. "Wait for Katie."

"Yeah, I will." It's all I can do anyway.

I guess these two do know what they're doing. I would have never put those pieces together. Hopefully, they're wrong, but it will be something I can easily deny and explain to Katie. It's going to be hard, and I'll probably go insane in the end, but I'll wait this out. I'll have to keep avoiding Katie though. It's the only way I'll be able to hold out.

Chapter Fourteen

Miles

By the time Friday rolls around, I'm emotionally drained. My nights are sleepless and I'm exhausted from doing nothing. It's my birthday, but I'm on duty and can't go home. My friends and fellow firefighters decided to throw me a party at the station to cheer me up. It's great but I'm far from cheery.

This party is not as extravagant as my dad's 50th birthday party last weekend. It's fine with me. My dad deserved that party and more. He's my hero. There's not another man like him. He worked hard to provide for his family. He loves my mom deeply, and to this day, he will boldly show it in public. Mom doesn't really mind. She secretly likes it. After thirty years of marriage, someday, I hope I'm still in love with my wife. So many marriages never make it to five years let alone thirty. Of course, I do need a wife first. My luck in the wife department is not going so great.

E did an amazing job organizing this little party today. The cake came from Sweet Treats. The Hayden Sisters brought the food. When those ladies from church get involved you never have to worry about running out of food. The guys at the station love it. We're going to have leftovers for days.

"Happy Birthday!" My little sister, Chloe, slams into me, wrapping her arms around my waist.

"Thanks, Shorty." I ruffle her hair, earning me her famous eye roll and groan. She hates anyone touching her hair, which means I'll never stop doing it.

"Too bad you had to work today." Chloe hands me an envelope. It's a birthday card. One she no doubtingly made. My little sister is big on crafting. I'll read it later.

"How's school?" I ask about her least favorite subject.

"Okay, I guess." Chloe shrugs. "I want to take dance classes next year, but Mom isn't sure yet."

"They offer dance classes at school?" That's new. I haven't really paid attention to the high school courses since I graduated.

"Next year." Chloe nods. "I hear the teacher may offer extra classes at the gym too."

The excitement on her face is something I haven't seen in a while. I'll talk to Mom and see if I can convince her to let Chloe take dance classes. If she really enjoys dancing, I'll pay for the extra classes at the gym. Chloe sees Marcie Calhoun and hurries over to her. Marcie is a couple of years older, but they've been friends for years. She and Avery are helping E with the party today.

After Chloe walks away, I put the card on the gift table. It's pointless to tell people around here to not buy you presents. They do it anyway. The flower arrangement and balloons on the table are nice. I know where they came from. I've been trying to not look at them for too long. Flowers make me think of her. Especially the ones I know came from her shop.

My eyes catch on something, and everything around me fades away. Gifts don't intrigue me like they do most people. Oh, they're nice, and I appreciate them. I'm more of a giver than a receiver when it comes to gifts. If it hadn't been for me putting Chloe's card here, I probably would have missed the gift hidden here. This might be considered a decoration to anyone else. But to me, this is way more than a gift or decoration.

I reach for the green vase hidden behind wrapped presents, balloons, and fluffy bows. It's simple. There's nothing fancy about it. If you didn't know better, you'd think it didn't belong here. To me, it's the greatest gift here. Money couldn't buy this gift. Inside the slim green vase are three daffodils. I gently rub one of the soft petals between my thumb and index finger. Hope. This is hope and nothing is greater. Plucking the card from the plastic holder, I close my eyes and swallow hard before pulling the card from the tiny envelope. What will these words do to me?

Happy Birthday

It's not a lot, but it's more than I expected. There's no signature, but it doesn't need one. I take out my wallet and slide the card behind where I keep her picture. The edges are tattered, but I haven't been able to pull it out in years. I don't need to. It's forever a memory. I only need to close my eyes to see her blonde hair and blue eyes.

"Thanks, Buttercup," I softly whisper.

My phone dings with a text. It's bound to be someone else wishing me a happy birthday. Pulling my phone from my back pocket, I open the text app. Both of my sisters have bombarded me with Happy Birthday messages and jokes since midnight. Those two didn't care I had to be at work at 8 am for a three-day weekend shift. They're two of my favorite people so I'm not mad.

These new messages surprise me. It's not from a number in my contacts. The first text says Happy Birthday. The two following it are gifs of a firetruck driving down the road and a fireman dancing in his turnouts. Whoever sent these obviously knows me. Three dots appear in the chat window, and a new message pops up.

Look up.

This person is here and watching me. Slowly, I look up, and my heart practically jumps into my throat. Katie is standing across the room just inside the doorway. She slightly lifts her phone up as her eyes dart around the room. Am I imagining this?

Me: Is this really you?

74

Katie looks down at her phone. Her eyes lift to mine for a moment before she types.

Yes.

It's real. She's giving me her phone number. After we had broken up, she changed her number, and nobody in town would give me her new one. Hope is like an ocean right now. Katie glances around the room again before coming back to me. A sad smile tugs at her lips. I sucked in a breath when she turned and disappeared through the door. I don't want her to go. Wait. Does she want me to follow her?

A few people wave and I nod to them as I hurry across the room. I don't want to skip out on my own party, but I need to know if she wants to talk to me. A hollow feeling settles in my chest when I don't see her in the hallway. When I get to the bay, I find Katie standing by the fire engine.

"Hey." I approach her cautiously, stopping a few feet away.

"Happy Birthday." She holds her head high.

She's fighting to be strong. Good for her. I want more. So much more. I want to close the distance between us, but I remain where I am. If this is all I get today, I'll gladly take it.

"Thank you." I hungrily take in every inch of her.

Cowboy boots? She only wears those for special occasions. I feel honored.

"Umm," she stammers and looks around.

We're alone, but someone could come into the bay at any moment. I'm not sure what's happening between us, and I do want to take things at her pace. Sadly, I'm a man, and we can be impatient at times. Okay. A lot of times.

"I'm glad you're here." I take a step closer to her. She doesn't move. "I…"

"We need to talk," Katie blurts out.

"We do," I agree and take another step. This time, she takes a step back. I hold this position. "Name the place and time."

"I'm working on that," she says softly.

Working on it? If she would tell me what the problem is, we could fix this. Waiting is destroying me, but it looks like I have no choice but to wait some more.

"Can I call you?"

She bites her fingernail while she considers this.

"Can we just text for now?"

Text? I want to shout and do a happy dance. It's not a phone call but it's close enough. It's darn sure more than I have now.

"Texting is fine."

"Good." She nods and starts for the door.

"Don't go," I call out.

"I need to." Her hand is on the door, but she doesn't turn around. "Miles?"

"Yeah?"

"I don't hate you." She shakes her head again but still doesn't turn to look at me. I can hear the tears in her voice. "I wanted you to know that."

"I don't hate you either." I never have, and she knows it. I just don't know what else to say without causing her to flee.

The breath she takes lifts her shoulders. What did I do to her? I don't get the answer today. Without another word, Katie opens the door and darts out into the rain. Moving to the doorway, I watch her get into her jeep and drive away.

"Miles!" Chloe calls from across the bay. "It's time to cut the cake."

Chloe rushes over and grabs my hand. Her eagerness makes me smile. Naturally, I drag back a little bit, forcing her to pull me up the stairs. My little sister loves birthday cake. Even with the hollowness in my chest because Katie left, this is the best birthday I've had in quite a while, and I can't skip out on everyone. Katie and I have a connection again. Hopefully soon, I'll know what went so wrong between us.

Chapter Fifteen

Katie

First thing Monday morning, I busied myself with changing the front window display of Petals. I loved the rainbow of vibrant colors in the new arrangements. Spring was one of my favorite seasons to decorate for. Even if the air was chilly, this was a sign of the warm days ahead. Summer was my favorite season. The warm months were filled with town events and family cookouts. Winter was a little depressing for me. With fewer things to do, I felt caged in. Summer was freedom and fun.

Stepping back from the front window, I admired my work from the sidewalk. It was perfect. The fact that I had hundreds of prom corsages to make couldn't dampen my happiness today.

The sound of an engine behind me had my feet frozen and my heart fluttering. It's odd how I recognize the sound. It's not the only Dodge truck in this town. Moving to the doorway, so I'm not totally obvious, I watch as Miles parks on the other side of the square. He gets out and practically drags himself into Beth's Morning Brew. He's exhausted.

It's almost eleven o'clock. His weekend shift should have ended three hours ago. News had already circulated around town this morning about a huge fire in Walsburg. One of the stores had caught fire and was burning the two businesses on either side of it. The call came in just before shift change causing both shifts to assist.

Friday, I gave him my phone number and said we could text. It was something Rachel and E thought I should try. I won't have another in-office visit with Rachel until the first week in May. Since she knew E, and due to how broken I was, Rachel scheduled phone visits with me each week until our next session. I made an emergency call to her Friday morning. She encouraged me to take a step if I was ready. I wasn't ready to talk with Miles face to face. Phone calls scared me too, so E suggested texting, She even gave me Miles' phone number. Surprisingly, it's the same number he's always had. It's odd how I still remembered his phone number.

Miles hasn't texted me yet. After the way I've pushed him away so many times, he's probably waiting on me to text first. I don't know why I'm being such a coward about this. It's just a text, only that's not exactly true. I'm not a weak person either. I am, however, broken and hurting but that's different.

Mrs. Murphy came in this morning to pick up a flower for the Hayden Sisters. She told us about the fire in Walsburg. Mrs. Barnes, the Sheriff's wife, was right behind her. With two fire-fighting sons, she had even more information on the fire. After they left, I went to my office and prayed for everyone involved. I prayed for Miles. If I can pray for him, surely I can talk to him.

Stepping inside, I close the door and pull out my phone. I move to the far corner behind the window display. There's a perfect view of Beth's coffee shop from here.

"Here goes everything," I mumble.

Me: *Hey. Are you okay?*

The reply comes within seconds.

Miles: *Morning, Buttercup.*

Miles: *Yeah, I'm just tired.*

Me: *I can tell.*

Three dots appear in the chat window and disappear. My heart drops until I feel his eyes on me. I always thought that was a romance novel cliché, but I swear I feel it. Lifting my eyes from my phone, I can see Miles standing in the front window of Beth's Morning Brew. He can't see it from there but I smile. I smiled, and because of Miles Hamilton. Sucking in a breath, I quickly turn and lean my back against the wall. I can't believe I smiled. What does it mean? Nothing. It means nothing. My phone dings with another test causing me to almost drop it.

Miles: *Would you ladies like a coffee?*

Me: *You're tired. You should get some rest.*

Miles: *I don't mind. I won't stay long.*

I should say no. He needs to go home and get some sleep. But I smiled. And heaven help me, I want to see him. It's just to assure myself he's really okay. Yeah, I'll go with that.

Me: *Only if it's not too much trouble.*

There. That gives him a chance to say no and go home. Like he would really do that.

Miles: *Donuts?*

Me: *Not today. Just coffee.*

Miles: *On my way.*

I step back in front of the window. Miles is already crossing the street to the center of the square. That man. He wasn't about to say no. I should probably run and hide, but I refuse to be a coward today. This is me taking one of those baby steps E's so fond of. Who am I kidding? I'm leaping a hurdle here. Before he gets to the sidewalk on this side of the street, I hurry to open the door.

"You didn't have to do this," I say as he walks in. There's a faint scent of smoke on him.

"I wanted to." He hands me a Peppermint Mocha.

Bailey squeals with delight when Miles takes her a Salted Caramel Latte into the workroom. I think she's missed these little treats from him. If I'm being honest, I have to. Little things like this are letting him past the wall I built between us. I've fought so hard for almost five years now to keep that wall intact.

"I just called in our lunch order at the diner. I'll go pick it up." Bailey waves and hurries out the door.

Lunch order at the diner? Yeah, no we didn't do that. There are bowls of beef stew from my grandmother in the fridge for our lunch today. Maybe I'll thank her later. It will depend on how this little visit goes and what she gets me for lunch.

"Do you want to go to the breakroom and sit down?" I motion toward the hallway.

"Yeah." Miles rubs the back of his neck with one hand and follows me to the breakroom.

"Thank you for this." I point to my coffee when we sit down. "After the morning you've had, I should be treating you."

"This is a treat for me." He settles in his chair and props an elbow on the table. "You heard about the fire?"

I nod my head. "Spencer and Beth's mother was here. Mrs. Barnes came in behind her."

"It was bad. All three businesses were destroyed. No lives were lost though. A few firemen got hurt, but that comes with the job." He rubs his forehead with his fingers. "It's going to take another shower or two to get the smell off."

Getting up, I grab a bottle of ibuprofen from the cabinet and drop a couple into his hand. He shouldn't be here. He's fighting his exhaustion on my account.

"Thanks." He pops the medicine into his mouth and takes a huge gulp of coffee.

"You need to go home and get some rest," I say.

"I will in a bit." His eyes meet mine. "I need this more."

Aiden was right. Miles is hurting too. Before I wouldn't have cared. The old me would want him to hurt because I was hurting. Ever since I broke down, and after my first visit with Rachel, I no longer wish to cause him pain.

"Still, I should have waited to text you. But you hadn't yet. Then I saw you. And…" I drop my eyes and shut up. I do tend to ramble when I'm nervous.

"I'm glad you did." His fingers gently tap the table in a rhythm. He's nervous too. "I've been waiting for you to text first. Now that I

80

know you're okay with it, be prepared for your phone to blow up." He smiles and his entire face lights up.

We sit quietly for a few minutes. The bell above the door breaks the silence. Bailey hurries in with a couple of bags from Davis' Diner. She sets one in front of Miles.

"It's a burger and fries. Miss Cora said you get it regularly," Bailey said to Miles and turns to me. "I need to call my mom back right quick. I'll be right back."

My assistant is acting strange today. She rarely ever calls her mom. We will discuss her behavior later. I do have to admit, she's helping me out here. Getting Miles lunch was sweet too. The shop phone rings, and I hurry to answer it. It's another order for prom.

Miles walks up behind me at the front counter. "You're busy, so I'm going to get out of your hair." He holds up the bag from the diner. "Bailey didn't have to do this. I can pay her back."

"It's my treat. Don't worry about it," I insist.

"Your treat?"

"I always pay for our lunch when we order out," I explain.

He starts to protest, but I firmly shake my head. What's lunch after what he's had to do this morning?

"Come on. I'll walk you out." I don't want him to leave yet, but he's practically dead on his feet.

"Thanks again for this," he thanked me again for lunch.

He raises his hand to touch my face. Unsure, I take a step back. It's as far as I can go without knocking over an arrangement. His face loses all expression as his hand drops to his side. Surprisingly to us both, I catch his hand in mine.

"You're off this weekend." I glance up and quickly look away. There's hope in his eyes.

"I am."

"Will you be at Aiden and E's gender reveal party on Saturday?"

It's a dumb question. He's one of Aiden's best friends.

"I wouldn't miss it." A wide smile crosses his face.

"I'll see you there." I smile back and gently squeeze his hand.

"We'll text until then?" His eyebrow raises.

81

"I'd like that." I shrug one shoulder. "And who knows, I might even see you around town this week."

"I'd like that." Miles squeezes my hand back.

"Will you let me know when you get home? So I know you made it," I quickly add. He really is exhausted.

"I'll text the moment I get home."

"And after you rest?" I chance another look into his eyes. "So I know you're okay."

Oh my gosh. I'm stalling him from leaving. What's wrong with me?

"I promise." He squeezes my hand again before releasing it. "Text you later, Buttercup."

"Bye." I wave as he walks out the door.

Who have I become? I'm definitely not the Katie Matthews who used to walk around with a chip on her shoulder. Instead of screaming how much I hate this man, I'm trying to keep him here. I clap a hand on my mouth. Oh my. I'm starting to forgive him

Chapter Sixteen

Katie

*M*iles made good on his promise to text often. We had good morning and good night texts every day. Throughout the day, there were *hey* and *how are you* messages, plus little tidbits about our day. Now, we've moved into a playful banter and even had a gif war. It was hilarious. I so won that. He thinks differently though.

Sadly, the only time I got to see him this week was when he stopped by Petals. He kept his visits short. I had a feeling he was trying to not crowd me or overstep. There were so many prom orders that Bailey and I worked late every night. Thankfully, I was able to get everyone to pick up their Saturday orders early so we could close up at four.

Mrs. Maxwell had already stopped by to pick up the flowers and decoration balloons for the gender reveal party. I was the only one in the shop when I opened the envelope with E's ultrasound results. No one but me and Doctor Larson knew if my friend was having a boy or a girl. After stuffing the huge black balloons with confetti and filling them with helium, I hurried out to my jeep. I couldn't wait to see Aiden and E pop these.

The party was in full swing by the time I got there. Aiden and E's yard was packed. It looked as if half the town was at their house. Steaks were on the grill and tables of food were set up on the back porch. More tables for guests were lined up in the yard. People were laughing and having a great time.

I was happy too until something strange and unexpected happened. One look at the happy loving parents and something slammed into me. It was like hitting a brick wall. Aiden had on a blue t-shirt and E was wearing a pink dress. It was a wonder I didn't let go of the balloon strings.

"Are you Team Boy or Team Girl?" Brady snaps me back to reality. He's holding up a blue and a pink rubber wristband.

"Brady." I point to the balloons. "I know the results."

"Okay. You get both." He shoves the wristbands into my hand before taking the huge balloons from me.

The wristbands are cute. They have Baby Maxwell on them. Rather than putting them on, I shove them into the pocket of my jeans. I hate the person I am right now. I'm happy for my friends. I really am. I just didn't expect this to hurt. Maybe it wouldn't hurt so much if I had dealt with my loss five years ago. Sadly, I latched onto hate and rage rather than going through the grieving process.

Some people might say I had no right to hurt and grieve like this. I had only known about my baby for five days. In those five days, I fell in love with my little one. I was going to tell Miles the Saturday night I heard Brittney bragging about the night she spent with him at the waterfall. It was the same night *it* happened. I'm not comfortable with saying the *m* word.

"Are you okay?" E hands me a glass of sweet tea.

I didn't realize she walked over here. Guess I looked kind of odd standing near my jeep all alone.

"I don't know," I reply honestly.

I don't want to ruin her day. She knows the truth, so I can't lie to her.

"If it's too much, I understand if you need to leave," E said.

"No." I shake my bad thoughts away and take her hand. I have to try for her sake.

E doesn't look convinced, but she squeezes my hand and pulls me over to where Sammie, Ally, and Beth are sitting. Things are still a little strained between her and Beth. I think we really should give Beth an intervention. Or, we could try locking her in her apartment on the weekends. It wouldn't work though. She would destroy the place trying to get out. I'm worried about her. She can't keep this up much longer.

"So, is she having a boy or girl?" Ally whispers.

"You'll see when the balloons are popped." I'm not telling anyone.

"Oh, you have to see the nursery." Beth grabs my hand and pulls me into the house.

"Beth, wait!" E shouts, but it's too late.

Beth rambles on about something and doesn't hear E calling her. She's practically dragging me up the stairs to the nursery. The other three come in behind us, but I don't hear them. The room is beautiful. I run my fingers over the railing of the oak crib. The room is painted light green with a baby animal border on the walls. The rocking chair by the window matches the crib. E's baby is already blessed in so many ways. I should have had this too.

"Let's go back outside," E suggested.

She slips her hand into mine, and we share a knowing look. I blink back tears and swallow the lump in my throat. It's her day. I won't ruin it.

"What's wrong?" Sammie asked when we get back outside.

I shake my head. I don't want to keep this from the rest of my friends, but I'm not ready to talk about it.

"Here girl." Beth shoves a beer into my hands. "Drink your problems away. It works for me."

She takes a long drink of her beer before bouncing over to where Luke Barnes and a few guys from the fire department are sitting on the tailgate of Luke's truck. Beth is starting to run with the wilder crowds in Hayden Falls. We should probably do that intervention right now.

"Come on, E!" Mrs. Maxwell is waving E over to the center of the yard. She's already gotten Aiden captured. "We can't wait any longer."

E looks at me. It's okay. I can do this. I motion toward her husband. She starts across the yard, but pauses, glancing at me over her shoulder.

"Go on," I insist. She can't cancel this because of me. Her Aunt Sara brings over the two black balloons.

My eyes land on Miles sitting across the yard with Spencer and Levi. He pulls on his bottom lip with his thumb and index finger. His eyes are locked on me instead of the soon-to-be parents. I should have looked away.

His gaze. The balloons. People shouted boy and girl, depending on which team they chose. The sound thunders in my ears as everyone starts counting down from ten. Slow deep breaths. In. Hold. Out. Hold. In. Miles' eyes narrow as he leans forward.

A chorus sound off of, "5, 4, 3, 2, 1!"

Pop!

Blue confetti fills the air. Team Boy for the win. Aiden picks E up and twirls her around. Happy shouts and congratulations come from everyone. Everyone except for me. I'm still mentally talking myself through breathing. Miles stands and takes a step. The first tear falls. I can't do this. Springing from my chair, I run to my car. Before I can open the door, I'm whirled around with my back pressed against the jeep.

"Breathe, Buttercup," Miles says in a soothing tone. "Deep breath in. Hold. Out. That's it."

We're quickly surrounded by our friends. Several of them speak, but I stay focused on Miles' voice and his instructions to breathe. After a few rounds, I blink back to reality.

"Hey." E squeezes my hand.

I pull my eyes from Miles' gray ones to look at my friend.

"I'm so sorry, E." I sniffle. "I didn't mean to ruin this."

"Shh." E steps in front of Miles and wraps her arms around me. "You haven't ruined anything."

She's lying, but I accept her words and fall against her. Sammie and Ally are wrapping their arms around us both.

"Let's go inside and call Rachel," E suggested.

"Take her around to the front door and up to one of the guest rooms." Aiden starts us around the side of the house away from the crowd.

I don't look at Miles, but I hear the frustrated scream he releases. How do I keep making things worse for everyone?

When we get to the guest room, my friends let me cry it out without saying anything. Sammie, Ally, and Beth sit around me and E on the bed. I don't want to tell them, but they need to know. Miles needs to know, and I'll have to tell him soon. Dragging it out is only making us both miserable. It's as if I'm ripping the wound fresh each time this happens. Maybe if I tell all the important people in my life what happened, I can finally truly begin to heal.

It hurt, but I told my friends everything. All of them were shocked Miles and I hid our relationship for a year. They all wanted to rip Brittney Douglas apart. Their hearts broke when I told them about the baby. I hope Beth doesn't go into one of her spirals and blurts everything out to the rest of the town before I can talk to Miles. She wouldn't do it while she's sober, but Beth has been drinking a lot lately. After falling apart today, I won't be able to keep this from Miles much longer. I should call him tomorrow and set up a day and time to talk with him.

Chapter Seventeen

Miles

I was raised to be a gentleman. Sadly, the one trait I never fully mastered was patience. I was doing okay so far, but today I snapped. It's why I'm sitting here on one of the swings in the gazebo in the center of the town square. My training as a firefighter taught me to keep moving when you're inside a burning building. The walls of my life were engulfed in flames. Sitting idle was hard. It was wrong. If I didn't move soon, I was going to die.

At Aiden and E's party, once again, all I could do was watch helplessly as Katie fell apart. When the girls came out of the house, Sammie put Katie in her car and drove away with Ally following them in Katie's jeep. Something was seriously wrong, and I was getting tired of people keeping me from her.

When I left the party, I went straight to Katie's grandmother's house. I didn't see her jeep in the driveway, but I knocked on the door anyway. Whatever was wrong with Katie, her mom didn't know about it. If she had, I wouldn't have been told where she was tonight.

My eyes dart up to the apartment window when a silhouette moves across it. It's Sammie, not Katie. I know she's in there though. Her jeep is parked in the alley behind the flower shop, one building over. I should have known they would come here.

The instinct to move consumes me. I can feel the heat of the imaginary flames around me. It's strange how they feel real. This instinct has saved my life more than once, warning me I only had seconds to move. I can't sit idle tonight. My actions may cost me dearly in the end, but I can't ignore this anymore.

Before I can talk myself out of it, I'm off the swing and storming across the street. The way I'm moving, if someone sees me going behind the jewelry store they'll call the Sheriff's Office. If I get arrested, it's Sammie's fault. She should have gotten an apartment somewhere else. This one might be a better studio for her artwork, but I don't care.

I need answers, and I'm not letting anything stop me tonight. This may backfire on me, but I have to try. I take the wooden stairs behind the jewelry store two at a time and knock on the door to the apartment.

Sammie's smile fades when she opens the door and sees it's me. She fills the doorway with her body, not allowing me to pass. I wouldn't enter without permission unless Katie's life was in danger, but I know she's safe here. Sammie folds her arms and glares at me. The once-over she gives me makes me feel as if she wants to break my legs. Well, she's welcome to try.

"You shouldn't be here," Sammie said.

"A lot of things shouldn't be happening," I snap.

Sammie's eyes roll up as she nods her head. I peer over her shoulder hoping to see Katie.

"She needs time," Sammie doesn't move from the doorway.

My eyes snap back to her face. "She's had five years."

"This is serious, Miles." Sammie's back straightens even more.

Seriously? Is this woman about to challenge me? That won't end well for either of us. One, I can't hit her. Two, because of reason one, she'll beat me to a pulp.

"I am well aware." My tone is harsh. "It's my life too. Someone needs to tell me something."

"Think about what you did." Sammie's tone is just as harsh.

This woman is fierce. Shocking. I've never seen her act this way.

"Samantha," I warn.

If looks could kill, I'd be dead. And not just a little dead. I'm talking totally and completely. There would be no resurrecting me when she was through. Sammie hates it when people use her full name. I don't want to argue with her, and I'd never hurt a woman. However, this stubborn one is in my way.

"It's okay," Katie says from somewhere in the room.

Sammie looks over her shoulder. "Are you sure?"

I can't see Katie, but she must have nodded her head. Sammie steps back and motions for me to enter. I give her a sideways glare. This could be dangerous. Still, I step into the apartment. This crazy woman probably has a torture room in here.

The kitchen and living area of the apartment is a huge open space with windows on the front and side. It's an artist's dream with natural lighting. The bedroom and bathroom are along the wall connected to the flower shop. The kitchen is tucked into the back corner with a counter separating it from the living area. Katie is sitting on this side of the counter on a stool. We stare at each other.

"We need to talk." I break the silence. She nods her head. "Do you want to walk to the gazebo?" She shakes her head.

"I need to walk over to the market for a few things." Sammie looks between us. Her eyes settle on me. "I'll give you thirty minutes." She grabs her purse and leaves.

Thirty minutes isn't a lot of time, but beggars can't be choosy. I have no doubt Sammie meant the timeframe. It's best to not waste it.

"I know you're hurting, but I need some answers." I lean back against the door.

I want to walk across the room and wrap my arms around her, but I can't. The floral scent surrounding her would consume me, and I would be so lost in her I wouldn't get any answers.

"I know," she admits. Her eyes drop to the floor.

"I can't help you if I don't know what's wrong." I try to keep my voice calm and even.

Her eyes snap to mine. Hurt, anger, and pain fill her eyes.

"What did I do?" Pleading, I hold my hands out.

"You know," she snaps.

"I don't," I snap back.

I take a step forward and stop. The way my body is shaking, the last place I need to be is near her. I would never hurt her, but I'd definitely grab her and lock my arms around her whether she wanted me to or not. Taking a deep breath, I rub the back of my neck.

"What does Brittney have to do with this?" I ask.

Wrong question. Fire blazes in Katie's eyes. I wait. Speaking would have daggers shot into me and not just the imaginary kind. Katie's shoulders lift and settle as she takes a few deep breaths.

"You cheated on me," she finally replies and drops her eyes back to the floor.

Spencer and Aiden were right. Brittney lied to Katie. These two weren't friends, and they didn't run in the same circles. Brittney is a little older than Katie. I've no idea how their paths crossed for this to happen. If Brittney had stayed in college, this wouldn't have happened at all.

"Look at me," I demand. I shouldn't demand anything, but I'm fuming. When her eyes lift to mine, I continue, "I never cheated on you. The thought never crossed my mind."

Katie sucks in a breath. She grabs the counter with one hand to steady herself. I hate she has believed this lie for nearly five years. I want to find Brittney and rip her apart.

"But…" Katie shakes her head.

"No buts." I'm not letting her argue about this. "I *never* cheated on you. You should have asked me about it. I've *never* touched Brittney Douglas. I wouldn't touch her if my life depended on it. I'd die first."

"She said you took her to the waterfall." She looks away again.

"I haven't been to the waterfall since I was sixteen," I tell her.

It's true. Phillip Crawford ruined the falls for me. One weekend, he takes Aiden's old girlfriend up there. The next, he took the girl I was interested in. Of course, it says something bad about Tara too. She was with me when I caught Phillip with Karlee.

"You said I was your first," Katie whispers.

"You weren't the first girl I kissed," I admit.

Her eyes lift to mine again. Something is still not right. Believing I cheated is not enough to cause her to fall apart like this. Katie is stronger than that.

"There's more?" I wait, and she nods. "Will you tell me what that has to do with?"

"Us."

"Us? Katie, I swear to you, I don't know what this is about." I run a hand through my hair.

"I know you don't," she admits softly.

I snap my head toward her. This is madness. She folds her hands on her lap. A tear rolls down her cheek. If she knows I don't know then what's going on? Why does she hold it against me? Nothing I do fixes anything. We both are losing our minds, and I don't know why.

"I don't understand." I hold her gaze for a long moment. "I love you, Katie." I choke the words out. Her tears are a steady stream now. I can't stop mine either.

"For almost five years you haven't given me a chance to fix anything. I know you're hurting. I see it. I get you need time. But, I'm human. I'm hurting too. I can't do this anymore. You need to heal? Fine. Since you won't let me help you, you fix you. I have to find a way to fix myself." I turn and grab the door handle.

"Miles," she calls out. The stool legs scrape against the floor.

I hear her pain, but I can't look at her. If I do, I'll break even more.

"Heal, Katie. Let me know when you figure it out. I hope it's not too late when you do because I do love you. I won't crowd you anymore." And just like that, Miles Hamilton the jerk opens the door and walks away. I'm the biggest fool on this planet.

Chapter Eighteen

Katie

For three weeks, my life got darker. I wouldn't have believed it was possible until it happened. It wasn't a gradual takeover, nor was it a head first thing. My entire body fell instantly and hard. Most days I spent curled up into a ball. Getting out of bed was too hard, so I rarely did. My nights were sleepless. Those I spent staring at nothing. Food had no taste. When it got dark outside, I didn't bother to turn a light on.

Work was impossible. Bailey took over and finished out all the prom orders. Mom and Grandma took turns working in my place and babysitting me. My little brother would sit and stare at me whenever I would make it downstairs to the couch.

Sammie had found me a crumpled mess on the floor the night Miles walked away. A group SOS message had all of my friends at her apartment within ten minutes. When it's important, we drop everything and go. My friends were the best in the world.

At first, they wanted to go after Miles. They aren't upset with him anymore because I thought he cheated on me. However, they are mad at him for walking out as he did. I'm not mad anymore. I'm numb. It took me over an hour to tell them everything Miles had told me.

I believed him when he said he didn't cheat on me. Now, my friends want to go after Brittney. Sammie, Ally, and E will be cautious and hold back because I asked them to. Beth, on the other hand, is a loose cannon. Because of her own troubles, I expect her to go off any minute.

My bedroom door hits the wall when it flies open. I don't move. I don't really care.

"Rise and shine." Beth bounces on my bed.

The curtains are yanked open, allowing way too much sunlight into my dark haven. I scrunch my eyes and pull the comforter over my head.

"It's too dark in here," E said.

"And it smells bad." Ally lifts the window.

"Grab her clothes. I'll get the shower going." Sammie heads to the bathroom down the hall.

"Go away," I mumble.

"That's not happening." E stands at the foot of my bed. "You have an appointment with Rachel today."

"I'm not going." I turn over and grip the comforter tighter.

"Yes, you are," Mom says from the doorway.

Great. My mom is in on this. Ally and Beth wrestle me for the comforter. It's two against one. Naturally, they win.

"Ugh!" I pound my fists on the bed.

"Oh. That's emotion." Beth sounds way too cheery.

"Emotion is good," Ally sounds pleased. With what? I'm not sure.

Ally, Beth, and Mom pull me from the bed and drag me down the hall to the bathroom. Sammie is ready and waiting.

"What are you doing?" I shout as they shove me into the bathroom and close the door.

Sammie doesn't leave the room. "You need a shower, girl."

"I'm fine," I insist. I'm not, but again, I don't care.

"When was the last time you took a shower?" Sammie asked. I narrow my eyes trying to remember. "Exactly. Now, strip and get in there, or I'll strip you myself."

"You wouldn't dare," I challenge.

"I could get a pair of scissors and cut those shorty pajamas off of you," Sammie challenges back. "But, since those have daffodils on them, I think you may want to keep them."

She's right. These are my favorite pajamas. Ms. Wallace, our local seamstress made these for me because there are not a lot of clothes available with daffodils on them. Reluctantly, I reach for the hem of my top.

I pause. "Are you going to leave?"

"Nope," Sammie replied. "But, I'll turn around."

"Geez," I mutter. "You guys are impossible."

"You need impossible today." Sammie continues to face the door.

This is ridiculous. Sammie obviously isn't leaving the bathroom. With a loud groan, I got undressed and stepped into the shower. Closing my eyes, I sigh as the warm water flows over me. I really did need this.

"Be sure to shampoo, rinse, and repeat," Sammie instructs. "That mop on top of your head will need a couple of washes."

If it wasn't true, I'd throw something at her, preferably the shampoo bottle. I wince as I run my fingers through the knotted strands of my hair. Do they make a detangler for adults? It takes nearly forty-five minutes before I feel clean and refreshed. I didn't really need to stay in here that long. The warm water felt so good I didn't want to get out. When I had used up all the hot water, and could no longer adjust the temperature, I turned the water off.

Sammie holds a towel out for me. I can't believe she stayed in here the entire time. At least she did step outside long enough for me to get dressed. The clothes my friends picked out for me weren't bad. The jeans and ankle boots were fine. The yellow sweater was a bit sunny and cheery, things I wasn't feeling. This was one of my favorite sweaters. Why? Daffodils were yellow, that's why. Until now, I didn't notice how much my life was surrounded by those flowers. I know the reason, but I won't admit it.

Once Sammie and Beth were satisfied with my hair, we all climbed into E's SUV Aiden bought her because she needed a safer car, or so he said. The ride to Missoula was going to be long and frustrating with all of my friends along. They put me in the backseat between Ally and

Sammie. Surely, they didn't think I'd open the door and jump out. Well, I wouldn't do it from a moving vehicle. With the way I felt, I couldn't promise I wouldn't at a stop sign.

Rachel wasn't sure about letting all four of my friends join us today. She gave in when I waved the matter away like it was nothing. I didn't want to be here in the first place, and my friends were so stubborn they weren't leaving. It was fine because I had no intentions of talking. If all of them wanted to, it was alright by me.

"Katie, you've missed our last three phone appointments," Rachel said.

I shrug. I don't know what she's complaining about. She got paid anyway. Besides, she's a professional. She should take it as a sign I don't want to continue with these stupid useless sessions. Just because E benefited from talking to a therapist doesn't mean I will.

"Do you want to tell me why?" Rachel asked.

I shake my head. As I said, I don't want to talk. I just want to go home. Don't know why that is, home is dark and depressing. I guess dark and depressing fits me right now. When you're numb to everything, nothing matters.

"This only helps if you let it." E's sitting next to me on the couch.

"Nothing can help me," I whisper.

"We're here to help you." Sammie's sitting on my other side.

"You can't help me. There's no hope because I can't do anything right. I lost Miles once because of a lie. I couldn't be a mom. I'm so broken, I lost him again," I cry.

Four sets of arms lovingly envelope me. Beth and Ally are standing behind the couch leaning into us. I hate the mess I am. It hurts. I'm so tired of hurting.

"You may be broken right now, but there is hope," E said softly. She has always been the positive one.

"It's okay to not be okay, but it's not okay to stay that way," Sammie said. Who knew she could be logical?

"Why does it hurt so bad?" I take the tissue Sammie hands me.

"Because you didn't grieve for your loss five years ago," Rachel replied. "There are five stages of grief, and they don't have a specific timeframe. Right now, I would say you're experiencing stage four."

"Grief has stages?" I raise my head to look at her.

"Yes." She nods her head. "Denial, anger, bargaining, depression, and acceptance. You can also experience more than one at a time, and you could even go back and forth between a few of them."

"I'm in stage four," I whisper.

Depression? How can that be right? No. This isn't possible.

"If I had to diagnose you today, I'd have to say you have severe depression, and you probably need a little help," Rachel confirms my fears.

"Help?" I ask. "I thought this was supposed to help."

"Our sessions will help, but only if you allow them to. I think you may also need an antidepressant," Rachel says the words I never wanted to hear.

"So, I'm crazy," I snap.

"Not at all." Rachel shakes her head. She's not affected by my little outburst. "You're sad and you're grieving. You're at a level you can't handle by yourself."

"So, your answer is to medicate me?" My voice rises.

"I'm not fond of medicating people." Once again, Rachel's voice is calm. "Sometimes, people need a little extra help. It's not forever if you work through your problems. I can give you a list of things you can do that may help you. They could drastically reduce the time you need the antidepressant."

"Like what things?" I would prefer natural solutions.

"Good sleep, avoid caffeine, vitamin D, good food." Rachel begins to list off things to help.

"Oh, we can have a girl's night making our favorite meals," Beth suggested.

"Beth, you can't cook," Ally bluntly tells her.

"No, but I can eat," Beth said, causing everyone to laugh.

I have to admit it, she made me smile, and she really can't cook.

"I've decided to offer Paint and Sip nights at the studio. Those could be fun," Sammie said.

"But, E can't drink wine," I remind her.

"You should avoid alcohol for a while too," Rachel adds.

"You and I can make virgin pina coladas." E takes my hand in hers.

"Yeah," I agree and lean against her. At least now she won't be the only one with no alcohol.

"Exercise is good too," Rachel adds.

We were going to take self-defense classes at Jasper Ramsey's gym but E can't take them until after the baby is born. I didn't think those classes were really necessary. After E was attacked twice by her ex-boyfriend, I quickly changed my mind.

"You and I can walk to the park or around the square a few times in the afternoons," E offers.

I nod my head. We should stick to the town square though. Going to the park would take us by the fire station.

"And Miles?" I wipe a tear away.

"He's trying to heal too," E replied.

"And, I don't think you've lost him," Sammie adds.

"Does Miles know about the baby?" Rachel asked.

I shake my head. I know I'm wrong for keeping it from him.

"You have a couple of options where Miles is concerned." Rachel crosses her ankles and tilts her head, but she never looks away from me. "You can tell him. If he does love you, it's going to break him. He will most likely need to grieve too. If your relationship is salvageable, you two could help each other through this."

I hadn't thought of it like that. He said he loved me, and he was going to try to heal himself. If I throw this at him later, he'll have to heal again. Will he hate me for keeping it from him? If the tables were turned, I think I might hate me.

"What's her other option?" Ally asked.

"She can walk away and make a clean break from Miles," Rachel replied. "If that's her choice, she should never speak to him again, and the things said here should never leave this room."

Hayden Falls was a small town. Miles and I could not avoid running into each other. One of us would have to leave. Miles' life was in Hayden Falls. He was never going to leave. If anyone leaves, it'll have to be me. I don't want to leave anymore. Never talk to him again? I didn't want that either. This choice sounded even more depressing than I already was.

"Whichever option she decides on, Katie needs to work on herself a little bit first. If she decides to tell Miles, I suggest that she does it soon." Rachel interrupts my thoughts. For the first time today, I look her in the eye. "If you're ready to walk out of this dark hole you've fallen into, you have lots of options and four amazing friends who want to help you."

Rachel described exactly where my life was at right now. I have fallen into a dark hole. I take a moment to look at each of my friends. She's right about them too. They are amazing, and I do want out of this darkness.

"Thank you," I say softly to all of them.

Once again, they wrap me in their loving arms. Each of them vows to help me in one way or another. For the first time in years, I see a flicker of light at the end of my long dark tunnel. I won't be alone anymore. Hope finally found a way through my darkness.

The girl's dinner nights will definitely be happening. Paint and Sip with Sammie is already scheduled for Tuesday nights. E, needing more exercise during her pregnancy, will walk with me around the square in the afternoons. Ally heard about the new dance teacher offering adult classes on Thursday evenings at the gym. E can actually take those with us. It sounds like they had a plan in place before they ever showed up at my house today. Because they hadn't given up on me, my life was changing for the better. I don't know what I'd do without these four.

After visiting Rachel's doctor friend two doors down for the antidepressant, I'm on my way back to Hayden Falls. I have to prove to my mom I can really do my job, and I have to heal. Somehow, and soon, I need to talk to Miles. He deserves to know the truth. If he never wants to see me again, I'll have no choice but to honor his request. It'll hurt, but after keeping this from him for so long, I deserve to hurt.

Chapter Nineteen

Katie

$\mathcal{B}$y Memorial Day weekend, I was becoming a different person. I was more like myself but not quite the girl I used to be. I would never be as carefree as I was when I was a teenager. The last couple of years of my teenage life was ripped from me.

Truth be told, a lot of the pain I felt for the past five years has been my own fault. I should have confronted Miles about Brittney that night. The lie would have been exposed right away. I should have told him I was pregnant, and if the doctors were right about the reason, Miles would have been with me when our little one wasn't meant to be.

Paint and Sip with Sammie has turned out to be a huge hit with the ladies in Hayden Falls. Every Tuesday night, Sammie opens up her studio apartment to a group of crazy women. I wasn't great at painting, but it was so fun I never missed one. The first one was just us five. I needed it that way to help break the dark shell around me. A few ladies asked Sammie to have Paint and Sip bookings for adult women's birthday parties. E's helping her work out a schedule to start hosting them next month.

Every Monday evening we meet up at one of our homes for dinner. These cooking sessions are the best. Beth still can't cook, but she tries. Baking cookies is not her thing. She burns them every time. She's getting better with crockpot dishes though. I think she works best with a mix it, leave it, and forget it type of recipe. The night we cooked at our house, my mom and grandmother loved it so much that the three of us cooked together several times a week now. My grandmother is over the moon about it.

E and I walk around the square every day we both work. Walking is so relaxing to me. I should have taken it up years ago. When one of us has the day off, I drive out to the lake and walk around the area the parties and bonfires are held. Since my little brother decided to play baseball this year, I go to as many practices and games as I can. We even started dance classes at the gym on Thursday evenings. It's so cute to see E dance with her baby belly.

I was such a mess at the beginning of the month. It worried Rachel so much, she now sees me every other week with phone visits for the weeks in between. I keep those this time. Rachel told us some people with severe depression never seek help and end up taking their own lives or have to be put in a mental hospital. That was not going to be me. Some days were harder than others, but I refuse to let the darkness consume me again.

I wasn't mad at my friends for dragging me out of bed, throwing me in the shower, and taking me to my therapy appointment. They probably saved my life. I've done some research on depression and found several people sharing their stories online. In many of their cases, the person didn't have anyone close in their life. In just about every case, their families had missed the warning signs. My mom had become so scared for me that she called my friends crying and begged them for help. All of them worked together to form a plan to get me to my appointment. I was one of the blessed ones.

At my appointment this week, it was just me and Rachel. Of course, Sammie and E were sitting in the waiting room. Beth and Ally couldn't get the day off. Because of my progress, Rachel thought I was ready to take another step. One of my goals was to tell the important people in my life what happened to me. Today, I was going to give it a try.

"Hey, Mom. Where's Elliott?" I pour myself a cup of coffee while Mom cooks breakfast.

"Brady Maxwell picked him up a little while ago. He's helping out at the ballfield today," Mom replies.

"Are they letting him play in the game tomorrow?" I ask.

My brother is a Junior in High School. This being his first year, he may not get to play in the game.

"I think he's just helping with this one but may get to play at the 4th of July game. He really enjoys baseball, so it's good practice for him." Mom sets a plate of pancakes in front of me.

Tomorrow is Memorial Day. We have a town picnic in the park and a charity baseball game between the high school teams and the men of Hayden Falls. It's hilarious to watch.

"Is Grandma home?" I take a bite of my pancakes as Mom sits down.

"In here, Sweetie," Grandma calls out from the living room.

Good. They're both here, and my little brother is out for the day. Now, I need a little courage.

"Can I talk to you two after breakfast?" I ask Mom.

"Of course," she replies.

She wants to talk now. I should have waited until after we ate to bring it up. Mom is only picking at her food now. My appetite is gone too. I only make it through half of my pancakes before I push the plate away.

"Come on." I stand and hold my hand out to her.

"Katie, you're scaring me." Mom takes my hand and follows me to the living room.

Grandma is sitting in the corner of the couch knitting. She's always making something for the Hayden Sisters. They make hats, gloves, and blankets to hand out during the winter. Today, it looks as if she's making a blanket. Mom and I sit down beside her with me in the middle.

"There's something I need to tell you. Please don't be mad at me." I drop my head.

"No matter what you're going through, we're here to support you." Mom puts her arm around me.

"I didn't mean to scare you." I look at mom. "Thank you for calling my friends."

"I didn't know what else to do." Mom's eyes glisten with tears.

"Something happened when I was seventeen." I drop my gaze to my lap. I can't look at them for this part. Their disappointment will break me. "I was pregnant."

"Katie." Mom sucks in a breath. Her voice is soft as her hand moves back and forth across my shoulders.

"What happened?" Grandma asked.

"I wasn't able to…" Squeezing my eyes shut, I shake my head. The words are too hard to say.

"You lost the baby," Grandma says the words I can't.

I nod and drop my face into my hands.

"Oh, Sweetie." Mom pulls me into her arms. "We could never hate you. I'm sorry we didn't see you needed help."

"How could you? I hid it." I wipe my tears away with my fingertips. "I went to the Emergency Room in Missoula. I gave them a fake name and paid them in cash."

It was wrong, but it was the only way I wouldn't leave a trace. Mom and Grandma may have understood, but my dad would have been furious. He hated Miles. Dad would have hated me even more for being with Miles.

"And Miles Hamilton was the father," Grandma said.

I snap my head toward her. "How did you know?"

"I'm old, child, not blind." Grandma cups my face in her hands. "That boy loves you."

"I'm not so sure," I say.

"I am," Grandma said firmly. "Not many men would approach Carson Matthews, but that boy did."

"What are you talking about?" I ask. This was news to me.

"A few months after your sixteenth birthday, Miles Hamilton knocked on the door and asked to speak to your father. I went to the kitchen, but I overheard it all. He asked for permission to date you. Your father went into a rage and cussed that boy with words I'd never heard before. He got his shotgun and ran Miles off. Threatened to have him locked up if he went anywhere near you," Grandma explains.

"Mother, you never said anything." Mom is as shocked as I am.

"I never heard anyone mention the boy's name again. I thought that was the end of it. Not many men will stick around when they're threatened like that." Grandma shrugs.

"Well, if they broke up because she lost the baby, she didn't need him anyway." Mom huffs out a breath.

"Miles doesn't know," I tell them.

"You never told that boy?" Grandma covers her mouth with her hand when I shake my head.

"I didn't tell anyone until a month ago," I admit.

"Are you going to tell him?" Mom asked.

"I am," I reply. "He'll hate me, but I'm going to tell him."

"Well, like your mom said, if he does hate you over this, you don't need him." Grandma reaches for my hand. "But I don't think you're giving that boy enough credit."

"I hope you're right." I take a deep breath. "Because I think I still love him."

"Don't worry, child. It'll work out how it's supposed to." Grandma sounds hopeful. I wish I did.

Needing some time alone, I decided to go for a drive. I loved driving around. Miles and I used to get out of Hayden Falls and just drive. I haven't been alone a lot the past few weeks, but I need it today. Knowing my mom and grandma are not disappointed in me took a huge weight off my shoulders. An odd peace washed over me.

I spent the entire day by myself. Of course, I had regular check-ins with my mom. I will never scare her like that again. I had no particular destination in mind today. It was just me, the radio, and the open road. Everyone in Hayden Falls was busy preparing for the picnic and baseball game tomorrow. A lot of people were partying at the lake. I waved to a few of them as I drove by.

Before I realized where I was heading, I was almost there. The sun had set and I should probably turn around, but I didn't. I was on the back road on the far side of the lake. I haven't been here in almost five years. The roads were better paved now, and a few houses had been built out here. With all the changes, I wondered if I'd recognize the spot. It was unmistakable. I was drawn to it like a magnet.

This was our spot. Miles and I slipped out here every chance we got. No one would get to use this spot as a secret get-a-way again. Someone had bought it and built a cabin here. Thankfully, the huge oak tree we spent so many nights under was still here.

I went a little way down the road and turned around. I shouldn't have, but I pulled over in front of the cabin and stepped out of the jeep. The log cabin was beautiful. It doesn't look like it's been here too long. It fit here with its wrap-around porch. I could see the lake behind it. There was a light on in one of the upstairs windows. When a figure appeared in the window, I got back into the jeep and left. The last thing I needed was to get arrested for trespassing. I was glad someone made this place into a home, but I was going to miss it. I missed him too. Hopefully, Miles would be able to find it in his heart to forgive me.

Chapter Twenty

Miles

The picnic and baseball game today are going to be a disaster. Well, for me anyway. The rest of the townsfolk were enjoying themselves. The picnic might go okay. I think I can handle grilling hotdogs and hamburgers with the guys from the fire department. It's funny how they always put us in charge of the grilling at town events.

The baseball game this afternoon was going to be another story. I didn't sleep at all last night. I should ask Aiden to move me to right field. There's no way I can cover first base the way I feel today.

Like every other town event in Hayden Falls, businesses are set up in booths around the square. Jake Campbell and his country band will take over the stage after the baseball game is over. The fire department has set up a couple of grills and tents at the edge of the park next to the station.

"Pit, Whatcha doing?" Luke calls out as Pit pulls his truck up next to us.

"I'm here to show you Sissies how to grill!" Pit shouts over his shoulder.

"We have grills." Levi motions to the two grills we're using.

"That's not grilling." Pit jabs his finger at our grills and turns around as if he's ending the debate. Sadly, the man's just getting started.

"And all this time we've been lying to ourselves." Luke rolls his eyes.

"You have," Pit agrees.

Four hops out of the passenger side. If I didn't already know how well Pit could grill, I'd be concerned. Levi and I help them unload the grill and tent.

"The cook-off isn't until the 4th of July," Levi reminds Pit.

"We're not competing." Pit shakes his head. "Chief Foster asked me to help out today."

Pit has stepped in a few times and helped us during town events. The man is a mystery to me. We don't usually see him around town during the week. On weekends, he's usually with Four at Cowboys. Both men get so drunk they can hardly walk on their own at the end of the night.

It takes Pit about half an hour to get set up. He puts on an apron that says *Pitmaster*. He rightly holds the title in Hayden Falls. If rumors are true, he holds it in a few other cities too. Four puts on one that says *Kiss the Cook*. Surely, he's not cooking, and I highly doubt any of the women here will kiss him.

"What's wrong with our grills?" Aiden asked. I knew it was eating him up.

"You're using gas." Pit points to the propane tanks. "At least you're not using charcoal."

"What's wrong with charcoal?" Luke walks around Pit's grill studying it.

"It's amateur." He points to the tanks again. "So's that, and it's basically bringing the kitchen outside. Grilling is an art, gentleman."

"Whatever, man." Aiden points a spatula at Pit. "I'm entering the cook-off this year and taking you down."

"You're welcome to try, One Arm, but you will lose." Pit's not concerned.

"My arm isn't broken anymore," Aiden points out.

Pit shrugs. He really doesn't care. He'll probably call my friend One Arm forever. Nicknames do stick in this town.

"You just take care of that pretty little wife of yours and leave the grilling to the professionals," Pit smirks.

Oh, we are about to have a fight. Several of us have to turn away to hide our grins.

"I take care of my wife just fine." Aiden glares at Pit.

Nobody moves. Our eyes bounce between the two men as we wait to see who comes out on top of this.

"How you take care of your wife is obvious to all of us." Pit just went there.

"She's just as cute with that little baby bump as she is without it," Four chimes in.

"Why you!" Aiden yells.

My best friend is now chasing Four through the park. The rest of us are either doubled over or about to fall out of our chairs laughing.

"Should we go help Four?" Luke asked.

"Nah," I reply. "That fool needs to learn to leave Aiden alone about his wife."

Four's not serious about anything with E. The two of them have been friends for years. He just likes ruffling Aiden's feathers. It'll probably get him killed one day. Four seems to learn things the hard way.

A sight entering the park catches my eye. The reason I can't focus and why I didn't sleep last night is walking toward the river. Katie's arm is looped through E's. She tilts her head back and laughs. Seeing her happy is a glorious sight.

I was a fool to walk away from her last month. After things ended between us almost five years ago, I don't know how to handle her. Everything I do is wrong, and on most occasions, the things I say and do around her just end up getting me punched. For some reason, I feel as if I've failed her, but I don't know why. Last month was my biggest failure to date. Hearing how she fell apart guts me.

It's been hard, but I've kept my promise to her. I haven't crowded her. I haven't texted or shown up at Petals either. I have kept tabs on her though. It's not as close as I'd like but it's better than nothing. It took some pleading but I finally convinced Aiden to toss me a little information about Katie. If E knew, she'd be mad at him.

Katie disappeared from town for a few weeks. She was so broken the day her friends pulled her out of bed and took her to see her therapist. It was the day Aiden decided to start helping me. I did that to her, and I hate myself for it. What kind of man breaks the woman he loves to the point she can't function? This fool apparently.

The only part of my promise I haven't kept is the part about healing myself. How can you heal from something if you don't know what the problem is? Maybe, I should completely walk away and leave her be. I'm obviously toxic for her. She seems happy today. I can't take that away from her.

I don't fully hear the conversation going on around me. Pit's giving some vague grilling tips. These guys are idiots. Pit isn't about to give up his award-winning secrets. I should probably listen, but my attention is focused on someone else. She's a lot prettier than Pit.

Four somehow ditched Aiden. It takes my friend another ten minutes to figure out where Four is. Aiden gives up his pursuit of Four when E and Katie start walking toward us. I should probably leave so I don't bring a frown to her pretty face.

The gentleman in me doesn't move. Instead, I hungrily drink her in. Her long wavy blonde hair was up in a ponytail. I preferred it down. The denim cut-off shorts she's wearing shows off her long tan legs. Thankfully, she's wearing a regular t-shirt. If she revealed any more skin, I'd be a bigger mess. Wait. Her t-shirt is one from the fire department. A smile tugs at the corner of my lips.

"Hey, Cowboy." E wraps her arms around Aiden's waist.

"Happy Birthday, Sunshine." Aiden gives her a kiss.

I had forgotten today was her birthday. Sometimes it does fall on Memorial Day. Naturally, the guys start singing *Happy Birthday* to her.

Four starts E's way until Aiden levels him with a glare. Four backed away laughing. As I said, this fool is going to die one day if he doesn't stop.

All of the guys greet Katie and E. I stay planted in my chair. Aimlessly, I move my thumb back and forth over my bottom lip. She is so beautiful. If only she were mine. When Katie looks at me, I drop my gaze to the ground. Apparently, I'm a coward now too.

Even without looking at her, I'm aware of every move she makes. My heart almost stops when Katie walks over to my chair. Still, this jerk doesn't acknowledge her.

"Hey," Katie says softly.

I look up at her. Her smile is small and tight.

"Hey." I'm so lame.

"I was wondering." She pauses and toes the ground with her shoe. "After the baseball game, can we talk?"

Talk? She wants to talk? Finally!

"We can talk now." I go to stand up.

"No." She holds out her hand to stop me. "After the game is fine."

She doesn't wait for my answer. Katie quickly turns on her heels and takes off toward the town square.

Chapter Twenty-One

Miles

Sadly, the gentleman still hasn't shown up today. The jerk, however, was working overtime. Springing from my chair, I followed after her. Before Katie reaches the square, I grab her upper arm and whirl her around to face me.

"Miles!" Katie shrieks. Her other hand flies up to her chest.

"Let's talk," I insist.

"After the game." She looks around nervously.

Megan Sanders is watching us from outside Frozen Scoops. She's not a problem. I made sure of it.

"I can't wait that long." I lean into her space. "Please, Katie."

She shakes her head. "I don't want to upset you before the game."

Upset me? So, she really does want to talk about what happened five years ago. There's no way I can wait now. Once again, the overtime jerk takes over. With my arm around her waist, I usher her into the square and around the sidewalk. People stop to stare, but no one says anything.

"What are you doing?" Katie asked when we reached the front door to Petals.

"We're going to the breakroom and talk." I nod toward the door.

The town square is packed right now. There's not another private place for us to go, and I'm sure she doesn't want to talk in public.

"What if I don't have my key?" She lifts her chin defiantly.

"Katie," I warn. "I've waited nearly five years. There's no way I can play in that game knowing you're ready to talk."

"You won't be able to play after this," she mumbles but unlocks the door.

When we get to the breakroom, she goes straight for the coffee pot. The pod she puts in is decaf. That's new.

"Do you want a cup?" she asked.

"No."

I don't want coffee. I don't want small talk. I want to get to the serious stuff. She's the world's greatest at stalling. Since she's finally willing to talk to me, I shouldn't push her. My last actions around her destroyed her. I can't repeat that. Thankfully, the gentleman stands up and pats the jerk down.

"I'm sorry for walking away like I did last month," I apologize. It has really been eating at me.

"Thank you." She takes a bottle of water from the fridge and sets it on the table in front of me. "I forgive you."

Whew. That's a relief and a bit easy. Should I be even more worried? I don't really want the water, but I open it. If us sitting here with drinks helps settle her, I'll do it.

"I just hope you can forgive me." She sits down across from me and stares into her coffee mug.

Forgive her? That makes no sense. Does she mean because she kept whatever this is from me? Did she act out in some way five years ago? She thought I cheated on her. Surely, she didn't go out and do the same. I've known both men and women who have done that very thing. Two wrongs do not make a right. I really need to quit speculating and wait for her to tell me what happened.

"I'm sure we can work through it." At least I hope we can.

"I'm sorry for not talking to you about Brittney" She rubs her thumb around the rim of her coffee mug.

"It's okay." I lean back in my chair and watch her closely. "We both know the truth about that now."

It's taken everything in me, and my friends holding me down a few times, to not go after Brittney Douglas. Somebody needs to put that lying heifer in her place.

"I'm even more sorry for keeping this from you. I shouldn't have. It was wrong of me. You deserved to know. I was hurt, scared, and young. I didn't know what to do and I handled it all wrong." She takes a deep breath and swallows hard. "I'm not making excuses. I'm just telling you what I went through."

"I understand." I take a drink of water while she gathers a little more courage.

If she cheated because she thought I did, it'll hurt, but I'll forgive her. I'll find the guy and rearrange his face for taking advantage of her when she was in a vulnerable state.

"I had something amazing to tell you that night. I was so happy." She drops her face into her hands and she starts to cry. "I should have found you, or at least called you. I don't think it would have made a difference though, but I should have."

Okay. This has me greatly concerned. How did something amazing turn into her hating me? I move to the chair next to hers and rub her back with my hand. She pauses to cry. I need more, but I don't push. The gentleman is in charge right now. I reach up and pulled the yellow band from her ponytail. Her blonde hair falls loosely over her shoulders. Unable to stop myself, I run my fingers through the long soft strands. I used to play with her hair like this. On a few occasions, she had drifted off to sleep in my arms.

"I left the diner that night and just drove." She finally continues, "I stopped and got sick. That part was my nerves. Then the pain started and I felt weak."

Pain? Weak? She didn't cheat. This is something physical. How could I have been such an idiot and not realized this?

"Buttercup, what happened?" I whisper.

"I was almost to Missoula anyway, so I went to the Emergency Room." Her sobs shake her entire body.

What do I do? How do I help her? What could have been so bad? I do the only thing I can think to do. Gently, I wrap my arms around her. She can punch me later. Right now, I need to comfort her. I sigh deeply when she falls against me.

After a few minutes, she sits up and looks me in the eye. The biggest tears I've ever seen in my life fall from her eyes onto my arm.

"I was pregnant, Miles." She covers her mouth with her hand and drops her head again.

Was pregnant? I run my hand through my hair and tug on the ends. Those words bring tears to my eyes. Getting to my feet, I pace across the room.

"What happened?" I could barely choke the question out.

"I lost our baby that night," she cried.

Those words ripped my heart from my chest. Of all the reasons in the world, this one never crossed my mind. It's heart-wrenching, but it explains everything.

"Why? Was it because of what Brittney said?" If it was, I'll hunt Brittney Douglas down and rip her apart. Prison would be worth it.

"No," Katie replied. "The Emergency Room doctor said I was about four or five weeks. When a miscarriage happens early on, it usually means something is wrong with the baby. Nature takes over and terminates the pregnancy. If it hadn't been for an at-home test, I probably wouldn't have known about the baby."

That explanation doesn't help. It keeps Brittney in one piece but that's it. It shatters everything in me into so many pieces there's not a number high enough to count them.

"You kept this from me." I roughly wipe the tears from my face.

"I'm sorry," she whispers.

"You had no right," I cry. "That was my baby too."

"I'm so sorry," she apologizes again.

I can't do this. I need to get out of here. I can't be around her right now. I'm too angry. I'm too broken. People aren't safe around me. Releasing a broken scream, I turn and head for the back door.

"Miles!" Katie catches me before I open the door. "I'm so sorry. I'm sorry I wasn't strong enough to carry our baby. I'm sorry I didn't tell you. I love you. Please forgive me."

I grab my head with both of my hands. *Tap the jerk down. Tap the jerk down. TAP THE JERK DOWN!* Thankfully, my mind has a little sense left to it. It's not much but it's enough. If I leave like I did last time, she could hurt herself. She was close to that point a few weeks ago. As broken as I am, I can't hurt her like that again.

"Please, Miles," she begs. "I'm sorry. Please forgive me. A part of me died with our baby that night."

She's right, a part of her did, and a part of me is dying now. Something was medically wrong. It wasn't her fault. I cup her face in my hands and rest my forehead against hers. She's broken enough, I won't add more to it.

"I need to process this, and I don't know how I'm going to be able to do that, but I don't want to lose it in front of you." I press my lips to her forehead.

"We could grieve and heal together," she whispers.

"Yeah," I agree. "I need to get this out. Give me a little time. Wait here. I'll be back. Okay?" She nods her head. "I promise I'll be back." I kiss her cheek. "Don't go anywhere."

Before I explode, I open the door and bolt into the alley behind the flower shop. Leaning my back against the brick wall, I pull out my phone. Going to my contacts, I find the number I need and hit send.

"Hey, man. Where did you run off too?" Aiden asked.

I'm still taking deep breaths to steady myself. "Aiden," I croak out his name.

"Miles, what's wrong?" Aiden is on high alert now.

"Ask E to call the rest of the girls and send them to Katie at Petals." My words rush out. "I need you and Spencer."

"Where are you?" I can hear Aiden running.

"Pick me up in the alley behind the flower shop," I tell him. "And hurry."

"We're on our way." Aiden ends the call.

Within minutes, he pulls into the alley with Spencer in the passenger seat. I jump in the backseat. Without saying a word, I fall over and completely lose it. Spencer somehow manages to get over the seat to hold me down.

Chapter Twenty-Two

Katie

$\mathcal{M}$y heart fell an hour later when Spencer and Aiden came to the back door of Petals without Miles. This was too much for him. He wasn't going to forgive me. If it hadn't been for Sammie, Ally, E, and Beth, I would have lost my mind completely sitting here by myself.

Aiden walked into the breakroom and wrapped his arms around E. Spencer stood in the doorway leaning against the frame with his arms folded across his chest. From the looks on their faces, I'm sure Miles had told them everything. They're mad at me too. Well, they can join the club. I'm mad at myself.

"Where's Miles?" I asked, breaking the awkward silence.

"He needs a little time," Aiden replied without looking at me.

"He shouldn't be alone," Ally said.

"He's not alone." Spencer finally looks my way. I can't read his expression.

"Is he okay?" Beth asked.

"No," Aiden replied. "And we're not talking about this." He finally looks at me. "This is between you and Miles."

"If you need to be with him, it's okay." E looks up at Aiden.

"No, Sunshine." Aiden gives her a kiss. "He's in good hands."

"He'll try to meet us at the ballfield. We should head out there." Spencer pushes off the doorframe.

"Where is he?" I asked again.

"With his parents," Spencer replied. He quickly looks away from me.

Oh, no. He's in good hands alright, but now, I'm sure his parents will hate me too.

"I'm so sorry," I whisper. Sammie puts her arm around me.

"As I said, we're not talking about this." Aiden looks me in the eye. "Miles is a good man. He's waited almost five years to know the truth. If he needs ten to get himself together, you'll give it to him."

Aiden doesn't wait for anyone to say anything. He ushers E out the back door and helps her into his truck. I deserve this. I kept something important from Miles. His friends aren't going to understand my side of this.

Reluctantly, I follow Sammie out to her car. We ride to the baseball field in silence. I don't want to be here, but there is a chance Miles will be, so here I sit on these cold bleachers. As much as I hate to admit it, Aiden's right. No matter how long Miles needs, I'll give it to him. If he never wants to speak to me again, I'll do what my father did. I'll leave Hayden Falls and never look back.

Miles doesn't show by the time the game starts. Eli Wentworth covers first base in his place. Chloe is sitting in the opposite bleachers with Marcie and Avery. At least she's being spared this pain. The rest of her family aren't here.

"It's going to be okay." Sammie reaches over and takes my hand. I give her a tight smile, but I don't believe her.

By the third inning, Brady walks out to take over as pitcher. Aiden is off his game today. It's my fault. He's worried about Miles. The high school team is winning by three runs. That wouldn't happen if Aiden was at his best.

"It's hot." E is sitting next to me fanning herself with her hand.

"You're really red. Did you forget sunscreen?" Beth is sitting in front of us. She starts fanning E. Something is wrong.

"You're not hot?" E asked as she stands up.

117

"E, I think we need to get Doctor Larson." I grab her waist to steady her.

She fanning her face with both hands now. Aiden is stepping off the pitcher's mound and notices her.

"Sunshine!" Aiden shouts.

E tries to turn toward him. Her hands slow and her eyes roll back. Ally, Beth, and Sammie help me catch her.

Everything happened fast after that. Aiden was there within seconds. Doctor Larson and the EMTs from the fire department surrounded E. Spencer, Brady, and Leo Barnes struggle to pull Aiden out of the way. They're going to need more help. Thankfully, they manage to hold him long enough for the medical team to get E onto a stretcher and into the ambulance. Doctor Larson and Aiden climb in the back with her. The rest of us follow the ambulance to the hospital in Walsburg.

The waiting room on the second floor fills up quickly. E's Aunt Sara, who is legally her mom, sits in a corner with Aiden's mother. They are surrounded by members of the Hayden Sisters and praying. Her Uncle Silas and Aiden's dad sit quietly in another corner with several men from town.

Both of Aiden's brothers are pacing across the room. Beth watches Brady close but doesn't move to speak to him. Chase, the teenage boy Aiden rescued, and Graham Bradley, the H. H. Maxwell Ranch foreman, lean against the wall near Brady and Colton. My friends are sitting huddled together in the chairs closest to me. The only words spoken in the room are a few mumbled prayers.

The room felt like it was closing in on me. I had to retreat to the corner by the windows. This isn't about me. It's about E, Aiden, and their little boy, but I can't help the mixed emotions running through me right now. E and Baby Boy Maxwell, they haven't decided on a name yet, have to be okay. She can't go through what I did.

I try to fight my own personal thoughts and feelings away. The battle is not one I can win. The memories of the night I spent in a cold Emergency Room come back slamming into my heart. I wipe the silent tear away with my fingertips and stare out the window. The window is closed but there's a feeling of openness standing here. I'm no longer comfortable with dark closed spaces. Rachel told me it was a good sign. I was starting to become aware of the things that could trigger my emotions. Finding a little hope, I mentally grab ahold of it and cling to it.

Sammie, Beth, and Ally look up at me several times. They're staying close because they don't trust me. Severe depression is painful. While I was going through it, I didn't really feel anything. I was too numb. Walking out of the darkness opened my eyes to not only my pain but the pain I was causing others. Watching someone you love drift away can destroy you.

Mom and I sat down and had a long talk and a good cry. She's been hiding her own pain over my dad leaving. Even though it was a bad marriage, she felt as though she had failed. She knows we're better off without him. She was falling into her own sad little world, and I didn't see it. Starting next week, she's going to help out part-time at Petals. I'm grateful she's trusting me with being the manager again. Even though we live in the same house, we rarely spent time together. I've always loved working with her. She needs this as much as I do.

A glance over my shoulder to the doorway reveals the same scene. It's empty. Waiting is so hard. Closing my eyes, I turn back to the window and bow my head. There's no such thing as too many prayers. Silently, I pray for E and her baby, the hospital staff taking care of her, and every person in this room. I pray for the man I destroyed a few hours ago, and finally; I pray for myself. Regardless if Miles ever forgives me or not, I have to learn how to forgive myself.

During my own research on depression, several articles mentioned spirituality. I admit it's something I've shied away from for years. Two weeks ago, I started going to church with my grandmother. She's beyond happy about it. E was there. I don't know why I was surprised. She went almost every week. Maybe it didn't fully register for me until I saw her there. We joke now about being future members of the Hayden Sisters.

My body goes still when a pair of strong arms wrap around me. It only takes a moment for my mind to know who this is. My body remembered him first and falls against him. He was really here with me. The silent tears start again.

Chapter Twenty-Three

Miles

Finding out the truth can destroy a man. It sure broke me. Telling everything to Spencer and Aiden broke them too. They were more than friends to me. They were the brothers I never had. They refused to leave me on my own, and I was in no shape to go back to Katie. Somebody needed to go to her because I had promised her I'd be back. It's why my friends took me to my parent's house.

Mom and Dad hadn't left for the ballgame yet. Thankfully, Chloe wasn't home. It broke my parents when I told them what happened. When all of our phones lit up with calls and messages about E, we pushed our pain aside and rushed to the hospital to be there for my friends. Dad had to drive us because my truck was still at the station.

Walking into the crowded waiting room, with still no word on E and the baby, was maddening. Surely, they knew something by now. Mom hurried over to E's aunt and Aiden's mom. Dad took a seat with the men in the corner of the room.

My eyes automatically went to Katie. She was standing alone by the window with her arms wrapped around herself and her head bowed. Her friends are sitting close by. I want to shout at them for leaving her alone.

I won't lie, I'm upset with her for keeping everything from me. It was something I'd deal with on another day. There were more important things happening right now. I had just found out about my loss, and it's a pain so sharp I'm not able to describe it. It's something I pray our friends don't have to go through.

Mom told me the pain of miscarriage will stay with a woman longer than it will with a man. She spoke from her own experience. It was something else I didn't know about until today. I was supposed to have a little brother and Chloe was what Mom called a Rainbow Baby. I have heard her use the term before, but she never explained it until today. Mom gave me more insights into what Katie was going through. Dad said he and I will talk later since Aiden and E needed us today.

Seeing Katie standing there trembling in the corner wrecked me all over again. I don't know what will happen to us, but I couldn't leave her like that. We had a lot to work through, but it could wait.

When my arms went around her and she fell against me, I felt a warmth flow through me I hadn't felt in years. It was her. Only she could fill the empty places within me. I don't know how this is going to end for us, but for today, we have this. We need to heal. Whether we do that together or apart remains to be seen. Today, at this moment, we have each other.

"Miles," she whispers and looks up at me with tear-filled eyes. "I…"

I place a finger to her lips. "Not right now. We'll talk later. Right now, I just need to hold you."

Without any complaint, she lays her head back against my chest. Resting my cheek on top of her head, we stare out the window. I do need to hold her and not just for her. There's a calmness here I can't explain. Less than an hour ago, I wanted to rip this world apart. Now, I need this. I need her. As angry and broken as I am, how does she calm me like this?

The feel of the entire room moving has Katie and me turning toward the door. Aiden and Doctor Larson are instantly surrounded when they appear in the doorway.

"They're both fine," Aiden informs everyone.

The entire room sighs with relief. Half of the women are now crying happy tears. I kiss the top of Katie's head and tighten my arms around her. Her arms tighten around my waist. Relief washes over both of us. Our friends won't have to know what we know.

"What happened to her?" Silas Hayes, E's uncle asked. A few moments ago the man was barely holding it together. E was a daughter to him.

"E and Aiden gave me permission to talk to all of you." Doctor Larson looked around the room full of people. He pats Aiden on the back. I could see why. My friends looked drained. He was relieved, but Aiden was exhausted. Worrying over someone you love takes a lot out of you.

"First." Aiden held his hand out to his mom and E's aunt. "Only two at a time can go back to see her for a few minutes. She's in room 210." Both ladies practically run from the room.

"E was dehydrated and got overheated. She also has Gestational Diabetes," Doctor Larson explained E's condition. "Mother and baby are fine now. E will be seeing a Nutritionist before she leaves the hospital. She could go home tonight, but Aiden insists she stays." Matt Larson rolls his eyes. "So, we will be monitoring her tonight and sending her home in the morning."

My body shakes from the laughter I'm holding back. E's condition isn't funny, and I'm not the only one laughing. Aiden is relentless when it comes to his wife's safety. My arms tighten around Katie again. I can't say I blame my friend for his actions anymore. I'm starting to understand him. If I could have saved my family, I would have.

"Katie." Aiden holds his hand out to her. "She asked to see you next."

She looks up at me and blinks a few times. I nod my head and release her. I was going to wait in the waiting room for her to return but Aiden motioned for me to follow him.

"Hang in there, man," Aiden said when we were alone in the hallway. "She needs you."

I nod my head. "I need her."

"I was hoping you'd figure it out." Aiden runs a hand through his already messy hair. He looks rough. "I think I lost ten years of my life in less than two hours."

"I haven't figured it out," I admit and look him in the eye. "But, I understand, man."

"I'm sorry it ended differently for you," Aiden said.

"Me too," I agree. "But, I'm beyond happy that Baby Boy Maxwell and his Mommy are okay. Man, y'all have to name your baby."

"I totally agree on that." Aiden lightly laughs.

With so many visitors waiting to see E, everyone only gets a few minutes with her. Her aunt and Aiden's mom leave the room, and Katie walks in. Aiden and I wait in the doorway. I'm not really sure why he brought me back here, but I'm grateful to be able to stay close to Katie. This has to be affecting her because it sure got to me.

"Hey." E smiles and pats the bed.

"I don't want to crowd you." Katie walks up to the edge of the bed.

"Nonsense." E pats the bed again. "I'm fine."

Aiden clears his throat. I swear E Maxwell has the loudest eye roll I've ever seen. Of course, her little giggle softens the blow causing Aiden to smile. Ever so gently, Katie sits down on the edge of the bed.

"Are you okay?" E asked.

"Me?" Katie puts her hand to her chest. I can't see her face from here, but I'm sure her eyes are wide. "You're the one in the hospital."

"I'm okay," E assures her. "I have some major diet changes to make, and I have to be careful to not get dehydrated again. But, I was scared of what this might do to you."

E does look okay. The IV she has I'm sure is for the dehydration. It's faster than having her drink a lot of fluids.

"I was scared," Katie admits in a soft voice.

"Promise me you won't stay in your room alone tonight," E said.

Her request has me concerned. I know Katie's friends had to make her go to her therapist appointment earlier this month. Aiden told me about her depression, but just how bad was it? Had I truly pushed her to the point she would hurt herself? If so, how could she say she loves me? Wait. She said she loved me at the flower shop today. Oh my gosh. How did I miss it?

"You okay?" Aiden asked.

"Man, don't ask me that right now." I shake my head. I'm more messed up than I thought.

Surprisingly, Katie walks out of the room. I missed the last part of her conversation with E. She loves me. I haven't heard those words in almost five years. Aiden motions for me to go into the room. Looks as if I'm about to get the best friend lecture.

Cautiously, I approach E's bed. She pats the spot Katie was sitting in a few minutes ago. My eyebrows shoot up. Is she insane?

"I don't think your husband will approve if he walks in here and finds me sitting on your bed," I tell her. I have no intentions of dying today.

"It's fine." E points to the door. "And he's literally standing right there."

I look over my shoulder and laugh. Sure enough, Aiden is standing against the wall where he can see into his wife's room. Katie is standing on his other side, but I can't see her face from here. One thing is for sure, this little mama has one over-protective husband.

"Don't be mad at him for it." I'm still not comfortable with it, but I sit down as she requested. "He waited a long time for you."

"I waited a long time for him too." E grins. Yeah, she did.

"Am I in trouble," I ask. I already know I am.

"No." She shakes her head. "I wanted to apologize to you."

Apologize? Has she known all this time? If so, I can't yell at her even if it makes me mad. I'm not fighting Aiden.

"For what?" I ask.

"I was the first person she told last month. I didn't even tell Aiden." She takes a deep breath and looks me in the eye. "After today, I see how important it is for the father to be there. Well, that is, if he wants to be there."

Like Katie, E tends to ramble when she's nervous. She has a big heart though, and I understand what she's trying to say.

"It's okay, E. And if I had known, I would have been there," I assure her.

"I'm not making excuses, but she was young and scared." E's eyes well up with tears. We can't have that.

"Mom has talked me through a lot about that," I say.

"You two can grieve and heal together," she suggested. Katie had mentioned this too.

I don't want to lie to E. I decided to tell her the truth. "I don't know how much of that we can do together, but we will try."

"She does love you," E whispers.

I risk the wrath of my best friend and lean forward to kiss his little wife on her cheek. Aiden Maxwell is one lucky man.

"And I love her," I whisper back.

E nods her head and I leave the room. I don't know how Katie and I will get through this. I do love her. I have for a long time. Hopefully, in the end, love will be enough to get us through this.

Chapter Twenty-Four

Katie

Knowing E and her baby were going to be okay settled me a lot. We all will pitch in to make sure the last half of her pregnancy goes well. I wasn't expecting her to want to talk with Miles though. When he came out of her room, he said goodbye to Aiden and took my hand. He quietly led me out to one of the small sitting areas around the hospital.

We sat in the area on the far side of the parking lot under a huge oak tree. The wooden benches here were nice. I wasn't a fan of the stone benches most businesses and parks around larger cities switched to. Looking up at the oak tree, memories of the last summer I spent with Miles flashed through my mind. I missed that tree and the times we shared under it. Too bad we couldn't go back there. Maybe one day, I'll ride back out there and take a picture of it. Hopefully, I won't get arrested for being a creeper.

Miles followed my gaze up to the tree. We shared a knowing look when our eyes met. He remembered too. I didn't think guys did things like that.

"I'm glad they're going to be okay," I say, breaking the silence.

I'm not sure what he wants. I look around nervously. This could go in so many directions. More than half of them scare me. One hard part was over. I'd finally told him what happened. Now, another hard part begins. Where does this leave us? What do we do now? Is there even an us?

"Me too," Miles agrees.

He settles back against the bench but doesn't let go of my hand. His thumb moves lazily back and forth over my knuckles. There's so much I want to say. Things I need to say, but the words were lost in my head.

"I'm sorry," I whisper. I'll say it until he forgives me. If he can forgive me.

"I'm sorry for so many things too." He puts a finger under my chin and lifts my face up until our eyes meet. "Don't apologize anymore because of what happened with our baby. I don't know or understand all the medical terms and reasonings, but it was something you had no control over."

I nod my head. I'm grateful he doesn't blame me. For a long time, I blamed myself. I always thought I did something wrong that caused it to happen.

"What do we do?" I asked.

"I don't know yet." His eyes stay locked with mine. "I won't lie, it hurts. I never felt a pain like this. I'm also having a hard time with the fact you kept this from me for so long. If I had known, I would have been with you. If our baby had made it, I would have married you and we'd be a family. I wanted to marry you. I was waiting for your eighteenth birthday. I was going to stand in the middle of the square and shout my feelings for you to the world."

I gasp at his declaration. He wanted to marry me even without knowing about the baby.

"You hid us because my dad threatened you." It's not a question.

"Yeah," he replies anyway. "I should have waited until you were eighteen, but I was already a goner."

"Well, I didn't exactly make it easy for you," I admit.

I wanted him as much as he wanted me. For years, I had watched him and learned all I could about him. When I was sixteen, I found ways to be around him more during town events and through our friends. Slowly, I got close to him. One day, it was as if he'd finally seen me as more than just a girl in the crowd.

"No, Ma'am, you didn't," he mutters. His lips turn up in a sweet smile.

Unable to stop myself, I reach up and place my palm against his cheek. He turns his face into my hand. A small sound escapes me at the feel of his lips on my skin. Gently, his large hand wraps around my wrist and pulls my hand away.

"We can't do that yet," he whispers.

Coldness replaces the warmth his lips left behind. It hurts, but he's right. If only we could forget all the bad things and go back to before I heard Brittney in the diner all those years ago. It doesn't matter what either of us would have done. It's pointless to dwell on it. My actions destroyed those chances.

I go to turn away and put a little distance between us. It's too hard being this close to him and not being able to touch him how I want to, how I should be able to. Miles cups my face in his hands, holding me in place. It's fine. I do not mind at all.

"Did you try to hurt yourself?" His question rushes out.

"What?" I shake my head. "Why would you ask me that?"

"E doesn't want you to be alone tonight. You were sad. Did I push you to hurt yourself?" His eyes plead for an answer that won't break him even more.

He's talking about my depression. There's no telling what rumor he's heard flying around about me. I haven't read Megan's blog in over a month, and my friends do not tell me about it. The nosy people of Hayden Falls need to shut up or find something else to interest them besides me.

"No," I reply. I can't let him believe this for even a second. "I would never hurt myself. I was really sad and numb. I was depressed, but I have great friends, and I see a therapist now." I hated admitting the last part.

His entire body relaxes, but he doesn't remove his hands from my face. He doesn't need to know I have to take medication. Maybe that's not true. Keeping things from him had destroyed us both. If there's any hope of fixing things between us, I need to be upfront and honest with him.

"I have to take an antidepressant for a little while." Shame washes over me from the admission. It makes me feel weak.

"I'm sorry I pushed you to that point," Miles apologized.

His muscular arms wrap around me. This is what I want, and I want to stay here forever. I was a fool to not trust him, to trust in us.

"It's not your fault," I tell him. "Everything piled up for so long it got to a point I couldn't handle it on my own anymore." Well, that's the way Rachel explains it.

We sit quietly holding each other for a long time. If only we could stay like this but we can't. Someone clears their throat, bringing us back to reality.

"Hey, man. No rush." Spencer is standing at the edge of the parking lot. "You're with me tonight. Take your time. I'll be waiting." He walks across the parking lot and climbs into his truck.

Miles doesn't leave right away. He pulls me back against his chest, and we continue to exist together in silence for a while. It's strange how the silence seems to be offering a little peace and healing. Maybe we don't need a lot of explaining and apologizing. Oh, we need to talk, but we need this too.

"Is there hope?" I ask softly.

"There's always hope," he replies.

Still wrapped in his arms, I look at him. "For us, I mean?"

He stares into my eyes for a long moment before answering. "I hope so."

"Me too," I whisper.

A smile tugs at the corner of his lips. "Are you saying you're tired of yelling at me and punching me in public?"

He's teasing, right? I'll take this as a good sign.

"Oh, I don't know." I roll my eyes. "I could still punch you if you'd like."

He chuckles, causing his entire body to shake. It feels good. I want more happy moments with him.

"We'll see," he says.

Well, it's not the answer I was hoping for, but it wasn't exactly a yes or no question. After everything that's happened, it's probably the best answer I could get. If he decides there's no chance for us, I'll have to accept it. It's my fault we're the mess we are today. If he wants to just be friends, that's great, but it's not something I could live with. I could never see him as just a friend. Sadly, for a while, I made him my enemy. He'd be crazy to try with me again, but it's what I want. If he doesn't, I'll follow my plan to leave Hayden Falls forever.

"You'll go home with Sammie tonight, right?" Miles asked.

"If she doesn't mind, I will," I replied.

"I don't mind," Sammie said.

She's standing in almost the same spot Spencer was a little while ago. She smiles and goes to her car. I can help her set up for tomorrow night's Paint and Sip.

"Is it okay to call you?" Miles releases his hold on me.

"You don't want to text?" I tease.

"Some." He shrugs. "But, I need more than texts."

"Yeah. Me too," I admit as I nod my head. Too much gets lost in texting. Hearing his voice will be so much better.

His hands move to gently grip my forearms as we stand up together. This is the part I hate. My heart hurts, but we have to go. Our friends are sitting in their cars waiting on us.

"Miles," I cry softly.

"I know," he says. "I feel it too."

My eyes close when he leans down to press his lips to my cheek. I don't want to cry, but I'm powerless to stop a few tears from falling. He leans closer with his lips next to my ear.

"I love you," he whispers.

Instead of warmth, coldness surrounds me and I know he's gone.

"I love you too," I say, not sure if he heard me.

When his steps falter on the small gravel stones around the sitting area, I'm sure he did. Still, neither of us says anything more. I want to run after him, but I can't. The distance between is my fault, and I'll have to live with the consequences of what I've done. Still, I want him more than I ever have.

Chapter Twenty-Five

Miles

I wish I could say I was strong, steady, and sure, but I wasn't. I was far from it. I didn't handle any of this gracefully. I imploded. Thankfully, Spencer, Aiden, and my dad didn't seem to mind. I wouldn't have gotten through it without all three of them. My dad's advice helped the most. He'd been through this, so I carefully listened to every word he said. He had been holding a lot in all these years. He didn't want to cause mom any more pain than she was already going through. I respect that. Mom was holding a lot of pain in too. We sat together and cried one night. In a way, it helped us both a little.

As great as my friends and my parents were, it wasn't enough. I was slipping, and I knew it. After hearing how bad Katie's depression truly was, I didn't implode this time, I exploded.

Aiden had invited me to dinner one night, and E told me everything. She felt as though she was betraying Katie, but I assured her she wasn't. Loyalty is strong among friends in our little town. I was grateful she told me because I needed to hear it all. Instantly, I knew I was on the same road to darkness Katie had been on. If I didn't get off of it soon, I was going to suffocate.

Aiden had to take me out to his family's ranch to the shooting range he set up with his brothers when they were kids. Hearing that Aiden had to come out here a few times last year made me feel like I wasn't alone. If he could survive his anger, I could use this to get through mine.

His brother, Colton, was mad at us. He stomped around mumbling something about us spooking his cows. I don't know what put that man in such a grumpy state, but he needed to lighten up. Colton was only two years older than we were. I don't remember him being like this when we were younger. He's definitely gotten the grumpy rancher life down perfectly now.

Some people might think I have no right to feel the way I do. If those people ever voice their opinions to me, I will gladly, and not politely, tell them where they can shove it. Aiden and his dad would lecture me about it, but I don't care.

By the time I was sixteen, I knew I wanted a family someday. Teenage boys don't think like that, but I felt it in my bones. After the disaster with Tara Adams, I decided to only casually date as friends. I wasn't a jerk. I was upfront with girls about it because I didn't want to lead them on. Honesty was always best. I was simply watching and waiting for the one I would someday have a family with.

I wasn't expecting Katie Matthews. When she floored me as she had, she turned my life upside down in a matter of minutes. I had known her for years. She was one of E and Beth's best friends. Since I was friends with Spencer and Aiden, I saw Katie a lot. Talk about knowing someone in a roundabout way. I look back now and laugh.

The summer she turned sixteen something happened. I can't explain it, but I was drawn to her like a magnet. Her cute little dresses and shorts revealed a pair of long tan legs, and I punched a few guys in the face for commenting on them. Her blonde hair seemed to catch the sun's rays and hold them. I loved how those soft strands framed her face and fell loosely down her back. Her dark pink lips begged me to kiss her. By the 4th of July festival, I had all I could take. I managed to whisk her away from everybody without them noticing. Before I let her go that night, I had claimed those perfect soft lips with mine.

After everything I've learned over the past few weeks, I did my own research on miscarriage and depression. I wasn't depressed. At least, I don't think so, but I needed to know how to help someone who was. If I was aware of the signs, I could keep myself from falling fully into it and help pull Katie out if she needed it. Since I was struggling, I agreed with my dad and sought help.

As a fireman, I've seen a therapist before. We all had. You couldn't see the things we do sometimes and not need help. This wasn't job-related, but it was affecting my ability to do my job properly and that put the other guys in danger. I went to Chief Foster and told him everything. He immediately reached out to some of the therapists the department used. Many of them strictly dealt with firefighting issues. A few had their own practices and took other patients.

Thankfully, the guy I've talked to before had an office in Walsburg. He had an opening, and I booked it right away. Since this wasn't a job-related issue, I had to pay for most of the visits out of my pocket. They were worth every dime. I was a man with responsibilities, and I took those seriously. I couldn't slide. Somebody needed me.

I didn't ghost Katie. I knew firsthand what that was like. I called and texted her often, every day in fact. I even stopped by Petals a couple of times. Those visits were always near the end of lunch so I could leave quickly. I wasn't trying to ditch her. I just needed a little time to get it together. She wanted more than I was giving her. I could hear it in her voice. I wanted more too, but I wasn't at a stage where I could make her any promises, and I didn't want to lead her on. All of that was about to change.

The jerk Miles Hamilton got over himself. I had to get the anger out, and I didn't want Katie to see it. Those two weeks were the longest two years of my life. My grandfather used to drive me crazy with his little saying. I didn't understand it until now. Next time I see him, I'll let him know he wasn't crazy after all. He'll get a kick out of it.

Today was a special day. June 10th four years ago was the day I was going to rightly claim what was mine. I'm a little late, and I can't rightly claim yet, but I'm laying the groundwork today. It was my day off, and I had plans.

The long line at Beth's Morning Brew put a slight damper on my morning. I should have known better than to show up here at 9 am and expect to hurry out. Unlike most of the stores in town, Beth opens her shop at eight. I think only the diner opens before her. I'm sure all of the working folks around here appreciate Davis' Diner opening at 7 am. Personally, I'm not moving that early in the morning unless I'm on duty and the tones ring out.

If this coffee wasn't part of my plan today, I'd leave. Since women and coffee go hand in hand, I take my place in line and wait. When I finally get to the counter, Beth steps up to take my order. I stare at the order board trying to figure out what I can get Katie because she's switched to decaf coffee.

"Card please." Beth holds her hand out.

"But I haven't ordered yet." I'm already reaching for my wallet.

"Oh, but you have." Beth grins and swipes my card.

I follow her down to the pickup counter. The gleam in her eyes has me worried. My feelings seem to be justified. The total today was a little higher than normal but I didn't question it. I have a feeling if I tell her the tray with four drinks she's pushing toward me isn't mine, she'll insist it is.

"Beth?" I adjust my baseball cap and stare at the drinks.

Beth huffs and points to cup one. "This is your regular boring coffee. This one is Bailey's. This special one with the sticker on the cup is Katie's Peppermint Mocha."

"But, she can't have caffeine," I interrupt.

"*Special*, Miles." Beth huffs again. "It's a decaf version just for her. I also have to make sugar-free ones for E."

Wow. That's really sweet of her. I should have known Beth would find alternative ways to make her friends' favorite drinks.

"So, is cup four E's sugar-free drink?" I ask. I don't mind dropping it by the inn for her.

"You need to get up to speed here, Dude." Beth jabs her finger at me. "Cup number four is a Vanilla Latte for Katie's mom. She works part-time with Katie now, and I just happen to know she's there this morning."

I didn't know that. Once again, I'm grateful Beth is looking out for me. Well, technically, she's looking out for her friends. Still, this works in my favor. The last thing I need to do is to show up without a drink for Katie's mom. So, drinks for everyone it is.

"Thanks, Beth." I hand her a ten-dollar tip and pick up the tray.

"Why didn't I get a tip every time?" Beth calls out.

The packed coffee shop goes quiet. All eyes are on me. It's fine. Let them look.

"Today's special," I reply.

"It's about time." Beth's smile matches my own.

"Yes, it is," I agree.

After leaving Beth's, I dart into Sweet Treats. I had placed an order yesterday for half a dozen assorted donuts. Knowing how Bailey loves donuts and with Ms. Matthews at Petals, I asked Sophie if she'd make it a full dozen. She happily changed my order. More is always better. Sophie smiled and blushed as she set the special box I asked for on top. I loved how the business owners in this town didn't mind helping a guy out.

When I get across the square, Grace is coming out the door with a spring vase. She sees I have my hands full and holds the door open for me.

"Thank you, Ma'am." I wink at her. There's really not much else I can do.

"It's good to see you, Miles." Grace's face lights up when she smiles.

I pause and watch her through the window as she crosses the street to the bookstore. She has her eye on someone in town, but she's too shy to make a move. She really is a sweetheart. I'm going to have to help her out with that one day. A slow smile crosses my face. That fool is not going to see her coming. He's going to fall hard too. Severs him right. I'm going to enjoy watching every minute of it.

The laughter from the workroom snaps me back to my plan. Since I slipped in as Grace was leaving, they don't know I'm here. This really will be a surprise.

"The convention in Seattle will be *amazing*," Bailey said.

"Are you sure you want to go?" Ms. Matthews asked.

"Yeah. It should be great," Katie replied. "I know it rains there a lot, but people say the area is beautiful. Who knows, if I like it, maybe I'll move there someday."

"I thought you wanted to remodel the upstairs here into an apartment?" Bailey asked.

"That's perfectly fine with me," Ms. Matthews said.

"I have been looking into doing that. I'm just not sure. It might be better if I move away for a while. Seattle could be nice." Katie's voice sounds sad.

What in the world? Has she lost her ever-loving mind?

"That's not happening," I inform her from the doorway.

"Miles!" all three women shriek at the same time with their hands over their chests.

Okay. Maybe I said that with a little more force than I meant to. At least I got their attention. Now, we need to settle this moving away crap right now. She's not going anywhere.

"What are you doing here?" Katie asked.

"Oh my gosh!" Bailey exclaims as she rounds the table. "Can't you see why he's here?"

Bailey grabs the to-go tray of coffee and sets it on the work table. In a swift movement, she's back taking the box of donuts. This woman and donuts. Geez. I'm going to lose a hand if I'm not careful. This is great, but we need to settle the moving thing.

"Coffee and donuts." Bailey grabs Katie's drink and points to the sticker. "And yours says *Happy Birthday*." She hands the drink to Katie.

I hold my hands out. "Happy Birthday." *Thanks, Bailey, for taking that from me.* It's best to keep that part to myself.

"Thank you." Katie happily takes a sip of her drink.

"This one is yours." Bailey hands me the one with my name on it before giving Ms. Matthews hers.

"This is really sweet, Miles." Ms. Matthews smiles at me.

I smile and nod to her before turning to Katie. "What time does your shift end today?"

"Any time you're ready to take her," Bailey said around a bite of her chocolate-covered donut.

"Bailey!" Katie exclaims.

Ms. Matthews and I laugh. Bailey shrugs as if this is a perfectly normal conversation. Her grin widens as she reaches for another donut.

"Ms. Matthews, may I borrow your daughter today?" I ask.

"Just for today?" Ms. Matthews lifts her chin and her smile fades.

Uh oh. Hopefully, she'll forgive my poor choice of words.

"I didn't mean it like that," I say quickly.

"Oh, I know." Ms. Matthews waves her hand and laughs again. She reaches for a donut. "And it's perfectly fine with me."

Well, that was cute and unexpected. She had me there for a moment. Not waiting for Katie to protest, I grab her hand and pull her out the front door. The birthday plan is well underway.

Chapter Twenty-Six

Miles

Without explaining my intentions, I led Katie to my truck parked in the town square. After helping her into the passenger seat, I handed her my coffee to put in the cup holder of the center console.

"Be right back." Before she can ask any questions, I close her door and jog across the street to Davis' Diner.

This stop was quick. My order was ready and waiting. I tipped Miss Cora well for her help this morning. When I got back to the truck, I handed the take-out bag to Katie and started the engine.

"You got us breakfast?" She sounds surprised. I nod my head in reply. "But, you got us donuts."

"Those were mainly for Bailey and your mom," I explain.

"You got a dozen," she reminds me.

"Have you seen Bailey eat donuts?" I shake my head and laugh at the thought.

Katie laughs too. "So true."

True? It's darn right scary. Bailey could give the guys at the station a run for their money when it comes to donuts. I wouldn't put her up against the Sheriff's Office though. Those guys are worse than we are.

"Where are we going?" Katie asked.

"You'll see." I go to put the truck in reverse.

"Are we hiding?" Katie asked softly with her head bowed.

Her question had me putting the truck back into park. I twist my upper body to face her more.

"No, Ma'am," I say firmly. "That will never happen again." I wave both hands, motioning around us. "We are sitting in the middle of town square and in my truck." I point to the ladies huddled together on the sidewalk outside of Sweet Treats. "They are taking pictures, and the one in the gazebo is recording."

Katie stares at each of the women gathering evidence. She makes sure they know we're on to them. She rolls her eyes and looks back at me.

"Hayden Happenings," we say at the same time.

"I'll call Megan later and make sure she gets all the facts straight," I say after our fit of laughter ends.

Megan and I met yesterday to settle our little agreement. I had been paying our little gossip blogger fifty dollars a week to not print anything about Katie. When the rumors about Katie's depression circulated around town, Megan realized how serious things were. She spread rumors and gossip. Plus, she reported on town events. Destroying someone's life was not her goal. Still, the annoying little woman gladly took my money.

Since Megan kept her word and promised to never write about Katie's past, I kept my word and gave her a final payment of two hundred dollars. The future sightings of me and Katie were fair game for her though. If she ever goes back on her word, I'll have Aiden destroy her little blog. Aiden had some serious connections. A few of them scared me, and I will never ask for details on them.

With the hiding issue now settled, I drove us out to the lake and parked near the tree line. It was early, but a few cars were parked near the firepit. Most weekends through the summer you'd find a few people out here camping and fishing. During town events and holidays, this place was packed. The Chief lets us bring the fire engine out here during the holiday parties. Even though we built a huge firepit, things have gotten out of hand a time or two. Four has no business building fires. The man is totally insane.

Within minutes of parking, I had the tailgate down and a blanket spread out in the bed of the truck. I took the to-go bag from Katie and helped her up. We settled back against the cab of the truck to enjoy our breakfast from the diner.

"Why are we at the lake?" Katie asked before digging into her pancakes.

"It's your birthday, and I wanted to take you somewhere special," I reply.

"The lake is special?" She glances up at me.

One look into her big blue eyes and I almost drown.

"Oh, Buttercup. This lake is *very* special." I wink at her and add, "Both sides."

She remembers all too well what happened on the other side of this lake. I'm reminded of those nights every single day. But surely, she hasn't forgotten this side.

"This is where it all started." I point off to her left into the forest. "The 4th of July, six years ago, we slipped right through there."

"You remember," she whispers.

"There's not a moment with you I don't remember." Her eyes lift to mine. "Are you finished?" I grab the edge of her plate. The food is almost gone anyway. When she nods her head, I set our plates to the side and slide out of the bed of the truck. "Come on."

She's unsure of what's going on, but she slides to the tailgate. Placing my hands on her hips, I hold her there for a moment. *Not here. Stick to the plan,* I tell myself. Before I blow the plan, I set her gently on the ground and close the tailgate. Taking her hand in mine, I lead her through the trees to the spot we slipped off to years ago. I came out here a few days ago and walked this trail. Okay. Honestly, I'm not sure if I have the exact spot, but I'm pretty sure I'm close.

When we get to the spot where the lake dips into a small cove, Katie lets go of my hand and walks to the center of the small clearing. She moves in a slow circle taking it all in. She remembers coming here. Brownie points for getting this right.

I give her a few minutes to remember. Before those memories take her further down the road to where we ended, and why, I close the distance between us. Wrapping my arms around her, I pull her close.

She looks up at me with a small smile on her face. The first time we were here, we only had the light of the moon to guide us. In full daylight, she's just as beautiful, and this is just as special. One hand remains around her waist while the fingertips of the other glide across her cheek and down to her neck.

"We started here," I say softly. "I thought it was only fitting that we did again."

Lowering my head, I gently press my lips to hers. The kiss starts slow and sweet. That only lasts for a few seconds. A hunger that has been buried for years comes to life. When Katie's hands slide up my chest and around my neck, I deepen the kiss. She moans into my mouth causing me to lose control. The kiss turns messy and sloppy as my fingers fist around the hair at the back of her head. She's everything I remembered, everything I need.

Neither of us breaks the kiss until we're gasping for air and have no choice. Wrapping her in my arms, I hold her to my chest as if my life depended on it. It probably does. No matter what happened between us in the past, I know I don't want to do life without her for another day.

I would say we needed to take things slow, but slow could cost me her again. Besides, my patience was worn out by this point. There was none left. We had some things to work through, but we could figure all that out later. There was one thing we needed to settle right now.

With my hands on either side of her neck, I tilted her chin up with one of my thumbs. Our breathing was still ragged, but this matter couldn't wait.

"You're not moving to Seattle," I tell her.

"Miles Hamilton, are you telling me what to do?" she asked.

I don't know if she's serious or not, but I am.

"I can't lose you again," I say.

"Again? What makes you think I'm yours?" she challenges.

"Tell me I'm wrong." I lift her chin as far as I can without hurting her. She tries to look away. "No." Her eyes come back to mine. "You look me in the eye and tell me you're not mine."

"I can't," she whispers.

Releasing my rough hold on her, I claim her gorgeous pink lips with mine again and kiss her until she's breathless once more. She will always be mine.

I have no idea how long we stay in the forest lost in a heated passion. I wasn't about to leave when the only woman I've ever wanted was clinging to me. When her knees give way, I figured it was enough for now. With an arm around each other, we walked back to my truck.

"Where would you like to go for lunch?" I asked.

"The diner," she replied right away.

"Front and center, huh?" I tease as I help her inside.

"Front and center," she confirms.

Well, it appears the good nosy citizens of this town were going to get a show today. Good. Beth was right this morning about a lot of things. It's about time everyone knows how much Katie means to me.

"You weren't really going to move away, were you?" I asked as we drove back to town.

"If you hated me or only wanted to be friends, I would have had no choice but to go somewhere else," she replies in a low voice.

I reach for her hand and bring it to my lips. Well, she has nothing to worry about there.

"Buttercup, you will *never* live anywhere but Hayden Falls." I bring her hand to my lips again. If she goes, I go with her.

"Is that so?" There's humor in her voice.

I glance over and wink at her. "Yes, Ma'am."

Thank goodness the moving away issue is solved. I can now concentrate on making Katie smile for the rest of her birthday, and longer if she'll let me.

We had to stop back by Petals for a while. In our haste to leave earlier this morning, I forgot her special ordered birthday cake with daffodils on it. It was fine because we got to share the cake with her mom and Bailey. Katie was thrilled her mother was a part of today. I tucked that little bit of information away for now. I'd make sure to include Ms. Matthews in future surprises for my girl. My girl. Katie Matthews was definitely my girl.

Chapter Twenty-Seven

Katie

This was the best birthday. Spending the day with Miles and rediscovering us was amazing. Not having to hide made it even better. Everywhere we went someone was holding up a phone. Megan was getting a lot of photos today.

The cake from Sweet Treats was beautiful. The daffodils had so much detail to them. I didn't want to cut it. Bailey, however, had no trouble with it. I must say, Sophie Lewis' baking and decorating skills were phenomenal.

My present from Miles wasn't just one gift. The day together was already the greatest gift. Well, that might now be exactly true. His kisses were the greatest gift. I didn't need anything more. Still, he handed me a huge box full of things. Naturally, everything inside had daffodils on it. The t-shirt was specially ordered online. There was a throw pillow, a journal, pens, magnets, towels, and what looked to be a handblown glass figurine. It was sweet of him to search the internet for all of this just for me.

We spent the afternoon riding down every road we could find. We talked, laughed, and sang along with the radio. For dinner, we went to Gino's Italian House in town. Antonio's Pizza Palace only served pizza. Gino's had every other Italian dish you could want. Miles was serious when he said we weren't hiding this time. I understand why we did when we were younger. Still, it's something I never want to do again.

"I wish I didn't have to take you home." Miles reaches over and takes my hand.

Sadness had surrounded us the moment we got into the truck after dinner. We've been sitting here in the parking lot for at least five minutes, and he hasn't bothered to start the engine. I understand why. This day has been so wonderful, I don't want it to end either.

"You're not taking me home," I say as calmly as I can. I have to look out the window.

"Uh, Buttercup." Miles gently tugs my arm until I look at him. "I want more, and I'm all for not going slow. But, we're not going *that* fast."

I can't hold my laughter in any longer. Covering my mouth with both hands, I lean back against the seat. I should probably say something because the look I'm getting from him says I'm in trouble.

"You're taking me to E's house," I explain when I can talk again.

"Oh, right. I forgot about that." Miles starts the engine and heads toward Aiden and E's house. "I'm picking Aiden up in the morning."

Spencer took Aiden to the airport last night. He flew to Tennessee to be a groomsman at a friend's wedding. Due to E's scare a couple of weeks ago, Aiden refused to let her fly. It probably wouldn't have been a big deal for her, but Aiden wouldn't take the chance. He was going to back out of being in the wedding, but E insisted he go. So, Aiden is only spending one night in Tennessee. Well, technically, it's two nights because last night he was on a plane. While he's away, we're having a girl's sleepover with E. A second member of the Dawson Boys band will get married at the end of the month, and we will do this again. I never understood why Aiden, with all his law enforcement training, ended up as the sound guy for a country band for a few years.

The drive to our friends' house only takes about ten minutes. It's way too short for my liking. Sammie, Ally, and Beth are already here. I had texted Sammie earlier and asked her to pick up my overnight bag from Petals. I was planning on riding to E's with Sammie after work today until Miles surprised me this morning. Trust me, I'm not complaining.

"Guess I'll be seeing you first thing in the morning." Miles helps me out of the truck and walks me to the front door.

"You will, but I still hate that this day is ending." I smile through my sadness. He went through so much trouble to make this day happen, I can't damper it for one second.

"Oh, Buttercup." He leans down and presses his lips to mine. "We're just getting started."

That's one promise I'm going to hold him to. Before I can say anything, the door opens, and Ally pulls me inside.

"Hey, ladies." Miles walks in behind us and waves to everyone.

Colton's dog, Bo, bounces over for Miles to pet him. Looks like Aiden has pulled out all his resources to make sure E's protected tonight. Like her four best friends aren't enough. Something tells me a ranch hand or two will be watching this house all night.

"Did you two have fun today?" Sammie asked.

I look up at Miles and smile. I'm pretty sure I'm blushing too. "Yeah, we did."

Miles winked at me again and turns his attention to my friends.

"Do you ladies need anything?" He asked.

"Trust me." E is sitting on pillows on the floor. She holds both hands out gesturing to the room. "We have more than enough."

One look around the room confirms just how right she is. There's already a blanket and pillow fort built in the living room. We will never outgrow those. Food and drinks are on the kitchen island and the coffee table. Of course, all of E's stuff is sugar-free and non-alcoholic. Movies, video games, board games, and puzzles are scattered around the room. It looks as if they started this party hours ago without me. Hey. It's perfectly fine with me. My day has been beyond amazing.

"Aren't you supposed to pick Aiden up in the morning?" Ally asked.

"I am," Miles replied.

"Then, it's time for you to go." Beth starts pushing Miles back toward the door.

"Beth!" I shout.

"Sorry. This is girl's night." Beth doesn't listen to me. "You gotta go," she tells Miles.

"Beth," Miles warns.

"Nope, Dude. You need some sleep so you can get to the airport on time. E wants her husband back," Beth said.

"She'll get her husband back and on time," Miles insists.

Beth still doesn't listen. She keeps pushing him toward the door. I'm going to hurt one of my best friends.

"Beth, wait." I hurry to the door and push her aside. She doesn't go far.

He can't leave without me thanking him for today. I wrap my arms around Miles' neck as his hands fall to my waist. He leans forward and I meet him halfway for a goodnight kiss. This is awkward with Beth standing so close, but I wasn't about to let him go without another kiss. I don't even care that my friends are watching.

"Happy Birthday, Buttercup," he whispers against my lips.

"Thank you for today," I whisper back.

"Ugh!" Beth exclaims as she pushes her way between us. "Sorry, Hamilton. Time to go." She finally manages to get Miles through the door. "You can have another kiss when you bring Aiden home."

I can't believe my friend right now. How can she be so annoying?

Miles looks around Beth and points at me. "I'll be collecting that kiss in less than twelve hours. Be ready, Buttercup."

"You two have sucked face enough today." With that, Beth closes the door.

"I can't believe you." I glare at Beth.

"But you love me." Beth puts her arm through mine and turns me to face the rest of our friends.

E holds her arms up and motions for me to come to her with her fingers. I settled down on the pillows in front of the couch with her. She looks comfortable enough. Bo curls up on her other side. Most of the time he seems like a big baby. No one would believe how much of

146

a guard dog Bo really is until you see him in action. I would not want this dog chasing me.

"Somebody is in love," Sammie said.

"You look so happy," E said.

"I passed happy hours ago," I admit. I know I'm blushing again.

"Okay." Ally wiggles on her pillow. "We need details."

"Yes!" Beth shouts and gets comfortable on a pillow next to Ally. "All the details, girl."

"We've been following it all day, but we need firsthand details." Sammie props her elbows on the coffee table and rests her chin in her hands.

"Following?" I ask. What are they talking about?

"Megan has been posting pictures and videos of you guys all day long," Ally explains.

"You two are her first live love story." Beth claps her hands.

Live love story? Oh no. You know what, scratch that. Good for Megan. Even better for me and Miles. I really love this no hiding thing.

"It started with coffee from Beth's and then donuts from Sweet Treats. Next, he's stealing you from Petals." Sammie starts recanting the events of my day.

"Lunch at the diner and dinner at Gino's," Ally adds.

"Did you two really have breakfast in the back of his truck at the lake?" E asked.

I cover my mouth with my hands and laugh while nodding my head. They sound like a bunch of teenage girls. I feel like a teenager again.

"And just what did you two do in the woods for over an hour?" Beth raises an eyebrow.

We all burst out laughing. They really knew every step Miles and I took. I'm so happy I can't find it in me to be mad about any of this. I hope Miles doesn't mind when he finds out what Megan has done.

"I don't kiss and tell," I say when I can finally breathe normally again.

"Tonight you do," E insists, causing us to laugh again.

Tonight, I do exactly that. Beth tells us about Miles picking up coffee this morning, and I fill in the rest. Sammie pulled up Hayden's Happenings, and I gave them all the details about every picture and video. The way this conversation was going, we'd probably still be up when Aiden got home. Miles' promise to claim another kiss in the morning had me giddy and blushing again. Twelve hours was going to feel like forever.

Chapter Twenty-Eight

Katie

Cowboys seemed to be overly crowded tonight. Of course, it was like this during the summer months, even on weeknights. My birthday was last week, but since Aiden was out of town, and we had the sleepover with E, my birthday celebration was moved to this weekend. E and I have the virgin pina colada she's so fond of. The others have beers and shots.

Beth had reserved our usual table on the far side of the dance floor. She seemed to be cozying up to one of the part-time bartenders Noah hired for the summer. I don't know what the new guy's name is, but the situation was not going to end well. A certain baseball player was watching every move Beth made tonight.

Brady Maxwell rarely ever came home after the secret of him being the one responsible for Old Man Wentworth's barn burning down years ago came out back before Christmas. He thinks everyone in town hates him now. He doesn't stick around long enough to really find out anything. He is on a downward spiral, just as Beth is.

I feel bad for the new bartender though. The guy is handsome, and he has more than half the women in here making eyes at him. The eyes the man needs to worry about are Brady's. Every time Beth leans across the bar to speak to the new guy, Brady turns another shade of red. I don't know why these two don't admit they like each other. Hopefully, they'll figure it out soon.

The only thing saving the new guy tonight is the fact that Aiden is sitting next to Brady. If things get out of hand, Aiden will get his little brother out of here. He seems to be on top of the situation. Aiden's eyes flick between Brady and Beth a few times. Oh my gosh. He sees it too. Glad to know I'm not the only one aware of it. Honestly, I think Brady and Beth are the only ones not aware of it.

My gaze moves to the man on Brady's left. My handsome sexy firefighter slouches in his chair with his elbow propped on the wooden banister around the upper level. He watches me as his thumb lazily moves back and forth across his bottom lip. A lip my lips need to be on. Oh, dear. What is happening to me? Miles chuckles and bites his thumb. The grin on his face is devilish. My eyes dart up to his. Oh my. He saw me lick my lips. He knows where my thoughts were just now. Miles winks at me and turns to say something to Spencer.

"Brace yourself," Sammie leans over and whispers in my ear.

Huh? Her eyes move past me. Turning around, I immediately see the problem. Brittney and Holly are walking this way. It would be too much to hope that they would walk right on by us without stopping.

"Hey," Holly said when they get to our table.

Yep. Hope is gone. Holly is wearing a bride's tiara. Ugh. Of course, Brittney, being Holly's maid-of-honor, couldn't plan a better bachelorette party. Well, to be fair, not that I should be where Brittney Douglas is concerned, we did bring E here for her sort of bachelorette party. E had a bit more class and wouldn't allow us to dress her up in the ridiculous outfit Holly was wearing tonight. Even if we had dressed her up, we would never go for a cheap tiara and a pink feather boa. I won't even get started on Holly's obnoxious leather pants and crop top.

"Hey." I smile back. "You look cute." It's a lie, and my friends know it.

Holly is cute, just not in this outfit. Her maid-of-honor makes me gag. The woman has no taste. Holly should ditch her.

"Did my mom settle everything up this week?" Holly asked. She's been out of town the past couple of weeks.

"Yes, she did. If you have any major changes, please let me know by Monday," I request with another fake smile. I think I'm getting good at doing this.

Holly's mother stopped by to pay her deposit this week, and she dropped off the photos of Holly's final choices for her wedding next month. This is one wedding I'll be glad to have over with. Holly is marrying a guy she met in college. After the wedding, she's moving to Boston. It would be great if she took Brittney with her.

"I will, but I'm pretty happy with my choices." Holly waves and pulls Brittney with her to the bar.

"At least the evil witch didn't say anything," Ally mumbles.

At least, my friends didn't tackle the evil witch. I would call this a good night. So far anyway. This is my life and things have a tendency to go wrong. Maybe it won't happen tonight. I scan the bar and freeze. The night may have just taken a turn for the worst. I should have known better than to think otherwise.

"What?" Sammie asked.

Yes, I was staring at the bar with my mouth open. Now, my friends are doing the same thing. Even from behind, there's no mistaking who the woman with long dark hair is. She turns around when Holly and Brittney approach her. Tara Adams. My heart drops to the floor.

I look across the dance floor to the upper level. Miles and the guys are lost in conversation. From where he's sitting, if he looks toward the bar, Miles will see Tara. I don't know what happened between him and Tara, but I know he dated her for a little while. That same summer, Tara left town to go live with her grandmother in another state. This is the first time I've seen her in Hayden Falls since. Sadly, jealousy rears its ugly head, turning me into someone I don't want to be. Will Miles want her? Was she the one who got away? Was I enough for him?

Hopefully, Tara and Brittney weren't friends. That would be a bad combination for me. Tara looks down at her phone. She waves by to Holly and Brittney before hurrying out the front door. There wasn't enough interaction between them for me to know anything about their friendship. Miles doesn't seem to have noticed her.

Jake Campbell and his band start playing a slow song. Couples pair off and make their way to the dance floor. Aiden comes and pulls E off her stool. Miles is there holding his hand out to me. With a smile, I place my hand in his.

"We've never danced in public before," I say as he moves us to the far side of the dance floor.

"We've never danced here before," he corrects me. "We danced at Aiden and E's wedding, and we've danced plenty of times under the stars."

Yeah, that's what I meant to say. We danced many times under the oak tree at the lake by the light of the moon. Being in his arms now, in front of everyone, feels so right, so natural.

"Are you enjoying your little party?' Miles asked.

"I am." I move my body closer to his. "You look like you're having fun too."

"How could I not? You make me happy," he whispers.

His head lowers and his lip press against mine. It's not the chaste kiss I was expecting in a public place. I moan when his tongue moves across my bottom lip. A small cry escapes me as his lips leave mine. His arms tighten around my waist causing me to sigh. I love everything about this man.

"I thought gentlemen didn't kiss girls on the dance floor," I say breathlessly. There's no way for me to kiss this man and not be affected by it.

"The first kiss should never be on a dance floor." One side of his mouth turns up in a sly grin. "All of our firsts happened at the lake, in case you forgot."

I'm pretty sure I'm three shades of red right now, but not out of anger as Brady is. Firsts. Miles. Me. The lake. Oh my gosh. Miles chuckles and gives me another quick kiss.

"I love where your thoughts are, Buttercup," he whispers in my ear. His breath is warm against my skin.

"You can't do this to me in public," I whisper back.

"Do you think you're not affecting me too? It's just easier for you to hide it, Sweetheart." He rests his forehead against mine.

I feel the rumble in his chest as Miles chuckles. He slowly moves us to the corner of the dance floor. A smile of satisfaction crosses my lips. Somebody is *very* affected. Releasing a long breath, he puts a little distance between us. Trust me, it's not enough.

"Are you okay?" I give him a playful grin.

"No, you little minx. You know I'm not," Miles grumbles.

When the song ends, Miles positions me in front of him and walks us through the crowd to the back door. He leads me to his truck and drives us the short distance to the alley behind Petals.

"What are we…"

My question is lost when Miles grabs the back of my head and crashes his mouth over mine. What we're doing is obvious, and I don't care what the whys are that brought us here.

"I can't kiss you like this on a dance floor," He says between kisses. "Or, in your front yard." His lips do not leave mine for long. "And, we're here because I couldn't make it any further."

I know exactly how he feels. Needing more, I unfasten my seatbelt and tighten my arms around his neck. Without breaking the kiss, I climb over the console onto his lap. I feel the seat slide back giving me more room. A make-out session in a truck may not sound ideal but this one is so divine.

After seeing Tara Adams tonight, I should slow things down and ask Miles about her. I don't know what type of hold she may have on him. He's never talked about her. Will she take him from me? I know I'm his, but is he truly mine?

I don't know the answers, but there's no way I can deny the passion I feel for this man. I'll take what he freely gives me and tuck the moments away as memories. If I have to, I can still leave Hayden Falls if he chooses Tara. Tonight, I want Miles Hamilton with every fiber of my being.

My hands slide under the hem of his t-shirt and up his chest. He has more muscles than he had five years ago. Not wanting a barrier between us anymore, I pull his shirt off. It's the only time our lips part. Right now, he's mine and I'm going to enjoy every second with him.

Chapter Twenty-Nine

Miles

Things with Katie were getting overly hot and heavy. On most days anyway. There were a few days when she gets quiet. We should probably talk about that. Hiding things destroyed us once before. I refuse to let it happen again. If she's slipping back into depression, I need to pull her out before she goes too far. I can't lose her for any reason.

On most days, Katie seemed to be getting stronger. I was so proud of her for fighting her way out of the darkness as she was doing. I didn't want to cause her any kind of setback. I'd give her a little more time and see if these odd quiet moments faded away completely. They could be nothing. Maybe they were just her adjusting to seeing things differently, or maybe I was imagining them.

Today was one of my favorite days in our little community. It was the 4th of July Celebration. The annual cook-off was well underway. The cook-off was scheduled to end at noon. Later this afternoon, due to the emergency that happened with E Maxwell on Memorial Day, there was a double-header baseball game. We were going to be worn out by the end of the day.

The Hayden Falls Fire Department was set up in our usual place in the park. We worked together as a team for the cook-off. Aiden and his brother, Brady, were set up under the tent next to us. Spencer is helping them out today. Pit and Four have a couple of tents set up on our other side.

Pit was once again wearing his *Pitmaster* apron. He was already set up when we pulled out our grills early this morning. I'm beginning to wonder if he's been out here all night. Aiden is wearing an apron that says, *The New Pitmaster*. Pit doesn't look worried though. In fact, he grins and shakes his head every time he looks at Aiden.

Four showed up around the time the sun came up. I don't think Pit actually lets him do any of the grilling. I'm sure the judges and everyone who gets one of his plates appreciates that. Four is wearing an apron that says, *Ask me a question. If I'm wrong, I get a kiss*. I guess the *Kiss the Cook* one didn't work out so well for him. This one is at least getting him a few laughs from the ladies today.

"When do you plan on locking that down?" Luke points toward the square.

Katie is standing at the walkway entrance of the park behind the diner. She's wearing cut-off shorts and the daffodil t-shirt I gave her for her birthday. I knew it would look good on her. She's talking to Mrs. Murphy and a couple more of the ladies from the Hayden Sisters.

"Man, you're a goner." Levi gives me a shove.

"Yeah, I am," I happily admit. I turn and glare at Luke. "And do not call my girl a *that* again."

"Whoa," Luke smirks and backs away with his hands up.

"Ignore my brother. He's a major pain." Levi waves Luke away.

"Hello, Beautiful," Luke says with his hand over his chest. His gaze is locked on his new target.

Levi and I turn to see who caught Luke's eye. Halfway across the park is a group of women with a couple of kids running around them.

"Is that Tara Adams?" Levi asked.

Luke studies the woman for a moment and nods his head. Apparently, the fool just recognized her. I haven't seen Tara in nine years. I knew her grandfather was really sick, but I hadn't heard anyone say she was back in town. It's good she came to see her grandfather. The reports I've heard about him aren't good.

Tara reaches for the hand of one of the little boys playing next to them. He's got the same dark straight hair she has. Wow. Tara is a mom. It's hard to tell from here how old her son is. He's a tiny little guy. I'm glad things worked out for her and she has a family. That's the ultimate goal for me one day.

"Never mind," Luke grumbles when he sees Tara walk away holding her son's hand.

I don't know if Tara is married or if she's a single mom. Luke Barnes is shallow though. There's no way he's going to bind himself in any way to a woman with a kid. The idiot would probably chase after a married woman if he thought he could get away with it. A mom would be a hard no for Luke.

"How are you two even related, let alone twins?" I asked Levi.

Levi shrugs. "I ask that same question all the time. Mom doesn't even have an answer."

"Man, you might want to get over there and get your girl." Devon Reed, one of our volunteers, points toward where Katie was talking with Mrs. Murphy.

If only she was still talking with the Hayden Sisters or anyone else in town for that matter. But no, not my luck. It had to be Phillip Crawford. I'm going to have to kill this fool. Bolting out of my chair, I storm across the edge of the park. Now I know how Aiden feels about Four flirting with E. Just the sight of Phillip Crawford near my girl makes me want to rip him in half. It's bad enough just seeing this jerk around town.

Well, this is not exactly the same situation Aiden has. Four is E's friend. I don't understand that friendship but it's real. Four only pulls his ridiculous stunts to aggravate Aiden. It's actually hilarious to watch most of the time. To everyone but Aiden that is. Phillip Crawford, on the other hand, has no friends and no morals. His intentions are dark and evil. He's got his eyes on the wrong girl. This one is all mine.

Stepping between them, I lock Katie in my arms and cover her lips with mine. Her little yelp of surprise is lost in the kiss. My lips devour hers until I feel her body sag against mine for support.

"Hello, Buttercup," I say against her lips. I smile when her lips press against mine. "Miss me?" She nods her head and kisses me again. "Good girl."

After another deep kiss, I put my arm around her waist and escort her to the fire department's tents where we receive a round of applause from everyone near us. I don't bother to look back to acknowledge Crawford.

"That was epic." E jumps up from her chair clapping her hands.

Aiden grabs her waist to steady her and points to her chair. She glares at him but only for a moment. I feel bad for E sometimes because of how strongly Aiden protects her, but she seems to take it all in stride. She kisses him and sits back down.

Grace Wentworth stops by Aiden's tent to talk with E. I notice she's stealing glances at someone. Once again, the fool has no clue. I need to make good on my silent vow to help her out.

"You and your friends should invite Grace to girl's night sometime." I motion toward Grace.

"We really should. She's so sweet, and I never see her go out," Katie said.

Aiden passes the spatula off to Brady and hands E a bottle of water from a nearby cooler. I can already tell he's offering her everything under the sun to make sure she's comfortable.

"Buttercup, why don't you go sit with E for a while?" I suggest. "Give her a little break from her overbearing husband."

"You don't mind?" Katie smiles up at me.

"Not at all." I cup her cheek with my palm and run my thumb across her bottom lip. "You'll be ten yards away, and any time my lips need these, I'll be right there."

"That goes both ways." She lifts her chin.

I hear the oohs and whistles from the guys, but I ignore them.

"Yes, Ma'am, it sure does," I agree.

To prove her point, Katie pushes up on her toes and kisses me long and sweet. This woman completely owns me, and I'm not ashamed to admit it. It's her kiss, so I let her end it. With a huge smile on her face, Katie walks away to go sit with her friend.

"You're one lucky man," Devon mumbles.

"About that locking down part?" Levi playfully nudges me.

"Soon, my friend, very soon," I reply with a huge smile of my own.

"Pit! Whatcha grilling?" Chief Foster calls out as he joins us.

"Baby backs," Pit raises a finger in the air while he concentrates on his grills.

Levi and I look over at Aiden. He looks happy and hopeful.

"Our friend is going to lose," Levi mumbles.

"Yep," I agree.

Pit never loses when he BBQs ribs. He almost lost one year with steaks and vowed to never use them in a competition again. I didn't see how he started everything this morning, but from what I've witnessed the past few hours, he's timing every step he makes. I would have never thought so many steps went into grilling ribs. No wonder Pit wins as often as he does.

The steaks the fire department and Aiden are grilling will be tender and will practically melt in your mouth. There's not a doubt in my mind though, Pit is going to win this.

"Do you think we should tell him?" Levi looks over at Aiden again.

"Man, we have a double-header this afternoon. I'm not ruining his day." I give my head a quick shake. "Let him lose fair and square and he'll accept it."

"If we're letting him lose fair and square, what was last night?" Levi whispered.

"Shh. Nobody needs to know about that," I whisper back.

Levi looks at Pit. "How is he still standing?"

"I don't think he's human," I reply.

Levi and I weren't exactly on the up and up last night. We hadn't intended on interfering, but the opportunity presented itself at Cowboys last night. We secretly bought Pit and Four three rounds of shots and a bucket of beer. I have no idea how much or what else those two had before we got there. They could barely walk when they left the bar.

"It's affecting him though," Levi nods his head.

Yeah, it's affecting Pit. He's downing water by the gallon and wearing sunglasses. I've seen him take some ibuprofen too. Sadly, it's not enough to help Aiden win this cook-off.

"Next year, you could try kidnapping him for twenty-four hours," Devon suggested.

Mine and Levi's eyes widen. We hadn't told anyone what we did.

Devon chuckles. "I saw you at Cowboys last night." He leans closer to us. "I even bought a round of shots for them."

All three of us double over laughing.

"We're a sad bunch." Levi can barely talk for laughing. "We can't even cheat."

"I don't think it's us." I can't stop laughing either. I point to Pit. "I think it's him."

Devon and Levi nod their heads in agreement. Oh well, we tried.

The sound of Katie's laughter has me forgetting all about Pit, Aiden, and this cook-off. Seeing her happy causes my chest to tighten. I run my tongue over my bottom lip.

"It's been too long," I whisper.

"What?" Levi narrows his eyes, but I don't notice.

"My lips need those." I point at Katie and bolt from my chair.

Chapter Thirty

Katie

Today has been amazing, for me anyway. For Aiden, not so much. He didn't win the BBQ Cookoff. Once again, Pit won the Hayden Falls Pitmaster title with his baby back ribs. Aiden came in second place with his mouth-watering steaks. He was a good sport about it though. He and Pit shook hands, shared a laugh, and vowed to compete against each other next year. Pit still does not look worried. I love the guy's confidence.

Aiden got a red ribbon, a small trophy, and a prize from the hardware store. The first-place prize Pit won wasn't as grand as some other cookoffs I've heard he's been rumored to have won. Some of those contests have high entry fees of three to four hundred dollars. Their grand prize of 10K is well worth the risk though. Pit won't admit to how many he's won. With those types of prizes, maybe Pit isn't the town clown everyone thinks he is. Pit got the clown title because of Four, I'm sure of it.

The participants in our little cookoff are mostly local guys. The grand prize in Hayden Falls isn't large enough to attract professional grillers. Until today, I didn't realize there were professional grillers. Pit shared a few of his competition stories with the fire department. The man has been all the way to Texas to compete in cookoffs. Again, he won't admit if he won or not.

For the guys around here, it's all about holding the Pitmaster title than the actual prizes. We all cheered when Pit proudly accepted his blue ribbon and larger trophy. Four did a celebration dance. We won't discuss that, but E almost fell out of her chair. Aiden offered to give her dollar bills to toss at him. The whole thing was beyond weird.

For the bonus grand prize, most of the businesses in town donated gift cards or certificates if they didn't have store cards. They ranged from fifty to a hundred dollars each. Petals donated a fifty-dollar one. I hear the hardware store always gives the largest donation of five hundred dollars, not bad for a small-town store. Still, there are a lot of businesses in our little town so Pit had a nice prize for his time and effort.

The man had a bigger heart than people realized. Most may have missed it, but I didn't. He gave the cards for Frozen Scoops and Sweet Treats to families with small children. A few others he gave to members of the Hayden Sisters. I had tears in my eyes when he gave the ones from the market and clothing store to a single mom I knew was struggling financially. Pit was definitely a mystery.

The baseball doubleheader was going well. The men of Hayden Falls won the first game. The second game was tied in the eighth inning.

Sammie, Ally, Beth, and I sat with E. The bleachers were not comfortable for her at this stage in her pregnancy. Not that the metal bleachers were comfortable to start with. Aiden took care of everything to make sure his little wife was as comfortable as possible today. He was making sure there was no repeat of what happened on Memorial Day.

We were set up in the shaded area near third base in foldout chairs. Aiden didn't trust the trees near us to provide E with enough shade today. Each of us had an umbrella attached to our chairs. We had cold drinks in our cup holders. A cooler of ice and more drinks were sitting on the ground next to E's chair. We even had battery-operated fans on nylon cords around our necks. E was hydrated, cool, and as comfortable as anyone could be on the 4th of July, maybe more so.

I also think we were purposely sitting next to third base because Doctor Matt Larson played the position. Matt would walk over to the chain-link fence in front of us to check on E often. Of course, Aiden came over or looked our way every chance he got. E would giggle and wave when he was on the pitcher's mound.

My friends and I were talking and not really paying attention to the game or our surroundings. Something startled me when it hit my shoe. Looking down, I find a red child's ball next to my foot. I pick it up just as a little boy with dark hair comes running over. He's really cute.

"Is this yours?" I ask.

"I'm sorry." He drops his head and twists the toe of his shoe in the dirt.

"It's okay. It didn't hurt," I assure him.

"Here you go." I hold the ball out.

He hangs back afraid to get close enough to take the ball from my hands. Good. His parents have taught him about stranger danger.

"It's okay," I say softly. "I'm Katie. I own the flower shop in town. What's your name?"

"Jeffery," he replies shyly.

"How old are you?" I ask, hoping our conversation will relax him enough for him to get his ball.

"Eight," Jeffery replied.

He's tiny for his age, but he's so sweet. Seeing that he's still not comfortable enough to approach me, I roll the ball to him.

"There you go." I smile at him. He squats to pick up the ball, never taking his eyes off of me. "If you and your mom ever stop by the flower shop, I'll give you a balloon."

He smiles back at me and nods his head. His long dark hair falls over his dark gray eyes.

"Jeffery!" a woman shouts as she runs up to him. "Are you okay?"

Jeffery nods. "My ball got away."

"I'm sorry if he bothered you." Tara Adams turns and apologizes to us.

"Not at all." My face loses all expression as I look up at her. My eyes automatically go to Miles at first base.

"Hey, Tara." E waves to her.

"It's good to see you," Sammie said.

"We're sorry to hear about your grandfather," Ally adds.

"Thank you," Tara said. "It's good seeing all of you again too." She looks at E. "And, congratulations." Tara motions to E's baby bump.

"Thank you." E moves her hand to cover her belly.

"Boy or girl?" Tara asked.

"Boy," E replied.

"Can I play with him?" Jeffery asked excitedly.

"You're a lot older, and he will be a tiny baby," Tara explains in a soft tone just for Jeffery.

"He'll grow," Jeffery pouts.

"We'll see, but we need to go for now." Tara ruffles his hair. She turns back to us. "Again, I apologize, and it really is good seeing you all."

"It's fine," I assure her. "Bring Jeffery by Petals one day, and I'll give him a balloon in his favorite color."

"Red?" Jeffery's eyes widen.

"I'll save a red one just for you," I promise.

"Thank you." Tara takes her son's hand, and they walk away.

When we saw her a few weeks ago at Cowboys, I didn't know Tara had a family. It was nice of her to come home for her grandfather. I should focus on that matter and not where my thoughts were going. Sadly, the selfish me was glad to know she had a family. She seemed happy. It would mean she wasn't a problem for me and Miles after all. Wait? Was she married? I didn't notice a wedding ring on her finger. Honestly, I didn't even look. Ugh! Jealous was an evil monster.

"Oh!" E exclaims.

Everyone's heads snap in her direction. She's sitting up straight with her hand on the side of her belly.

"Are you okay?" I ask quickly.

Doctor Larson is already making his way to the fence. Aiden isn't far behind him.

"I'm fine!" E shouts and waves to them. "He just kicked, and really hard."

It takes Matt and E a few minutes to convince Aiden that everything is fine. Finally, he goes back to the pitcher's mound, but his eyes keep darting over to his wife. He's not going to be able to finish out this game. Sure enough, after giving up two runs, Aiden hands the ball over to his brother. Chase and my brother, Elliott, are now heckling Brady. Boys are so weird.

E is fidgeting in her chair trying to get comfortable with her hand pushing against the right side of her belly. I can't take my eyes off of her. It's strange, and I can't explain why, but I cautiously reach over and place my hand next to hers. E stills. I haven't touched her baby bump before. The others have, but I've held back from doing this.

A small gasp escapes me when I feel the baby's movement. My tear-filled eyes lift to hers.

"It's amazing," I whisper as a tear spills over and down my cheek.

"Oh, Katie." E goes to move my hand.

I shake my head. "It's okay."

"Katie, I'm…"

"Don't say you're sorry," I interrupt her. "This little guy is a miracle, and you need to experience this time to the fullest."

"But…"

"No buts." I won't let her feel bad because of me. "I didn't get this part. Share it with me?"

She nods her head and moves her hand so I can lay mine over the area where her little boy's foot is moving. Closing my eyes, with a tear or two running down my cheek, E's head falls against mine. She doesn't rush me or complain. My friend sits quietly, letting me have this moment. I can't explain how special this is.

A familiar hand moves slowly over my back as his other hand rests on my thigh. I don't have to open my eyes to know it's Miles. If he's noticed this, I'm sure others have as well, but I don't care. I need this moment.

"I'm here, Buttercup," he whispers. I nod but stay where I am. He had pulled up a chair next to mine.

The tiny foot stops pushing against my hand. I'm so grateful E let me have this moment. She and I release a breath and sit up.

"Thank you," I whisper. "I can't wait to meet him."

She puts a palm against my cheek. "You're going to be an awesome Godmother."

Baby Boy Maxwell, they really need to name this baby, will have an abundance of Godparents. Aiden and E couldn't decide on one, so they chose all of us.

Leaning to my other side, I fall into Miles' arms. The last inning of the game goes on, but we don't notice. The high school team won by three runs. All in all, it was a great day.

"I love you," Miles whispers in my ear.

"I love you too."

Rachel told me moments like this would sneak up on me. Until this moment, I didn't realize how right she was. Rather than shutting down as I used to do, I embraced it the best I could and felt my way through it. Maybe someday, I'll get to be a mom. Today, no matter how hard things are for me, I'm beyond happy for my friend.

Chapter Thirty-One

Miles

The next couple of weeks were great. Katie and I were getting closer every day. This was the relationship we should have had to start with. If her dad hadn't been a class A jerk, things would be different now. We would already be married with a kid or two.

It was Friday, and I had the weekend off. Today, Katie had an appointment with her therapist. Instead of one of her friends, she asked me to go with her. I was a little nervous about going, but if it helped Katie, I'd gladly do it. Rachel Montgomery was great. She and Katie had a calm relaxing connection. After seeing her today, I was sure she was exactly who Katie needed to walk her through her depression.

We had lunch in Missoula and were now on our way back to Hayden Falls. We had the windows down and were singing along to the radio. This was one of our favorite things to do when we were younger. We were on our way to my parent's house for dinner. This would be Katie's first family dinner with us. My mom and Chloe were beyond excited. They've messaged me all week about it.

A couple of miles outside of town, something darted across the road in front of us. Slamming on the brakes, I held my arm in front of Katie to brace her as the truck slid to the shoulder of the road.

"Are you okay," I quickly ask the moment we come to a stop.

"What was that?" Katie asked between ragged breaths.

"I don't know," I admit.

We were on a long stretch of road with no traffic. I was paying more attention to the beautiful woman beside me than to my surroundings. I knew better, but my girl was hard to resist.

"Did we hit it?" Katie unfastened her seatbelt and lifted up on the seat with her knee.

"No." It's the one thing I am sure of right now. "But you stay here. I'll check it out."

Getting out, I grabbed my shotgun from behind the seat before closing the door. I didn't get a good look at the animal, but I'm pretty sure there was more than one. They darted from the right side of the road, where my truck now sits. Crossing the road, I come to a halt on the other shoulder. I stare in shock or awe, I'm not sure which, for a few minutes.

An old man in worn overalls and a tattered hat stands just inside the tree line staring back at me. Some kind of animal sits next to his left leg.

"Mags, are you okay?" I call out.

"Yep," he replies. He doesn't move.

My girlfriend doesn't listen and climbs out of the truck. Katie crosses the road and moves to stand behind me when she sees who I'm talking to. Well, Mags isn't the problem. The creature sitting next to him greatly concerns me.

"What are you doing out here?" I ask.

"Chasing rabbits." Mags reaches down aimlessly to pet the creature on the head.

"Was that you we almost hit?" I asked.

Mags nods his head. I guess the old man can move faster than I thought. My eyes remain on the thing by his leg.

"What is that?" Katie asked.

"I don't know," I whisper over my shoulder. She really needs to get back into the truck.

Mags looks around as if he's trying to figure out what Katie is talking about. He doesn't comprehend that it's the thing sitting next to him. The creature bears its teeth causing me to step back a few paces taking Katie with me.

"Mags, what is that?" I point to the creature.

"Oh, this?" He rubs the animal's head. "He's one of my dogs."

"I don't think that's a dog," Katie whispers.

I don't think so either. Mags is crazier than I thought if he befriended this thing.

"Does your dog have the mange or rabies?" I eye the animal curiously. A better word to describe it would be deformed.

"I'd have to shoot him if he did." Mags looks at me as if I'm the crazy one.

I don't even want to know if this man has a gun. The best thing I can do is to get Katie out of here. I don't care what Mags says, that's not a dog. Whatever it is has started a low growl. Thankfully, I have backed us to the driver's side of the truck. If the creature moves toward the road, I won't hesitate to shoot it, rabies or not.

"Buttercup, slowly open the door. Get in and climb across," I instruct over my shoulder. I'm not taking my eyes off that creature for one second.

"Yeah," she whispers and does as I ask.

"Mags, you sure you're okay? I ask again.

"Yeah, just heading home," he replies.

"Be sure you take that thing with you." I point at the strange creature still sitting by his leg.

"Come on, boy." Mags turns and starts walking into the forest. Thankfully, the creature follows him. "We gotta get home and set out Mrs. Big Foot's snack."

Mrs. Bigfoot? Snack? What in the world? I shouldn't be surprised. He has a deformed creature he believes is a dog walking beside him. Mrs. Bigfoot and snacks sound totally normal at this point.

I get into the driver's seat, keeping my shotgun across my lap, and watch until Mags is out of sight. There's no way to explain what just happened.

"Did he say Mrs. Bigfoot?" Katie asked.

"Yeah, he did." Shaking my head doesn't clear any of the past few minutes away.

"I wonder what kind of snacks he gives her." Katie narrows her eyes and tilts her head.

Surely, she's not taking this seriously. I gape at her. This is so unbelievable. I can't even move.

"I bet it's Ramen." She holds up a finger and nods her head.

What alternate universe did I just fall into? I'm going to need medication after this, some strong medication at that.

"Ramen noodles?" I continue to stare at her as if she's insane.

"Yeah. Mags buys several packs when he comes to town," she replies as if this is all normal.

"I don't know." I run a hand over my head. This is giving me a headache.

"I wonder which flavor is her favorite." Katie bites her thumb and looks toward the tree line where Mags disappeared.

I follow her gaze and turn back to her. What happened to my beautiful normal girlfriend? Oh, she's still beautiful, but nothing about this is normal. Unable to hold a straight face any longer, Katie bursts out laughing and covers her mouth with both hands. Okay. There's my normal girlfriend. I join her laughter and shake my head. Somebody is a comedian today.

"Are you okay?" she asked.

"No," I quickly admit. "That was the strangest encounter I've ever had in my life."

"Well, that was Mags," Katie points out.

She's right about that. The old man gets weirder every year. After seeing what he thinks is a dog, I never want to get lost in the woods around here. Surely, there aren't more of those things wandering around here. Thank goodness we didn't hit either of them.

It might not be a good idea to let Mags live up on the mountain in that shack by himself. Of course, that's the sheriff's department's job, not the fire department. Thank goodness. Chief Foster does have us chop up a load of firewood every fall for Mags. I'm now beyond glad that his son, Samuel, is the one who has to deliver it.

"What kind of animal do you think that really was?" Katie sits back and buckles her seatbelt.

"A Chupacabra," I reply, and I'm not being sarcastic.

"I thought those were a myth." Katie locks her door. Yeah, she's not believing that anymore.

"Nope. Mags has one." I lock my door too, just to be on the safe side. We both burst out laughing again.

"Can you get us out of here, or do we need to call for a tow?" She holds up her phone.

I give her a sly grin. "Buttercup, we might have to go through that field." I point to her right. "But trust me, we aren't stuck."

After starting the engine, I hit the four-wheel drive. We go through the field just because we can. I might have to pay Eli Wentworth for tearing up his grandfather's field but hearing my girl laugh was worth it.

Hearing my family laugh at dinner as Katie and I recanted our strange encounter with Mags today was worth it too. It would have been better if I could have shot that strange creature though. The thing was darn right scary. I will definitely be letting Spencer and Aiden know it's out there just in case there are more of them.

My family almost falls out of their chairs when Katie told them about Mrs. Bigfoot. All I can do is sit beside her and smile. She fits in so well with my family. She belongs here with us. My mom gives me a little nod from across the table. She sees it too. Maybe someday soon I can do something to ensure she's always here with us, with me.

Chapter Thirty-Two

Katie

Saturday nights out at Cowboys with friends were the greatest. This was becoming the new normal for all of us. Every other week when Miles wasn't on duty you could find us here for a few hours. As always, my friends and I sat at a table on the far side of the dance floor, and the guys had their usual table on the upper level. I think Aiden and Spencer reserved these tables on purpose so they could keep an eye on everything.

My friends almost fell off their stools when I told them about seeing Mags outside of town yesterday. If Ally hadn't caught Beth, she would have fallen. Beth isn't doing any better. She's still drinking too much and flirting heavily with the new bartender.

My visits with Rachel are now just once a month, and I only have to call her if I have an emergency and need her. I was glad Miles went with me yesterday. His support has really been a building block for me. No, I'm not dependent on him. I just like having him by my side. It's what couples are supposed to do. When I heard he had to see a therapist too for a few weeks, it helped me to feel better about my own situation.

Having my first official family dinner with Miles' parents and little sister last night was everything I had hoped it would be. Too bad his sister, Natalie, couldn't be there. Tomorrow, Miles would be joining my family for lunch after church. We haven't officially labeled what our relationship was yet. He hasn't asked me to be his girlfriend, but it sure feels as though I am, and I love it.

Every time the band played a slow song, Miles and Aiden would come down to dance with me and E. Beth, after having a few drinks, pulled the new bartender out onto the dance floor, earning her a hard glare from Noah. The guy was supposed to be working after all. Sammie and Ally surprised us and danced with a couple of guys, but they weren't interested in anything more with them. I was happy and in love. I wanted to see all my friends happy too. Relationships can't be rushed or forced though. I'm sure they'll find their guys when they're meant to.

Grace is here with us tonight, but she's not dancing with anyone. She claims she's just saving our table. I'm glad she accepted our offer to join us for girl's night. She's sweet but way too shy. If she hangs around with us long enough, she won't be.

Every now and then, she glances across the bar and blushes. She tries to hide it, but I saw where her eyes went. There are six men at that table. Two are taken, and one might as well be. Which of the other three causes Grace to blush like this? This is intriguing. I really do need to get to know her more. I can drop a few hints with either one of those guys.

"Hey!" a woman shouts behind us.

I turn to find a drunk Brittney Douglas glaring at me. My peaceful wonderful night has just been destroyed. Brittney is alone tonight. Holly's wedding is next weekend. One more week and I won't have to deal with this hateful woman again. If another order comes through Petals that was connected to her in any way, I'll let my mom and Bailey handle them.

"You got a problem?" Beth snaps.

Oh no. Beth is as drunk as Brittney seems to be. This is not going to end well for any of us. All of my friends said they wouldn't seek her out, but if the opportunity ever presented itself, they were going to get Brittney. Tonight appears to be the night.

"Do you have Holly's flowers ready?" Brittney ignores Beth and focuses on me.

"Everything is in order and will be delivered to the church Saturday morning." I smile and turn back to my friends. I have no idea what I ever did to this woman.

"See to it you don't mess them up," Brittney said, slurring her words.

"Katie will do a fantastic job for Holly. Now, shoo." Sammie motions Brittney away with her hands.

Beth starts to get off her stool, but I grab her arm and shake my head. The woman isn't worth our time. I wiggle my fingers in a little wave at Brittney and turn back to Ally and the story she was telling us. Brittney's drunk. It's best to ignore her.

"You can wave me away, but you can't wave Tara Adams away so easily." Brittney lightly laughs.

I snap my head toward her. "What?"

I shouldn't engage in any conversation with this woman. However, she just hit on a subject that had me concerned. It was really jealousy, but I was fighting it. Sadly, thoughts of Tara with Miles found ways to creep in.

Brittney staggers closer to me. "Tara Adams isn't just back in Hayden Falls for her grandfather."

"Go away, Brittney," Ally demands.

"Nobody wants to hear anything you have to say," E tells her.

"Katie should." Brittney's grin widens. "She should be very worried."

"Why?" I ask. It was a big mistake.

"Tara's here for the father of her son." Brittney's eyes flick toward the upper level of the bar and back to me.

I don't bother to follow her gaze. I know she means Miles. I should have already asked Miles about Tara. I don't want to entertain this idea, but I can't help it. Miles dated Tara in high school. Could it be true?

"That's enough, Brittney." Sammie's off her stool in a flash and pushes Brittney away.

"Don't you dare believe her for one second." E points her finger in my face.

Too late. That one second already happened, and a few more. Tara has been gone for about nine years. Her son, Jeffery, is eight years old. The timing sounds about right. It could be possible. Did she leave town all those years ago because she was pregnant?

"Is she always rude like this with you all?" Grace asked.

"She's not like this when she comes to the bookstore?" E asked.

"She's never been in Page Turners," Grace replied.

"She probably can't read," Beth mumbled.

Brittney manages to push her way back to our table. "Look at his hair and eyes. You know I'm right."

Ally hops off her stool and helps Sammie pull Brittney to the front door. They talk to one of the bouncers and have Brittney thrown out for the night. Sadly for me, it wasn't soon enough.

It's too late. My mind is already reeling. Jeffery has dark hair, and so does Miles. Jeffery has dark gray eyes. Miles' eyes are more of a steel gray. Still, both of them do have gray eyes. Personally, I thought Jeffery looked a lot like his mother. Could he really be Miles' son? Has Tara given Miles the family I couldn't? It's too much, and it hurts.

Slowly, I lift my eyes to the upper level. Miles is watching me. His eyes narrow as he looks to the front door and back to me. Ally and Sammie return to our table, but I can't hear anything my friends are saying to me. The only sounds I hear are the thumping of the music and the pounding of my heart. Miles shakes his head, but I don't understand what he means.

It's too much to process. I can't stay here. Hopping off my stool, I bolt for the front door. Hopefully, Brittney isn't still out there. I don't trust myself around her right now. Why is she so bent on destroying my life?

The moment I run through the door the cool night air hits my skin. It's not enough to settle me in the least. I have to get away from here, but where do I go? I came here with Miles. I can walk to Petals from here. It's only a couple of blocks.

Before I reach the edge of the parking lot, someone grabs my upper arm and whirls me around. Miles locks his strong arms around my waist pinning me to his body. I push against his chest, but he refuses to let me go.

"What just happened?" he asked.

I shake my head. How do I explain what happened? Does he know about Jeffery? Do I want the truth? Can I handle the truth? I'm not so sure I can.

"Katie." Miles grabs my chin and forces me to look him in the eye. "One minute you're happy. Brittney shows up and you crash and bolt for the door. What happened?" he demands.

"She. You." I take a deep breath, but still can't comprehend it all. "It can't be real."

"If it came out of Brittney Douglas' mouth, it's probably not real," Miles said. "If it has anything to do with me and her, it most definitely isn't real."

"It's not her," I cry.

"Then take a deep breath, Buttercup." Miles loosens his grip on my chin, but he doesn't let me go. I do as he asks. "Now, tell me what she said to you. I'm not letting you go. I'm not letting you hide and slip back into darkness. I need to know what she said."

The pleading in his voice gets through the fogginess in my head. Brittney's words caused me to hide and fall into darkness before. I never want to repeat that.

"Tara." I manage to get the one word out.

"Tara Adams?" Miles narrows his eyes. I nod my head. "What about her?"

"She's here for you." I can't hold back the sob any longer. "You're the father of her son."

Miles' face goes pale, and he loses all expression. It only takes him a moment to compose himself again.

"No, Katie." He slowly shakes his head. "I'm not."

"She's been gone for almost nine years. Jeffery is eight," I tell him.

"It doesn't matter how old he is. Tara's son isn't mine. It's not possible," Miles insists.

"But…" I don't get to finish my protest.

Miles takes my hand and pulls me over to his truck. He opens the passenger door and motions for me to get inside. He's angry now. I've pushed him too far.

"Get in," he said, still holding the door when I didn't move.

"Miles."

"I don't ever want to lose my temper in front of you. I need you to get in the truck." He continues to wait, but I don't move. "Katie, please."

His pleas have a way of gripping my heart to a point I can't deny him. I don't fully trust the situation, but I get in and fasten my seatbelt.

Chapter Thirty-Three

Miles

"Where are we going?" Katie asked as we headed out of town.

"To clear this up," I reply.

She remains quiet for a few more minutes until she realizes where we're going. Katie shifts uncomfortably in her seat, but I don't turn around. I can't. My world and my future depend on this answer.

"Miles, we can't do this," Katie protests as I pull into the driveway of the Adams' family home place.

We shouldn't have to be doing this at all. However, doing this is the only way to settle the problem. I'm not a heartless man. I know Mr. Adams is sick, and Tara has a young son. It's only eight o'clock. Hopefully, we won't disturb either of them. I only need a couple of minutes at the most. One question is all I need to ask. A simple *'no'* will send me on my way.

"Miles, please." Katie tries again, but I'm set on doing this.

There's no point in arguing about it, so I don't bother replying. I get out and open her door. She's upset with me, but this won't wait until morning.

As we walk up onto the front porch, I can see the dim light of a lamp and the flashes of light coming from the television. I knock softly on the front door, fearing the doorbell would wake Mr. Adams or Tara's son if they are already in bed. The porch light comes on just before Tara peeks through the curtain. She opens the door and steps out onto the porch.

"Miles? Is something wrong?" Tara looks between me and Katie.

"Hey, Tara. I really hate bothering you like this, but there's a little issue I need you to clear up, please. It wouldn't wait until morning," I said.

"Sure." Tara shrugs. "If I can."

"Am I the father of your son?" I bluntly ask, getting straight to the point.

Tara's eyes narrow, and her mouth opens and closes a few times. Finally, she finds words.

"Miles, I don't know why you're asking me that. You know it's not possible," Tara said.

"Oh, I know," I admit, nodding my head. "I just needed you to confirm it."

I glance over my shoulder to Katie who has been slowly slipping behind me. She's embarrassed, but this was the fastest way to clear things up. Tara follows my gaze and realizes what's happening here. She has always been good at putting things together.

"You thought Jeffery was Miles' son?" Tara asked Katie.

"I'm sorry," Katie apologizes.

"It's not her fault." I step in before Tara gets the wrong idea. "Blame Brittney Douglas."

"Ah. That explains a lot." Tara folds her arms over her chest and nods her head.

"We're sorry to bother you, but thank you," I apologize and start to leave.

"Wait." Tara stops us. She takes a deep breath and steps forward. "I think I can help a little more, and there are some things I need to say to you anyway."

Now, Tara has me concerned. She doesn't need to help me more. She just solved the problem. However, I don't understand why she needs to say something to me? I have no idea what it could be about.

Tara turns her attention back to Katie. "There's not even the slightest possibility that Miles is Jeffery's father. Nothing ever happened between us. Well, I did kiss him a couple of times, but that was it. My heart was a fool for someone else."

Okay. So far so good. This is all true, and I like how she's concentrating on Katie's feelings.

Tara looks me in the eye. "I owe you an apology, and I really am sorry." She turns back to face Katie. "I wasn't interested in Miles. I had a crush on someone else, and I used Miles to make him jealous."

Okay. I wasn't expecting that, but good to know, I guess.

"There was no chemistry between Miles and me." She turns to me again. "No offense, Miles."

"None taken." I hold up a hand. I have no problem with any of this.

"I saw the two of you together during the 4th of July festival. You belong together." Tara looks between me and Katie as she speaks. "Don't let Brittney, or anyone else, take that from you."

"I'm sorry," Katie apologized again.

"Don't be. I know how conniving Brittney Davis is. Never trust her," Tara said. "Holly is great, but Brittney is evil. She obviously wanted Miles, or she wouldn't be trying to cause you problems. I might have had a role to play in that. If I hadn't used Miles all those years ago, there would be no connection between us that Brittney could use against you two now."

"It's nobody's fault but Brittney's. No one forces her to do the things she does," I say.

"Well, I do hope this cleared things up for you." Tara smiles at Katie. She nods in reply.

"Thanks." I pause for a moment. I shouldn't ask, but I am a little curious. "Does your son's father live in Hayden Falls?"

Tara lightly laughs. "I'm not comfortable with talking about Jeffery's father. He knows Jeffery exists. He was born a few weeks early, not too early though. He was born with asthma and is sick a lot. He's not as strong as most little boys his age. Apparently, a kid was a hard no for his father. He signed his parental rights away when Jeffery was three months old."

Katie gasps and places her hand over her heart. "Oh, Tara. I'm so sorry."

"Don't be." Tara shrugs and gives us a tight smile. "I'm not. I admit that I wasn't the best person when I was a teen, but that little boy changed my life. He forced me to grow up and kept me from getting mixed up with the wrong crowds. I'm a different person because of him, and I have an amazing son." Her face turns sad. "I wish his father could have seen it that way." She swallows hard and adds, "For Jeffery's sake."

There's more to her story, but I won't pry. She's done more than enough for me tonight.

"I'm sorry about that, but thanks for clearing this up," I say.

"It's not a problem." Tara shrugs again. "After what I did to you, I kind of owe you that."

She's right, but I don't look at it the way she does. Hearing you were used to make another guy jealous should hit a man hard, but it doesn't bother me. I have to agree with Tara, there was no chemistry between us. Things didn't work out for a reason. I'm just sorry things didn't work out for her in the end. Well, she has Jeffery, so maybe they did.

"If you ever need our help, all you have to do is ask." I look down at Katie, and she nods her agreement.

"I appreciate that, but if things are settled here, I'm going to call it a night." She motions over her shoulder with her thumb. "One of those two amazing guys in there could wake up before the sun rises."

"Goodnight, Tara." I take Katie's hand and head back to the truck.

Well, this night sure didn't go how I had planned. When we got into the truck, I reached over and took Katie's hand in mine. We rode back to town in silence. I was glad the situation was cleared up, and it hadn't taken years to do it, but this was a setback for us. I wasn't sure how things stood between me and Katie right now. I know she's not okay so there's no need for me to ask.

"Where would you like to go?" I'll take her anywhere she asks. Hopefully, it's somewhere we can talk.

"Home," she replies softly.

Okay. No talking tonight. We continue to ride in silence. I don't want to leave things like this, but I don't know what to do. So, I do the only thing I can do. When we get to her grandmother's house, I walk her to the front door and kiss her goodnight. I don't want to let her go, but maybe she needs a little time to process everything. My heart falls when Katie unlocks the door. Surprisingly, she grabs my hand and pulls me inside.

"What are we doing?" I whisper.

"We're going to start a movie and cuddle on the couch," she whispers back.

The movie I care nothing about but this cuddling sounds great.

"Uh." I look up at the ceiling. Her family is upstairs sleeping.

"It's fine," she assures me. "Grandma said if we ever want to sit here and watch movies all night rather than going out, it's fine with her."

"Really? All night you say?" I grin and lift an eyebrow. Maybe things weren't as bad as I thought they were.

"Yes. She said she was young once so she knows, but please," Katie points at me. "do not ask her for details. Trust me, it's embarrassing."

She motions toward the couch before disappearing into the kitchen. I sit down and wait. Surprisingly, she comes back with a beer for me and a glass of sweet tea for her. I hold the bottle of beer up questionably.

"It's another thing you do not ask my grandma about." She picks up the remote and starts a random movie. Neither of us pays much attention to it.

"Your Grandma sounds like my kind of woman," I tease. "I sure hope that spunk of hers runs in the family."

Katie punches me in the arm. Looks as if I'm back to getting punched by this cute little woman.

"Hey. I'm totally in love with her granddaughter. I'm just hoping she has some of her grandmother's traits." I defend myself as I settle into the corner of the couch.

Katie laughs and falls into my open arms. I could get used to nights like this. Things went south fast earlier, but thankfully, it was ending on a happier note.

"I'm sorry I let Brittney get to me," Katie apologized again.

"It's okay. We figured it out." I gently brush a few loose strands of her hair away from her face.

"I thought Tara might have been the one that got away," she whispers.

I cup her face in my hands. "Buttercup, *you* were the one that got away."

She sucked in a breath at my admission. It's true. She's the only woman I've ever wanted. Wrapping my arms around her, I pull her to me.

"I promise to come to you first before I freak out like that again." Her fingertips roam over my cheek.

"That's all I ask."

Softly, I press my lips to hers. If she comes to me first, it will save us a lot of heartache in the future. She is my future, and I'll do whatever it takes to make sure she's happy.

"I love you, Miles."

"I love you too, Buttercup."

Katie grabs the blanket from the back of the couch and tosses it over us as she settles into my arms. We stay this way for hours. I want more nights with her cuddled in my arms like this. In fact, I wanted all of my nights to be like this.

Chapter Thirty-Four

Katie

$\mathcal{H}$ayden Falls Baptist Church was beautifully decorated today if I have to say so myself. And, I do say so myself. Holly had chosen simple yet elegant designs for everything. The live pink floral arrangements enhanced her theme, plus their sweet fragrance was calming. I hate it when brides decide on using silk flowers, It's just not the same. Standing at the back of the sanctuary, I took one last photo of the final layout to add to the portfolio at Petals. This will be a nice addition to our designs.

"It's perfect," I say as I admire the flowers one last time.

Sammie and Bailey nod their heads in agreement. Sammie insisted on coming with us today. She's helped me deliver and set up for weddings before, but I knew she wanted to be here today because of Brittney. So far, I've been able to avoid her.

Mrs. Laine stepped into the sanctuary. She walked around lightly touching every decoration. Her bright smile had us smiling too. She came in two weeks ago and paid the final balance of Holly's order. I was so glad she took over the details of this wedding. At first, I feared Brittney was handling everything as part of her maid-of-honor duties.

"Everything is perfect," Mrs. Laine praises. "You ladies did an amazing job. Thank you."

"Thank you for letting us be a part of this special day." I hand her the final box with the bouquets for the bride and bridesmaids.

"Let's get out of here," Bailey said as Holly's mother walked away.

She has the right idea. We can now officially mark the Laine wedding off the books for Petals. This means goodbye to Brittney Douglas for me.

I'm glad Holly is having the wedding here and not at The Magnolia Inn. I wouldn't want E to have to deal with Brittney. Of course, Aiden would step up and shut Brittney down in a heartbeat if she upset his pregnant little wife.

"You're pathic," Brittney sneers from the hallway.

So close. I groan *very* loudly, not caring if she heard me. We were almost out the front doors. Brittney must have been waiting in the shadows for the right moment to strike. Sammie starts to say something back to her, but I hold up a hand to stop her. This is my fight, so to say. It's just words. We're not throwing punches here, well, not yet anyway.

"You should really look up the definition of that word," I tell her. Yeah, not my best comeback, but she's not the best person.

Brittney's not fazed in the least. She doesn't care about anything except for hurting others. I see through her hateful tactics now.

Miles and I had a long talk last week as we cuddled together on the couch. I may not be the strongest woman in the world, but I think I'm finding my backbone and can stand up straighter now.

"Miles will come to his senses soon enough and drop you like he does everyone else." Brittney smiles slyly.

The pink gown she's wearing is elegant. The bouquet she will carry today is beautiful. Too bad she has an ugly heart and a rude personality.

"If he's crazy because he's with me, I'm fine with being crazy with him for as long as it lasts. Forever sounds great with me." I turn to go. There really is no point in arguing with this woman.

"He'll leave you for his son!" Brittney shouts. Her voice is no longer confident.

I should keep walking. I really should, but I can't resist one final jab. Brittney takes a step back when I turn to face her. My facial expressions no longer hide the anger I feel toward this woman. She's not sure of herself anymore, but I'm sure of who I am.

"The only children Miles Hamilton will be having are the ones I will give birth to. You cost me Miles once, I won't let you do it again." That's it. I have nothing more to say to her.

As I grab the door handle to walk away from this evil woman once and for all, someone enters the other side of the church foyer. Yeah, I know. I shouldn't have gotten snappy in a church.

"What's this about?" Mrs. Douglas asked.

Brittney's mom is kind and sweet. As much as I want to leave, I won't resort to being rude to her. I also won't lie to benefit Brittney. Sadly, Petals may be about to lose one of our longest and best customers.

"Brittney has lied to me about Miles a few times," I reply.

I don't know how much Mrs. Douglas heard, but that's all she needs to know about the situation. I could spill all of her daughter's hateful deeds, but I won't. If the tables were turned, Brittney wouldn't hesitate to out me of my misdeeds. My refusal to fully share the awful things she's done is the only blessing Brittney will get from me. I do this for me, not her.

"Has she now?" Mrs. Douglas glares at Brittney while she continues to speak to me. "Tell your mother I said hello. You ladies did a fantastic job today, just as I knew you would. Enjoy your day. I'll deal with my daughter."

I wasn't expecting that, and I don't wait around to hear any more. She is more than welcome to deal with her rude daughter. From Mrs. Douglas' tone, she's already aware of how troublesome Brittney is. Well, this is Hayden Falls after all. Someone has bound to have told her how conniving her daughter has been over the years.

"That was amazing," Bailey shouts once we're inside the Petals Florist van.

"I'm so proud of you." Sammie is actually beaming with pride right now. "How would you like to celebrate?"

How would I like to celebrate? My lips turn up into a smile. "Would you ladies mind if I ditched you for a little while?" I asked.

"Ditch us?" Bailey sounded offended. "After that epic performance?"

"I'll get you coffee and donuts first," I offer.

"Something tells me the fire department is about to get a few sweet treats as well." Sammie's huge smile matches my own.

"One firefighter sure is," Bailey adds.

After getting my friends their favorite coffee from Beth's Morning Brew and a dozen donuts from Sweet Treats, I sent them back to Petals with the van. I got a couple of bags of coffee from Beth for the fire department since I wasn't sure if any of the volunteers would be there today or not. I got the house blend because it's Miles' favorite and a bag of vanilla-flavored coffee. Beth assured me most of the guys at the fire department loved her special vanilla blend. She should know.

Before going back into Sweet Treats, I went to the edge of the square to check the parking lot at the station. There were only a few vehicles there, so I got a dozen cupcakes and a dozen assorted donuts. Hopefully, Miles wouldn't mind me showing up out of the blue like this. I was happy and wanted to see him.

When I got to the station, Luke was in the bay. He happily took the boxes from Sweet Treats from me and I followed him upstairs. In the dayroom, Devon Reed took the bags of coffee and started a fresh pot of each. Devon was hired as a full-time firefighter this week. Miles and Levi were sitting in recliners across the room.

I was expecting Miles to walk over to greet me. Instead, he remained in his chair watching my every move. His eyes danced with delight as his thumb moved lazily back and forth across his bottom lip. This is the look he gives me just before his lips devour mine. Even with him across the room, my body remembers the feel of his hands and those sexy lips. Do I want him to kiss me here in front of the guys? You know what? I believe I do.

His heated gaze has me licking my lips. One corner of his mouth turns up in a half-grin as he lifts a finger and motions for me to come to him. I could tease and play defiant here, but the seductive gleam in his eyes pulls me across the room. The power of knowing this sexy firefighter belongs to me is intoxicating.

Miles doesn't stand up when I reach him. Instead, he grabs me around the waist and pulls me onto his lap. My yelp is lost when his fingers fist into the hair at the back of my head and his lips claim mine. This always happens when I get *the look,* and I'm not complaining.

Levi chuckles. Luke and Devon whistle, but Miles doesn't break the kiss. Chief Foster comes in to see what the commotion is about. He helps himself to a cup of coffee and a couple of donuts before speaking.

"Thanks, Katie," Chief Foster calls out before heading back to his office.

Miles finally breaks our kiss. I should be embarrassed for kissing him in front of the guys, but his sexy grin has me wanting his lips on mine again.

"So," he drags the word out. "How many kids are we having?"

"What?" That's surprising.

"Buttercup, I'll happily give you all you want." His grin widens.

We've never talked about having kids before. It's great, and I'm all for it, but where is this coming from? I look to Levi for answers. Levi is holding his phone with the screen turned towards me. The website for Hayden's Happenings is pulled up. Oh, no. What has Megan done? Levi hands me his phone. I'm going to die of embarrassment.

The Lady Knows What She Wants – BABIES!

Today, our little florist put the town troublemaker in her place. It appears that one of our handsome firefighters is officially off the market. Sorry, Ladies. He's ALL hers! In her own words, She will be the ONLY one having HIS BABIES! I guess our fire-fighting hero needs to be creating some seriously HOT flames in the bedroom!

I'm going to tackle Megan Sanders in the middle of the town square. She's no longer safe from me. I wouldn't really do it, but I can sure imagine it. How did she get this information so fast?

"Uhm…" I hand Levi back his phone.

"Do you want to explain that to me?" Miles asked.

I really don't, but it looks like I have no choice but to do so. *Thanks, Megan.* I glance at Miles from the corner of my eye. He stares at me with his cocky little grin. He's not mad. He's enjoying this. I shake my head.

"I'd rather hear the truth from you. Someone in this town is bound to share a dressed-up version later," Miles said.

If this is already in Hayden's Happenings, it's circulated around town at least ten times by now. And, Miles wouldn't just get a dressed-up version later. The wonderful people of this little town will have a tie-dyed version going round by sunset.

"Brittney said you would leave me for your son." I hated to admit this part.

"Buttercup, we cleared that up already," Miles said.

"Oh, I know," I agree. "That's when I told her the only babies you'll be having are the ones I will give birth to."

"Whoa! Girl!" Levi leans forward to give me a high five. "I'm getting a cup of coffee and a cupcake. Man, you need to kiss your girl again for that one."

After Levi leaves, I give Miles a cheesy grin. He sighs and shakes his head. He seems proud and has a seductive gleam in his eyes. Looks as if we're both thinking about making all of those babies.

"Well, I guess the lady really does know what she wants," Miles teases.

"You're not mad?"

"Oh, no, Buttercup. I love this side of you."

"Bailey and Sammie wanted to celebrate," I tell him.

"And you chose to come here?" His thumb slides across my bottom lip. I nod in reply. "This is you celebrating?"

His eyes move over to the kitchen area where the guys are enjoying the cupcakes and donuts.

"Part of it," I admit.

"The other part is right here, Sweetheart," Miles whispered.

He motions with his finger for me to come closer. His thumb is replaced by his lips. This is definitely the other part. The best part. The part I want to do over and over and over again.

Chapter Thirty-Five

Miles

*E*ven with all the devastation I've seen over the years, I love my job. What I do matters, and it comes with a lot of responsibility. Being a fireman isn't as easy, or as glamorous, as a lot of people believe. It requires hours of training, hard work, and complete dedication. I give it everything I have and then some.

We don't get a lot of calls in the middle of the night around here, but we do practice them often to keep us prepared. Sadly, this morning wasn't a training exercise.

Just after 4 am, the tones rang out pulling us from our beds. Within minutes, we were fully dressed in our turnouts and ready to go. Our volunteers and first responders descended upon the station. Those who couldn't make it by the time the engine and ambulance pulled out would meet us on sight. The station in Willows Bend needed assistance with a house fire.

House fires and car accidents were the worse for me. This was where things got raw and real. Ordinary people's lives could change in a matter of seconds. During the situation, we were focused and did our jobs to the best of our ability. Many times, we go above and beyond what's required of us to ensure lives are saved.

By the time we arrived at the two-story farmhouse, Willows Bend Fire Department was already battling the blaze. Smoke billowed into the night sky, and flames were starting to pierce through the front roof. From the looks of things, I could already tell there wasn't much we could do. Older homes such as this one burned fast. The Walsburg Fire Department wasn't far behind us. Two departments would concentrate on putting the house out, while the other one soaked down the barn and outer buildings in hopes of saving them. It was the best we could do.

Neighbors had arrived and were helping to keep the family out of the way. A few people held tightly to three small children wrapped in blankets. A man in pajamas was pacing and shouting. I couldn't hear him over the roar of the fire and all of the departments working. Finally, he grabbed a fireman from Walsburg. The next call to come over the radio was the one a fireman never wants to hear.

"The mother is still inside!"

All focus turned to the main house. Levi and I were on the backside of the house. Without a second thought, we raced up onto the back porch and broke through the door. This side of the house wasn't in flames yet, but we didn't have a lot of time.

"Did anyone say what room she could be in?" Levi shouts over the radio.

"No!" I shout back.

"Stay together!" Levi ordered.

He's been at this longer than I have, so I follow his orders and let him take the lead. In situations like this, Levi has a sixth sense. I make sure to stay two steps behind him as we make our way through the kitchen. Getting separated in a burning building has cost a few firemen their lives. Thankfully, it's never happened to anyone in our department.

"Boys! You don't have a lot of time!" Chief Foster says over the radio.

Levi and I nod to each other as we reach the far side of the kitchen. The living room is engulfed in flames and they're taking over the second floor. Going upstairs is a bad idea, but we have no choice. At the top of the stairs, Levi trips over something. I quickly pull him to his feet. Looking down, my heart drops, but I'm grateful at the same time. The mother had almost made it to the stairs before collapsing. We've found her, but don't have time to assess her injuries. I help Levi hoist her over his shoulder, and we hurry back down the stairs.

The flames were now less than two feet from taking stairs. The ceiling in the kitchen was starting to be overtaken. Somehow, we make it off the stairwell in time. Now, we have to make it to the door.

"The roof is going to go!" someone from Willows Bend Fire Department yells through the radio.

"Miles! Levi! Get out now!" Chief Foster shouts.

"We found her!" I shout.

"Get out!" Luke's panicked voice comes through the radio.

"We're trying for the back door!" I shout.

No further requests are needed. I already know every fireman who can is headed for the backside of the house. The groans of the roof giving way behind us can be heard over the roar of the fire. Time's almost up. The back door seems a million miles away. The front side of the house begins to crumble. This mother has one chance of making it out of here alive. There are three small children waiting for her. We cannot fail this family.

The sound behind us gets louder. There's no need to look over my shoulder, I know the roof and second floor are falling. Levi and the mother have to get out of here. My heart thunders in my chest. I fear we aren't going to make it.

"Levi!" Luke shouts desperately for his bother.

"Miles! Get out!" Devon shouts.

With the back door now a few feet away, I give Levi and the mother all the help I can. With my hands on Levi's back, I shove them as hard as I can through the door. They're out! That's all that matters.

The kitchen ceiling starts falling. With the last of my strength, I push toward the door. As I get close, hands reach in and grab me. The doorframe and back porch collapses around me, but somebody keeps pulling me. Tumbling to the ground, more hands grab us and pull us farther away from the house. Well, from the flames, the house is gone.

My helmet is removed and tossed carelessly to the side. I look up into the wild eyes of one crazy Devon Reed. Without this man, I would be dead right now.

"Thanks, man," I say between ragged breaths.

Devon pats my chest with his hand. "Don't scare me like that again."

Devon has been full-time for less than two weeks. I don't want to tell him, but I was just as scared as he was. Hopefully, this won't cause him to quit on us. He's one of the best firemen I've seen.

Looking to my left, Luke Barnes is hovering over Levi the same way Devon is me. Levi looks my way and nods his head. He looks up at his twin brother and says something I can't hear.

Luke looks at me. "Thanks, man."

I nod. Levi must have told him how I shoved him and the mother through the back door. I have never seen Luke Barnes with tears in his eyes before. Levi and I have never been that close to death before either. We've had close calls plenty of times, but none as close as tonight. I can't say I ever want to do that again.

The unconscious mother is put in an ambulance and rushed to the hospital in Walsburg. I don't know if she'll make it, but I pause to say a prayer for her. The father makes his way over to thank us. Levi and I lift a hand and nod, still trying to catch our breath. A fireman from Willows Bend walks the man to his truck so he can follow his wife to the hospital. Neighbors volunteer to take the children home with them.

One of the reasons I became a firefighter was because of a house fire in Hayden Falls when I was a kid. They got the family out, but the parents didn't make it. They died later at the hospital from smoke inhalation. Three young kids became orphans that night. They were sent to live with family members in another state. I never heard what became of those kids. A couple of them were close to my age. I was only in the fourth grade back then, but I knew when I heard the horrible news, I would one day be a fireman.

Chief Foster and several EMTs surround me and Levi. We were given a routine assessment before the Chief ordered us to the hospital. After the close call we just had, Levi and I know better than to argue. We needed to be checked out by a doctor. Besides, my left shoulder and arm hurt. I'm pretty sure the doorframe or part of the back porch hit me.

Luke refused to leave his brother's side. He climbed in the ambulance with Levi. Since there were more than enough firemen here, Chief Foster sent Devon with me. Honestly, it was comforting to have a face I knew and trusted by my side.

Since I made it out, and I knew I was going to be fine, I asked the Chief to not call my parents or Katie. There was no need in waking them up to scare them over nothing. I'll call them from the hospital to let them know I was alright. Only, I didn't realize until we were halfway to the hospital that my phone was in the engine. We didn't have a ride back to Hayden Falls either. With Luke and Levi being the Sheriff's sons, I'm pretty sure he, or one of their brothers, will come to get us.

"Thanks again," I say to Devon when we get to the Emergency Room in Walsburg.

"I would say any time, but man, I hope that never happens again." Devon blows out a breath.

I happen to agree with him. We sit quietly for a while. When the curtain next to us opens, I expect to see a nurse or doctor. Luke is there pointing a finger at me. He's still struggling. It takes him a few minutes to speak.

"Neither of you better do that again." Luke has already lectured his brother. We heard him through the curtain when we first got to the hospital. Now, he's getting us both. He hands Devon and me a coke from the vending machines. "Here. They wouldn't get me a beer."

Levi, Devon, and I laugh. Luke glares at all of us. He's right though. We probably could use a cold beer right now, or something a lot stronger.

"Dad's on the way," Luke said. We all nod.

By the time Sheriff Barnes arrives, Levi and I have been cleared from all our tests. My arm isn't broken, but I was given a sling and told to follow up with Doctor Larson in a few days. Levi didn't have any injuries, but he was told to see the doctor if he felt lightheaded or experienced any pain later on.

Chief Foster gave the four of us the rest of the day off. Our other full-time crew stepped up and agreed to finish out the day for us. Plus, several of our volunteers would be there during the day to help out. The way I felt, I didn't want to go home alone to an empty house. I had the Sheriff drop me off at my parent's house. They needed to know I was alright. I could call Petals from there and talk to Katie. I'd get my phone and truck from the station later this afternoon.

Chapter Thirty-Six

Katie

The first thing I do when I get to Petals is to head straight for the coffee maker. We have a Keurig and an auto-drip coffee maker. I use the pods to get a quick cup and start a pot of vanilla-flavored coffee. Beth was right about her vanilla blend, it's the best. Thankfully, she was able to get me a decaf bag. Bailey will be here soon, and she will devour the vanilla coffee.

Sitting down at my desk, I turn on my computer and open my books from yesterday. I left yesterday without logging the daily reports into my spreadsheets. I love my job, but the paperwork is my least favorite part.

I take a sip of my coffee and rub the back of my neck. It would be nice to have some caffeine to help wake myself up a bit more, but I'm not willing to risk drinking it yet. Maybe one day I will again. For now, I'll just keep pretending there's caffeine in here. The mind of matter thing doesn't always work, but I'm not willing to slide backward here.

If I have another night like last night, I'll have to look into ways to have better sleep. Several times this morning, I jolted awake for no reason. Each time it happened I couldn't remember what had woken me up. At first, I thought one of my family members was up moving about, but the house was quiet. When I finally fell back asleep, I ended up oversleeping. It was just my luck, and it was a tiring way to start my day.

I was in the middle of typing in yesterday's numbers when my phone started dinging from several text messages. By the time I got to a place where I could stop and reach for my phone, Bailey came rushing into the office.

"Oh my gosh!" she exclaimed. "Is he alright?"

"What?" I asked.

"He must be alright, or you wouldn't be here," Bailey adds quickly, mostly to herself. "Whew. That's a relief."

"Bailey, what are you talking about?" I'm too tired this morning to talk in circles with her.

"Miles," she replied.

My hand flew to cover my heart. Miles?

"You don't know?" Bailey asked. I shook my head. "There was a fire in Willows Bend this morning. Miles and Levi were sent to the hospital."

Those are the words the family of a firefighter never wants to hear. I'm not technically Miles' family, but he's mine just the same. I bolt from my chair causing it to hit the wall.

"Which hospital?" I ask, already moving toward the door.

"Walsburg, I'm sure, but it looks like everyone is back at the station." Bailey follows me out of the office.

If he's at the station, he's fine. I, however, do not feel fine. I have to see him. Bailey's words are lost to me as I rush out the front door. People hurry to move aside as I run down the sidewalk. The fire department is at the edge of the park just below the diner.

Bursting through the side door and into the bay, I bend over to catch my breath. Several firefighters turn to stare at me. I know them all, but this isn't Miles' crew. Where is he? His shift doesn't end until 8 am in the morning.

"Katie?" Chief Foster hurries over to me.

"Miles?" I can barely get his name out between ragged breaths.

"Miles is fine," Chief Foster assures me. "He and Levi were checked out at the hospital and released. I gave all four guys the day off and sent them home."

"Home," I whisper.

Once again, I take off running without listening to everything being said to me. I run back to Petals and turn the shop over to Bailey. She can call my mom if she needs any help today. Grabbing my purse and keys, I hurry out the back door to my jeep. If took the time to stop long enough to check the messages on my phone, I might find out what was going on. I'm such an emotional mess, my mind doesn't comprehend that until later.

All I can do while driving is check the first few messages to see who they're from. None of them are from Miles. I pull up his name and call him. Hearing his voice would settle me down really fast. I don't understand why he hasn't called me already. His phone goes straight to voicemail. Things are not working out in my favor today. Tossing my phone on the passenger seat, I concentrate on getting to Miles' house as fast as I can.

Pulling up into the driveway of the cabin Miles rents from the Calhoun family, I don't see his red truck. Come to think of it, I think I saw his truck parked at the station, but I can't be sure. He probably got a ride home from the hospital with one of the guys. The black BMW sitting outside the cabin has me concerned. No one in Hayden Falls drives a car like that.

Stepping onto the small porch, I take a few deep breaths. The last thing I need to do is startle Miles. He's probably exhausted. Standing here, I realize I've never been to his house. Strange how that is. Hopefully, he won't be mad at me. I mean, I am his girlfriend, right? It's okay for his girlfriend to show up unannounced. Isn't it?

The Calhoun Cabins are cute and cozy. The family owns a small ranch. It's nowhere near the size of the H. H. Maxwell Ranch. What the Calhoun family lack in livestock, they make up for in cabin rentals. Miles is their only year-round renter. Most people come here for a romantic weekend or summer vacation. Sometimes they get long-term renters, but those last no more than six months.

When my nerves are settled down enough, I knock on the door and step back to wait. I'll just make sure he's alright and go back to work. He probably wants to rest for a while anyway.

"Coming!" a man calls out.

Alarm shoots through my entire body. That wasn't Miles' voice. The door opens and a man I've never seen before smiles slyly at me. I sucked in a breath and clamp my hand over my mouth.

"Hello, Beautiful," he said.

"I'm sorry." I quickly turn away.

It was too late though. I had already gotten an eye full of Mr. tall, dark, and handsome. His wet hair fell just above his eyes. His bare chest was covered in water droplets. A towel hung low on his hips. This man had just gotten out of the shower. This fits right in with the day I'm having.

"Miles. I'm looking for Miles Hamilton," I hurry to explain why I'm here.

"I don't know Miles Hamilton," the stranger said. "He's a lucky man if you're looking for him. He's also a fool."

"What?" I snap, turning my head towards him.

The stranger stands in the doorway with his shoulder leaning against the frame. He makes no effort to cover himself up. He's one of those guys who know they're handsome and built.

"A man would be a fool to not give you the right address, Sweetheart," he replied.

"He didn't give me an address," I continue to snap at the man. "Miles has lived here for years."

The stranger looks over his shoulder into the cabin and back to me. "I've been here for a couple of days. I can assure you, Sweetheart, he's not here."

"I'll find him." I wave and start down the steps.

"If you don't, Sweetheart, please do come back," he said.

I can hear the humor in the man's voice. I'm glad he thinks this is funny. The man is cocky and sure of himself. I'll admit, he is handsome and sexy too. Still, Mr. BMW in a Towel needs to turn his charm down a notch or two.

"I'll find him," I say again.

Without looking back, I wave again and climb into my jeep. Pausing at the end of the driveway, I try to figure out where Miles would be. I don't understand why he isn't here. Maybe Jessie or Four would know where Miles is. Perhaps Miles moved to another one of their cabins for some reason. My best bet would probably be Miles' parent's house. They only live a few miles down the road from here.

When I pull up at the Hamilton home place, Chloe comes running out to greet me. She's such a sweet girl. Miles was able to convince their mother to let Chloe take dance classes when school starts in the fall. They're still trying to talk her into the extra classes at the gym. Chloe would love the classes. My friends and I sure do. The teacher is really good. I don't know why she's bothering to teach in a small town. The woman has enough talent to belong with a dance company.

"There you are." Chloe wraps her arms around me. "We were wondering when you'd get here."

"Miles is here?" I asked.

"Yeah," she replied. "Sheriff Barnes dropped him off this morning."

He was here. That meant he was really okay. If he wasn't, he would still be at the hospital. I sighed with relief and followed Chloe to the door. Walking inside, I found Miles sitting on the couch. His face lit up when he saw me.

"Finally," Miles said.

He motions with one hand for me to come to him. I hurry over to the couch and settle into his right side. I'm careful to not touch his left side. His arm is in a sling. He's hurt, but he's alive. The thought of losing him has me tightening my arms around his waist and burying my face into his neck.

"I was so scared," I whispered next to his ear. "Are you okay?"

"I am now, Buttercup," Miles whispered.

He kisses the top of my head before resting his cheek there. We sit this way for a long time, just breathing each other in. The faint scent of smoke still lingers on him. When we can finally speak, he tells me about the fire in Willows Bend. He shares a lot of details, but something tells me he's holding back just how bad it really was. My heart breaks for the family and for Miles. He has to endure situations like this and risk his life to do his job all the time with little praise.

"Is there a safer job?" I asked.

"Not one I'd be happy with," he replied. "This is who I am, and I don't want to change it."

"I know," I say. "And I understand. I would just feel better if your job was safer."

The fire department takes the safety of its firefighters seriously. The guys go through routine training excises all the time. The station supplies them with the best up-to-date protective equipment available. Still, even with all of those precautions, some of them get hurt and a few even lose their lives.

"I second that," Mrs. Hamilton adds from the kitchen.

Miles chuckles, but there's no humor to it. This morning was serious. Still, he's a fireman, and that's not going to change. He's also a hero whether he believes it or not, and I'm so proud of him.

Cupping his cheek with my palm, I rest my forehead against his. I love this man so much. I almost lost him today. Knowing he puts himself in danger to do his job will never get easier for me. I'll have to accept this part of his life, and he'll have to understand I'll fall apart every time it happens.

"When Bailey told me, I swear my heart stopped, and I panicked when I couldn't find you," I tell him.

"No one told you I was here?" Miles asked.

"Chief Foster said you all went home. I called your phone, but it went to voicemail. Then I went to your house, but some man in a towel answered the door," I replied.

"Wait." Miles leans back and narrows his eyes. "My phone was in the fire engine, but a man in a towel answered my door?"

"Yes."

"Mom!" Miles called out. "I need a phone!"

"Is everything okay?" Mrs. Hamilton brings Miles her phone.

"No." He searches through her contacts. "Apparently, there's a man in my house. I need to call Spencer and Aiden."

"It was strange." I think back to my conversation with Mr. BMW in a Towel. "He said he didn't know you, and you didn't live there. There was a black BMW parked outside."

Miles gives Spencer all the information. About twenty minutes later, Spencer calls back to report there's no one at Miles' house.

"That's really weird. Maybe you should call Jessie," I suggest.

"Jessie Calhoun?" Miles looks confused.

"Yes."

"Buttercup, where did you go?"

"To your cabin just down the road." I point in the direction of the cabin.

"I haven't lived there in over a year," Miles tells me.

"Oh, well." I sit up straight. "Oops. I went to the wrong house."

Miles laughs and kisses my cheek. Oh, dear. I went to the wrong house and interrupted a stranger's shower. Jessie will have a hard time explaining my madness to his tenant.

"I'll let Spencer know, but I'm definitely calling Jessie. He needs to make sure his renters open the door with clothes on. I don't like the idea of my girlfriend being greeted by a man in a towel." Miles is already dialing one of them

He called Spencer first. They had a good laugh over my mistake. He then called Jessie Calhoun. Unlike Spencer, I could hear Jessie's laughter through the phone. Miles let him know right quick that the situation wasn't funny.

Even though I made a mistake, I'm beyond happy right now. Miles just called me his girlfriend. I guess that confirms our relationship status. Before he ends the call with Jessie, I lean over and kiss his cheek. Wrapping my arms around his waist, I settle back against his side. I'm the happiest woman in the world right now.

Chapter Thirty-Seven

Katie

August was a warm and happy month for nearly everyone I knew. The fall school term would be starting soon. Labor Day weekend was only a couple of weeks away. People were already planning their camping and parties at the lake. The Hayden Falls Fall Festival was the following weekend. Bailey and I would make hundreds of small bouquets for the event. They seemed to sell faster than the bigger arrangements, and of course, the colored balloons we gave out to all the small children during festivals were always a huge hit.

Even with all of the wonderful things coming up, I hated this month. For the first couple of days, I retreated into my sad quiet little world. This month hurt, but I couldn't live in darkness anymore. I wanted to move forward, not backward. Rachel helped me to see that a few sad moments weren't a setback. Denying what had happened to me wasn't going to help. Instead, I needed to find a way through it.

When Mrs. Maxwell decided to throw a party for Brady this month, I decided to focus on that. Parties were wonderful happy celebrations. This party was a double celebration. Brady had graduated college a couple of months ago, but he was away a lot. He will be playing for the Seattle Mariners next year. It was a dream come true for him, and Aiden. Today, we were celebrating both events. We were all proud of Brady.

Everyone was laughing and having a great time, except for me. Oh, I smiled and laughed, but it was mostly fake. Today was the worst day of my life. I couldn't be upset with Mrs. Maxwell for planning Brady's party for today. My best friends were the only ones who knew what today was. I told them during girl's night a few weeks ago.

My fake smiles weren't fooling those four amazing women. Every now and then, they would look my way. Their expressions were silently asking me if I was okay. I would nod to them and move on. Miles gave me the same look a few times. Had he figured out what today was?

Chase and my brother, Elliott, were playing catch. Wait, playing catch is a childish term, according to my brother. They were throwing the ball around. Same difference to me, but not to Elliott and Chase. Those two had become good friends this year. Chase really brought Elliott out of his shy phase, and my brother helped Chase settle into living in Hayden Falls. Both guys had really needed a friend.

Chloe and one of her friends were sitting on lounge chairs a few feet away from the guys. The girls were giving them a hard time. All four of them would be Seniors in high school this term. That's so hard to believe.

Beth had me worried today. She was once again drinking too much and too fast. It's hot out here, but it's not that hot. Brady discreetly pulled her away to a spot across the backyard. From where I was sitting, they were out of hearing range. I could still see them though. The two were in a heated conversation.

At one point, Brady stepped into Beth's personal space. If you didn't know any better, you would think he was about to kiss her. Beth obviously didn't like what Brady said to her. With her hands on his chest, she shoved him away before storming off. She went straight to E and they disappeared inside for a few minutes.

Brady was left rubbing his forehead with one hand while throwing the other up in frustration. His friend, Dalton Edwards, hurried over to him. The party today was for Dalton too. Somehow, those two managed to end up on the same Major League Baseball team. They have been best friends since they were toddlers. They did everything together in high school, college, and now in their careers.

After helping Aiden grill steaks and burgers, Miles came over to sit with me while we ate. He kept watching me from the corner of his eye. If his memory was good, he probably could almost pinpoint what day things happened. This was something I shouldn't keep from. He has a right to know what today is. When we're alone later, I'll tell him.

After eating, Miles took my hand and pulled me over onto his lap. Normally, I wouldn't be comfortable doing this with so many people around, but today, I need this connection with him.

"How are you really doing?" he whispered in my ear.

Our eyes meet and I almost lose it completely. He's figured it out. With a sigh, I drop my forehead against his.

"You know," I whisper.

It wasn't really a question, but Miles nods his head anyway. His arms tighten around me, pulling me closer.

"Can I have everyone's attention?" Aiden calls out.

Everyone stops what they're doing and gives Aiden their full attention. He and E were standing in the middle of the back deck holding hands.

"We are happy to announce that Baby Boy Maxwell has a name," Aiden said. Cheers erupted all around.

"If this is too much for you today, we can go. Our friends will understand," Miles whispered.

"No." I shake my head. "I can do this, for E."

E, being sympathetic to my situation, had already told me they were planning on revealing the baby's name today. I really do appreciate her talking to me about this first. She didn't have to do that, but she has such a big heart. I should have known she would put my feelings first. This day would probably always hurt for me, but I couldn't let it dimmish my friend's wonderful news today. She could have told me the baby's name, but no, she made me wait like everyone else.

Miles presses his lips to mine for a quick kiss. Gently, I brush the long strands of his dark hair from his forehead. My fingertips slowly slide around the corner of his eye down to his cheek. His gray eyes hold so much love. I give him another quick kiss before leaning back against his chest to wait for the baby's name to be revealed. It's about time our friends agreed on a name. Their little boy was due next month.

"At any time you need to go, just say the word," Miles said. "Just know I'm here."

"Thank you so much," I whisper over my shoulder. He has no idea how much his care and concern for me mean right now.

"After months of debating." E rolls her eyes and smiles up at her husband.

"We have decided to name our son, Caleb Alexander," Aiden announces. The cheers start up again.

The Alexander part was understandable to everyone. It was Aiden's middle name. E had told us months ago the baby's middle name was all they could agree on. She has a notebook of the long list of rejected first names.

"Why Caleb?" Mrs. Maxwell asked.

"Well, I have to admit that Memorial Day was scary for me." E paused to smile at Aiden again. "Because of that, I really wanted our son to have a Biblical name. Moses sent men into the Promise Land to spy it out. Out of the group, only Caleb and Joshua believed they could take the land."

I figured that was where she had gotten the name. Pastor Coleman had mentioned this in a sermon last month. It now explains why E was so interested in the story.

"I wanted to name our son after my father or grandfather." Aiden winked at E. "My sweet little wife's reasoning for the name Caleb won me over, especially after she said I could use the names I wanted next time."

From the look on Aiden's face, there would definitely be a next time for them. Everyone laughed. E rolled her eyes again and gives Aiden a playful shove. Those two are so good together. They have a special way of balancing each other out.

"We hope the story of the Promised Land gives meaning to the name Caleb for our family. We want our son to believe he can do the impossible things, especially when the odds seem to be against him," E adds.

Awe, that's so sweet. Her reasoning is a whole lot better than Aiden's. In approximately four weeks, we will get to meet little Caleb Alexander Maxwell, my Godson. I love his name, and I already love him. We all hurry over to give E and Aiden a hug.

"Hey." Miles gently pulls me away from our friends. "Let's get out of here."

"Miles, I promise I'm okay." I wipe a tear from the corner of my eye. "It's a happy tear."

"I know." His fingers caress my cheek. "I have somewhere I want to take you."

I glance over my shoulder at all of our friends. Hopefully, they won't think it's rude for us to skip out on them like this. Whatever this is, it seems important to Miles.

"It's okay," Miles assures me. "Aiden and E already know where we're going."

"Okay," I agree and let him lead me to his truck.

We ride in silence for a while. I have no idea what he's up to. We pass the party field side of the lake. Several tents are set up around the area, and a huge bonfire has already been started. When he takes the road that leads to the other side of the lake, I know exactly where we're going. Only, we can't go there.

"Miles." I reach over and place my hand on his arm.

"Mmhmm." He glances at me and then back to the winding road.

"We can't go here," I tell him.

He slows down but doesn't turn around.

"Is it too hard for you?" His face drops. He looks really hurt.

This side of the lake is very special for us both. Our favorite spot is here. The times we spent together here are wonderful memories for me. I wish we could share more memories under the oak tree, but sadly, we can't.

"No," I reply.

"Then why can't we go here? You used to love it here," he reminds me.

"I did," I admit. "And I'd love to be able to go to our spot, but we can't."

"Why?"

"Someone bought it and built a cabin there," I explain. He must not know this.

"Oh." He nods his head. "Did they now?"

I guess he hasn't been back to this side of the lake since things ended with us years ago. I've only been here a couple of times over the summer. Before, it was too painful, but something in me led me here a few months ago. I had to see it, and now, I have a physical memory of it. I sucked in a breath when he pulls into the driveway at the cabin.

"Miles, what are you doing?"

"We're going to our spot," he replied as though it was no big deal.

He gets out and opens my door. There are no vehicles here, but the garage doors are closed. It's hard to tell if anyone is home. Maybe this is just someone's summer home. The first time I was here, I did see someone in one of the upstairs windows. Miles means well, but I have a feeling this is a bad idea. Our luck, Spencer will be here shortly to arrest us for trespassing.

"I don't like this." Still, I take his extended hand and hop out of the truck.

"I think you will." He brings my hand to his lips and kisses my knuckles. "Now, come on."

"Fine," I give in. "But, we need to hurry before the owners call the Sheriff."

Chapter Thirty-Eight

Miles

The Sheriff? She's cute, but nobody is going to call the Sheriff's Office on us. I can't believe she doesn't know where we are. This is Hayden Falls. How can she not know? It was never a secret. Maybe my life had only become worthy of gossip the past few months because Katie and I were not hiding our relationship this time.

Usually, I only ended up in Hayden's Happenings when it had something to do with my job or about one of the town festivals. I didn't mind the relationship gossip now. I wanted everyone to know Katie was mine.

Hand in hand we walk across the driveway to the oak tree we spent countless nights under. She sucks in a breath as her other hand moves to her chest. Her eyes dart between the wooden bench and the stone marker on the ground. When her breathing quickens, I fear this was a bad idea.

"Miles? Why? How?" she asked between ragged breaths.

"Is it too much? Did I overstep here?" I asked.

Katie lets go of my hand as she kneels to place her hands flat against the marker. At the top, in the center, is a small vase with three daffodils. Next to the vase is a small terracotta-style pot. I lift the battery-operated candle out and turn it on. On one side of the marker, near the bottom, daffodils blooms are carved into the stone. On the other side, there is a fire engine. In the very center is today's date, five years ago, and the name, Baby Matthews Hamilton. Between the name and date is a baby angel.

"Miles." Katie's tears fall to the granite marker. "You did this."

"Yeah, but I didn't mean to make you cry." I kneel beside her and wrap my arms around her.

"Today hurts, but this is a good cry," she said.

There really is no way to describe what this day feels like. It's harder for her than it is for me. There are no words for what either of us feels, so I don't try to find them. Right now, it's only us and we will love each other through this.

"Thank you for this," Katie says between sobs.

"My mom and grandmother firmly believe that our little one is in Heaven waiting for us." I wipe a tear from the corner of my eye. "I need to believe that too."

"I like that." Katie rests her head on my shoulder.

"Since it was too early to know if our little one was a boy or girl, I had both of our last names carved into the marker. I hope that's okay. He or she was a part of both of us," I explain. "You like wooden benches, so this one is here anytime you wish to sit here."

"And the candle?" she asked.

"My mom suggested it. She said some people like to light candles for their loved ones. I made sure it was battery operated because we can't burn down this tree." I place a kiss on her temple.

We will still have to remove the candle each time we use it. Rain and snow will destroy it. I thought my mom's suggestion was a great idea, so I included it.

"It's beautiful." She gives me a sad smile.

I stand pulling her up with me. With my arm around her, we walk toward the driveway. Katie pauses and takes everything in one last time. She looks up at the huge oak tree, at the marker, the wooden bench, and the lake. There are so many memories of us here.

"What about the owners?" She looks toward the cabin.

I lightly laugh. "You really don't know?"

"Know what?"

"You've been here twice this summer. Two weeks ago, you took a picture of the oak tree," I tell her.

"How did you know that?"

"I saw you both times." I take her hand and pull her up onto the porch. "Katie, this is my house."

Her eyes widened as her mouth falls open. She didn't know. She looks over her shoulder at the oak tree again.

"You bought this?" she asked.

"I bought the land about a year after things ended between us. The cabin was finished a little over a year ago." I unlock the door and motion for her to go inside ahead of me.

She walks through the living room and kitchen taking everything in. From the look on her face, she's impressed. That makes me feel good. Opening the French doors, Katie steps out onto the back porch that overlooks the lake.

"I can't believe you bought this place and built all of this." She turns in a slow circle taking everything in again.

"Well," I shrug. "I couldn't let someone else own the one place that holds my greatest memories."

"Greatest, huh?"

"Buttercup, you hold every memory I do of this place." I lean back against the porch railing and pull her into my arms.

"That's not true." She narrows her eyes at me. "You've lived here for over a year."

"True, but I was just getting it ready for you to come home." Deep down, that was what I had always hoped for.

"Home?"

"Home," I confirm.

I tighten my arms around her waist and kiss her until she's clinging to me. She's finally here, and I never want her to leave.

"Stay with me here tonight," I whisper between kisses.

"Here?"

"Yes, Buttercup."

"Okay," she replies breathlessly as I kiss my way down her neck.

After another long kiss, I give Katie a tour of the cabin. We spent the rest of the afternoon cuddled up on the couch together watching movies. This was definitely one of my new favorite things to do with her.

For dinner, we worked together to prepare spaghetti, breadsticks, and a salad. This was my little sister's favorite meal. Since Chloe visited often, I made sure to keep all the supplies on hand. It was the first meal Katie and I prepared together. I could already tell I was going to love domestic life.

After dinner, we went back out to the oak tree for a while. Katie asked for a few minutes alone. I was reluctant to give it to her. My mom had gone into great detail about how hard this day was for a woman. Trust me, I paid close attention to every word she said. If Katie had been allowed to go through the grieving process five years ago, she would be stronger today. Oh, she would still be hurting, but it wouldn't be as hard on her.

Unsure of how this day would fully affect Katie, I sat on the back porch and watched her while she sat on the wooden bench. I wasn't trying to be controlling. If she needed me, I wanted to be close so I could get to her quickly.

At one point, I noticed she bowed her head. Realizing she was praying, I settled back in my chair again. While she prayed, I bowed my head and prayed for her. She was the most important person in my life.

Katie didn't have a change of clothes with her. Being here had created a private little bubble for us today. We both needed this. Neither of us had thought about going to her house for an overnight bag. She could use a pair of my boxers and a t-shirt to sleep in tonight. We would need to get some of her things here soon because if I had my way about it, she was going to be here often.

Since she was fidgeting, I had taken my shower first. Mentally, I kicked myself for her uneasiness tonight. I should have brought her here before now. It was obvious she liked it here. I wanted her to be comfortable, to feel at home.

While she took her shower, I waited on the balcony outside the master bedroom. I loved it out here. The balcony was on the side of the house. From here you could see the front drive in one direction. The oak tree was straight ahead. Yeah, I had it designed this way on purpose. I had taken a lot of trips down memory lane sitting out here late at night. You could also see the lake from here. It was the perfect spot.

When I heard Katie come out of the bathroom, I got up and went back inside. The sight of her in my clothes halted me in my tracks. I will never be able to look at my gray fire department t-shirt again without picturing her in it. I had to tear my gaze away from her tan legs.

"Where do I sleep?" Katie asked.

Taking her hand, I led her over to my bed. I had turned the covers down while she was in the shower. I could have given her one of the guest rooms, but she belonged here, with me.

"There's only one place you'll ever sleep in this house." Pressing my lips to hers, I gently guide her onto the bed and climb under the covers with her.

After turning off the bedside lamp, I pulled her to me. It only took a few minutes for my eyes to adjust to the moonlit room. My fingertips caress her cheek. So many times I have envisioned her laying here beside me. This was a dream come true. My hand slowly moves down to her waist. She was the only woman, other than my family, to be in this house. She's the only woman I want in this house.

"Thank you for today," Katie whispered. Her hand moves slowly across my cheek.

"Thank you for staying." Turning into her touch, I kiss her palm.

I first made her mine under the oak tree outside. This was the only place we gave ourselves to each other. I wanted to make her mine again, but it wouldn't be happening tonight. Today was a hard day for her. No matter how much I wanted her, I refused to push my advantage when she was vulnerable.

Tightening my arms around her, I inhaled her sweet floral scent. Even after using my soap and shampoo, her flowers were still there.

"Sleep, Buttercup," I whispered.

She settled closer to me, entangling her arms and legs with mine. Every memory of her body close to mine like this came rushing back.

I've missed her so much. No more words were said, none were needed. Our bodies drifted closer together until there was no space left between us. We held each other like this until our breathing evened out and we drifted off to sleep.

Chapter Thirty-Nine

Miles

$\mathcal{D}$aybreak was one of my favorite times. It was peaceful and calming for me. I loved watching the morning sky overtake the night. I often sat on the back porch to witness this miracle. You wouldn't realize how many different shades of blue there were until you had watched the process happen a few times. Throw in some pink, orange, yellow, and red then you'll see a painter's canvas of colors. Right now, the sky was still a deep blue. The morning light should start peeking through any time.

I woke up about an hour ago from a peaceful sleep. It was the best I've slept in years. Katie was sleeping soundly, and I didn't want to disturb her. After watching her for a while, I gently kissed her forehead and slipped out of bed.

I was on my second cup of coffee when I heard Katie moving around in the kitchen. I hadn't planned on asking her to stay with me last night. It kind of just worked out that way. Thankfully, I was prepared for the coffee situation, just not her clothes. I had gotten a small box of decaf pods from Beth's Morning Brew a few weeks ago for Katie when she was here. Sadly, I hadn't brought her here until yesterday. No wonder she thought I still rented the cabin from Jessie Calhoun's family. Guess I still had idiot moments.

Her beautiful smile when she walked through the open French doors was enough to light up my morning. She had found the box of coffee and the mug I set out for her by the coffee maker. She looked like a goddess standing in the doorway sipping her coffee. She was still wearing my t-shirt. My boxers were under there. Automatically, my eyes fell to her bare legs. Closing my eyes, I groaned. Her light laughter was music to my ears. The little minx knows how much she gets to me. I pat my thigh and she comes over to settle on my lap. She belongs right here.

"Good morning." I lightly kiss her neck.

"Good morning. It's beautiful here." She looks out toward the lake.

"You're beautiful." I trails kisses back up her neck. "And, I never want you to leave."

"I wish I didn't have to." She turns her head and presses her lips to mine.

"Then don't."

"What?" Katie leans back and stares at me.

"Don't leave," I say. "Stay with me."

Yeah, I'm jumping about ten steps here, but I don't care. I don't just want her, I need her.

"You want me to live here with you?"

"I do," I admit.

"Wow." She sits up straight and looks toward the lake again.

We sit quietly for several minutes. She doesn't look offended. In fact, she looks as though she's seriously considering it.

"Do you really want that with me?" she asked.

"Only with you." I pull her to me and kiss her again.

"Miles." My name is a whisper on her lips.

That's it. She's completely undone me. I nudge her to let me up. I wasn't planning this for today, but it looks as though we're going here.

"Wait here. I'll be right back." I set my coffee on the outdoor table and hurry inside.

When I come back, Katie is standing at the porch railing. The view of the lake behind her has me captivated. The lighter blues are starting to overtake the morning sky. If I thought she was a goddess before, I'm sure of it now. This is a view I've waited years to see.

In three long strides, I'm in front of her. Taking her coffee cup, I set it on the table by my lounge chair. Standing in front of her again, I open the small box in my hand. Katie gasps when she sees the ring. It's a rose gold daffodil I had custom-made from the Sutton's Jewelry Store in town. Landen was either talented or he had some serious connections.

"Miles, it's beautiful."

Taking her left hand in mine, I slide the right just over her fingernail and hold it between my thumb and index finger.

"I have loved you since you were sixteen. We got a little sidetracked, and I'm sorry for that. Since I couldn't ask your father for permission, I spoke with your mother and grandmother. They want whatever makes you happy," I say.

"Miles?" Her blue eyes search mine.

"This is not an engagement ring. When you're ready for that step, I'll buy you the diamond you want. This is a promise," I explain.

"I want you to live here in our spot with me. I want to make this a home and not just a house. I want a future, kids, and to grow old with you. I want the good, the bad, and everything in between." I want everything with her.

"You want all of that, with me?" she asked.

"Only with you," I vow.

"What if I can't have kids?" She drops her eyes to the floor.

I hadn't thought of that. My mom said some women never go on to have other children after a miscarriage. She was one of the blessed ones because of Chloe. Kids or no kids, I know I want Katie.

"That doesn't matter to me. If you can't have children and want them, we will adopt," I tell her.

"You'd do that?"

"For you, I'd do anything," And, I mean it.

"I don't see Doctor Larson for female matters. I go to a doctor in Missoula. She doesn't see any reason why I can't have children." Her eyes search mine again. "I'm just scared."

"I understand." I give her a quick kiss. "When you're ready to try, I'll be with you every second."

"Thank you," she whispered.

"This ring is my promise to you. Promises of this home, our family, our future, and my love. Any time you're sad, or you doubt, or if some outside force tells you we don't belong together, you to look at this ring and remember everything we've promised today. I want you to always remember, no matter what happens, you and I belong together." I mean every word I'm telling her and more.

"You really want all of that? You want to live here, have kids, build a life togcther, light candles." Her eyes glance over to the oak tree. "Cook dinner together, cuddle on the couch, fall asleep in each other's arms every night, and grow old together?" she asked.

"I want all of that," I tell her. "And, *only* with you."

"Even if I get mad and punch you?" she teases. She is teasing, right? I nod my head. "You really want me to move in with you?"

"I've spent too many years without you." I rest my forehead against hers. "I don't want to waste another day."

I'll start moving her stuff today if she says yes.

"Then, Miles, I don't need time to figure out when I'm ready to take the next step with you. I want all of that too, and *only* with you. I don't want a diamond. I want this ring." She motions with her head toward the daffodil ring I'm still holding over her fingernail. "It's perfect."

"Katie Matthews." I lift an eyebrow. "Are you saying you want to be engaged to me?"

She nods her head and grins. We're jumping about a hundred steps here. Well, she's my girl, and I did promise to do things when she was ready.

"I guess we need to do this a little differently then." Trust me here, I'm all for this.

Still holding the ring over the tip of her finger, I kneel on one knee. Katie's smile widens and her eyes dance. The sunrise over the lake has never been this beautiful. The light seems to catch in her long golden messy strands. Even morning hair looks beautiful on her.

"Katie Matthews, will you…"

"Yes."

"I didn't finish," I say.

"It's still yes."

"I need to finish," I insist.

"Oh." She wiggles before standing up straight. "I'm sorry. Go ahead."

"Will you do me the honor of becoming my wife, and let's make all of those beautiful babies of mine that you vowed only you would be giving birth to?" My eyes dance as I look up at her.

She laughs. There was no way I could leave out her famous words from a few weeks ago, and my babies will be beautiful because of their mother.

"Yes, I will."

I slide the ring down her finger.

"Well, Buttercup, consider yourself officially engaged." I'm the happiest man alive right now.

I kiss the ring on her finger before standing up to claim her lips with mine. My world had never been this perfect and it was only because of her.

Debbie Hyde

Letter from the Author

Welcome to Hayden Falls!!

I hope you enjoyed Miles and Katie's story. I really loved writing this series. As you can see we have a quirky little town with lots of characters. I hope you found several that you love and can connect with. This is just the beginning for our dear little town. We're only two stories in.

If you missed book one, please read Aiden and E's story in Forever Mine. If you'd like to know more about the country band, Dawson, that Aiden used to work with, you can find that story in The Dawson Boys series. You can fall in love with Harrison, Bryan, Calen, Grayson, and Evan as they try to handle music and relationships. Start the series with Harrison Shaw in *Holding Her ~ Book One*.

https://www.amazon.com/dp/B09LCH821Y

Please consider leaving a review for Only With You on Amazon and Goodreads, or other book sites you have. I would really appreciate it.

Check the Follow Me page out for ways to connect with me. I'd love to see you on my social media sites. Be sure to sign up for my Newsletter. Stay tuned, there's lots more to come from Hayden Falls, Montana!

Blessings to you,
Debbie Hyde

Follow Me

Here are places to follow me:

Sign up for my Newsletter:
www.debbiehyde-author.com

Facebook:
Debbie Hyde & Nevaeh Roberson - Authors

Facebook Groups:
Debbie Hyde Books
For the Love of a Shaw
Debbie Hyde's Book Launch Team

Instagram:
www.instagram.com/debbie_hyde_author

Twitter:
Debbie Hyde5

Other Books by the Author

For the Love of a Shaw series:
Historical Romance
When A Knight Falls ~ Book One
Falling for the Enemy ~ Book Two
A Knight's Destiny ~ Book Three
Capturing A Knight's Heart ~ Book Four
A Duke's Treasure ~ Book Five
A Knight's Passion ~ Book Six
A Mysterious Knight ~ Book Seven

The Dawson Boys series:
Contemporary Romance
Holding Her ~ Book One
I Do It For You ~ Book Two
Books 3-5 Coming Soon!

Forest Rovania series: Middle-Grade Fantasy
Written with: Nevaeh Roberson
Jasper's Journey ~ Book One

Women's Christian:
Stamped *subtitle:* Breaking Out of the Box
   Her *subtitle:* Beautiful, Loved, Wanted, Matters, Priceless

Debbie Hyde

Cover Background Art

Cover Background Photos are provided by Carrie Pichler
Photography ~ located in Montana!

Debbie Hyde

Acknowledgments:

A VERY special Thank You goes out to Pit! Yes, Pit is real! I can't say he's one of the town clowns as our Pit in Hayden Falls is, but he is definitely THE PITMASTER! Thanks for all the grilling tips, my friend! I must say, I do know how to grill some amazing Baby Back Ribs! And, thanks for being my Toon Blast Captain!

Thank you to my awesome *Toon Blast* gaming friends, Four!, Pit, and Mags! You guys gave me some great character names for this series. Stay tuned! I'm sure those guys will be doing a lot more throughout the series!

Thank you to my friends Nancie Blume and Wendy Sizemore, my daughter Neleigh, and my granddaughter, Neveah, for all your help with suggestions and for making sure I stay on track with these stories. I couldn't do this without you!

Thank you to the members of the Facebook group The 406! I do appreciate those of you who liked and/or commented on my post for stories from Montana. I have included your names here. It meant so much to me.
Tim Reiter, Ann Pertile, Idonna Harke, Kevin Kallen, Barb Blankenship, Ruth Santorno, Paige Raby, Joe Wiggins, Clark Linn, Peter Mast, Robyn Hofstad, Pam Arvidson and the Home Café!

Thank you to the members of the *Facebook* group *For All Who Love Montana.* Your stories are so great! If you liked or commented on the post for stories I have included your names here. It meant a lot to me that you took the time to share with me.
Christine Migneault, Tammie Duran, Jim and Coleen Larson Done, Andrea Phillips, Joy Rasmussen, Kelli Vilchis, Sandra

Stuckey, Sarah Jobe, Gracene Long, Dennis Fabel, Deb McGann Langshaw, Janice Berget, Ruth Collins Johnson, Roxanna Malone McGinnis, Shawn Wakefield, Alan Johnson, Judy Shockley, Danielle Mccrory, Larry Campbell, Maureen Mannion Kemp, Nancy Ray, Jerry Urfer, Kris Biffle Rudin, Holly Good, Vic Direito, Mozelle Brewer, Joseph Hartel, Cheri Wicks, Stephanie Schuck-Quinn, Travis Frank, Kamae Luscombe, Dianne Eshuk Ketcharm, Patty Ward, Tina Griffin Williams, Steve Kline, Jim Lidquist, Christina Mansfield, Glen Hodges, Teri St Pierre, Lalena Chacon-Carter, Eric Wolf, Jennifer Ahern Lammers, Marilyn Handyside, Lynnette Graf, Arianna Dawn Fake, Cody Birdwell, Doug Jeanne Hall, Mary Thomas. Janet L. Fischer, Dan Rhodes, Jodi Anderson, Denise Byard, Kenneth J. Marrow, Susan and Dan Stocks, Monica Garrahon, Debbie Garrison, Debbie Couch, Joe Wiggins, Mary Poole.

About the Author

Debbie Hyde is the author of the Historical Romance series For the Love of a Shaw. The seven-book family saga begins with Gavin in When A Knight Falls. She is currently working on The Dawson Boys series and the Hayden Falls series.

Debbie has a love for writing! She enjoys reading books from many different genres such as: Christian, Romance, Young Adults, and many more. You will always find wonderful clean stories in her fictional writings.

When not reading or writing, she enjoys using her talents in cooking, baking, and cake decorating. She loves using her skill as a seamstress to make gowns, costumes, teddy bears, baby blankets, and much more.

Debbie started Letters To You on Facebook after God put it on her heart to "Love the lost and lead them to Jesus". This wonderful community of amazing people allows her to continue her mission to Just #LoveThemAll.

Debbie would love to hear from you and see your reviews!

Made in United States
Troutdale, OR
10/23/2024